The Burden of Our Sins
Avenging Angel - Book Two

Tony C. Franklin

Paperback ISBN: 979-8-9896147-5-2
Written By: Tony C. Franklin
Cover design by: Getcovers

Chapter 1

Angel

The air was crisp, and the sun shone bright. My hair was flying behind me. What a great eighteenth birthday! I had a promise ring on my hand, and my very own Jeep, which I had wanted since I was ten. I was driving my jeep with Dad beside me and my boyfriend, Dan, in the back jump seat.

A pickup passed us and blared its horn. The truck pulled into the lane in front of us and slammed on its brakes. The old pickup had a back sliding glass window. A man leaned out, holding a shotgun.

I heard Dad scream, "Look out!" He leaned over and grabbed the steering wheel, pushing it left to avoid crashing into the rear of the pickup truck.

Then I felt the sensation of multiple stings and flying upside down. Was I remembering this? I couldn't remember what had happened after. Was it a memory? It went away, and things went black.

It had to be a memory. Why couldn't I focus and recall everything? I blacked out again.

*****

Dan

I thought drive-by shootings only happened in the big cities until I was in one. We were taking Angel's birthday present, a rebuilt Jeep CJ5, for a drive down a quiet country highway when a pickup passed and began shooting at us. Angel and I were lucky to survive. Her dad wasn't so lucky. We were physically and mentally bruised from the wreck. The physical injuries will heal. I wasn't sure about the mental injuries.

My family was in and out of the hospital checking on me, Angel, and her mom, Mrs. Cotton. My family and the hospital staff looked for me in my room but found me in Angel's room, sitting with her and Mrs. Cotton.

I was constantly being chastised by the hospital staff and my parents for leaving my room. I responded, "Put me in the room with Angel. That's where I'll be, and where I will return until you make me leave again."

Their response was to release me from the hospital early and send me home. Only I wouldn't go home unless Mrs. Cotton was at the hospital with Angel. One of us needed to be there when Angel woke up. The cuts from the glass shards were healing, but the bruises from being thrown around inside the rolling jeep were turning black and purple.

The wreck had occurred on Friday afternoon, and the doctor wanted to wake her up on Sunday. That hadn't gone so well. The Doctor wanted to wake her again on Monday morning. I slept in my own bed Sunday night and woke up tired, stiff, and bruised. Sleeping with a broken arm annoyed me because I couldn't sleep in my usual position.

Mom and Dad didn't argue when I told them I wasn't ready to return to school and I wanted to be there when Angel woke up.

Dad said, "Dan, you can miss today, but you need to go back to school tomorrow. You need to get back into a routine."

I was about to argue when Mom spoke. "Lloyd, I'm not sure I want either of them going back to school. I'll homeschool them if need be. They might not survive the next time."

It was unusual for Dad to remain quiet when Mom disagreed with him. But Mom's "next time" comment must have caught both of us by surprise.

"Do you think it's over just because Jonathan is dead?" she asked, looking at Dad. "Dan and Angel witnessed a murder. They aren't safe, even in the hospital. I want you to call Bull and have him post a guard at Angel's door."

I was speechless; the possibility of us still being in danger hadn't occurred to me. It was over; I thought. Dad still said nothing, but he took a deep breath and slowly exhaled. I knew he agreed with Mom when he reached for our hands, bowed his head, and began to pray.

"Next time," kept ringing in my head as I walked to my truck, only to realize that I couldn't steer it and shift it with a broken arm. I walked to the Cotton's house and drove the Mustang I had loaned Angel. I controlled the steering wheel with my knees while shifting gears.

Angel didn't wake up right away. It wasn't until I opened her hand and used my finger to draw a heart in her palm that she reacted at all. She squeezed my fingers. A nurse had been waiting and watching to make sure she didn't go hysterical again. I had a feeling she had been awake for several minutes and was waiting for the fog to clear and gather her thoughts. I prayed I was prepared for whatever those thoughts brought us.

Chapter 2

Angel

When I opened my eyes, I saw two doll-size children sitting on the hanging light fixture above my bed. Their feet were hanging off the edge, and they were swinging their legs back and forth, causing the light fixture to move like a swing on a school playground.

I must be going crazy.

One of them noticed me open my eyes.

"She's awake!" It whispered to the other.

"Oh, hello, Angel," the second one said.

I didn't respond. I just stared at them. How did they get up there? I couldn't speak. I wanted to tell them to get down; they would fall and hurt themselves.

"Don't talk, just listen," the first one said.

"You have been chosen to be a living, avenging angel," the second one said.

"We will be back to tell you about your assignments when you get better."

"Get well and get strong," one said.

"Bye!" they said and flapped their wings and flew out the window. It was more like going through the window, because the window was closed.

I closed my eyes, wondering what they meant by a living avenging angel. Were they angels? How am I an angel if I am living? How did they fly through a closed window? Were they children, angels, or hallucinations, I wondered as I drifted back into the darkness of sleep.

It wasn't long before I felt people holding my hands. I heard a murmur of voices, but I couldn't understand them. I felt like I was returning from a deep abyss.

My body ached and my head pounded. I remembered the children. They were so realistic, and I heard them clearly, unlike now. I heard people talking, but their voices sounded distant and muffled. But the longer I listened, the clearer they became. Mom was here, and Dan.

Why couldn't I open my eyes? Where was I? What did the children say? Don't talk; rest and get well.

I felt someone open my palm. I felt a finger moving on my palm. It wrote something. No, it drew a heart. I squeezed the hand that did it. That must be Dan. Things became clearer. He gave me a promise ring the night before my birthday.

My birthday. Mom and Dad gave me a Jeep for my birthday. We went for a drive in my Jeep. I couldn't remember anything after that. Except for the dream, my mind was so foggy.

Where was I? I was afraid to open my eyes, but I opened them a little. I wasn't at home. I saw Mom. She was holding my left hand, and she was crying. I wanted to ask why she was crying, but my mouth failed to work.

I looked to the other side and saw Dan. It hurt to move my eyes. At least the guy looked like Dan, but he had a black eye and the side of his head was black and bruised. What happened to him?

I looked around the room. A woman wearing scrubs stood at the foot of the bed. Was I in a hospital?

I closed my eyes again when I felt dizzy. My brain was like the fog on the river at home. Everything was still there, but I couldn't see it through the cloud-like mist.

"She opened her eyes a little," Mom said.

The woman spoke. "I'll get the doctor. She may get nauseous, so keep the bedpan close."

I squeezed Mom's hand, but the thought of moving my fingers made my body ache, so I relaxed.

I heard some shuffling sounds and then a male voice asked, "How's our patient this morning?"

"She opened her eyes," Mom responded

"That's good. Take the oxygen mask off. She doesn't need it, and it will get in the way if she gets sick."

I felt gentle hands around my face, removing the mask. When the hands finished, I opened my eyes. As soon as I did, the room began spinning. I went from cold to hot, and I gagged. Hands turned me on my side, and I felt the cold pan against my head as I vomited.

*****

Dan

Angel dry-heaved into the container. I held her on her side, with my one good arm, while her mom held her head and brushed her hair back. In between the dry heaves, she moaned in agony. I realized she was lying on her bruised side.

"We need to roll her onto her back as soon as possible. She's on her bruised side," I said.

As soon as she caught her breath, I rolled her onto her back. Her eyes were closed, and she took short, ragged breaths.

The Doctor stepped forward and touched my arm and pushed me away from Angel. I wanted to protest, but realized he wanted room to examine her. He spoke gently, telling Angel she had been in a wreck, and that he was going to examine her. He explained everything he was going to do before he did it.

The nurse turned to me and asked, "We are going to do a full exam. Will you step outside, please?"

I stepped into the hallway to find a deputy sitting in a chair by the door. Dad and Sheriff Bull Tatum had worked fast. I moved to the window and whispered a quiet prayer for Angel.

The nurse left the room and rushed down the hall, away from the room. I went back to the door and eased it open. "Is everything okay?"

The Doctor looked at me and frowned. "Mrs. Cotton will tell you shortly."

"Yes, sir."

I closed the door and moved to the window.

The nurse returned with a small tray. A few minutes later that they rolled Angel out of her room and down the hallway.

I stepped back into the room and sat beside Mrs. Cotton and put my arm around her shoulders. She leaned in to me and started crying. How much more could she handle, I wondered? How much more could any of us handle?

"He found shotgun pellets in her back. They are taking her for an X-ray to see if there are any more."

"She's going to be okay," I said. "She's a fighter."

I wished Mom and Dad were here because they knew the right things to say and do. Then they entered the room. Mom took over with Mrs. Cotton, and I stepped out of the room with Dad.

"What's happening, son?"

"The doctor found shotgun pellets in Angel's back during a routine exam earlier. He's taken her for an X-ray to see if there are any more."

"We are all very concerned, son," he said.

"I'm drained, Dad. Physically, she will be fine. Mentally, I'm concerned about us both. How many more times will they attempt to kill us before they succeed?"

The deputy overheard our conversation and said, "The sheriff has been on the phone all morning. He's called every contact at every state and federal agency he knows. He's getting help to sort this out."

"Thank you," Dad said and pulled me into a hug. I stared out the window at the mountain rising beyond. Dad will want to pray after our hug. I knew I needed to pray, because I felt the anger boiling inside. The urge to seek revenge was rising to the surface of my tumultuous life.

Chapter 3

Dan

It was a long day. I stayed with Angel while Mom and Dad helped Mrs. Cotton with the funeral arrangements. The state crime lab had released Officer Cotton's body. The cause of death was determined to be multiple gunshot wounds.

Angel opened her eyes occasionally and then went back to sleep. The Doctor explained that would happen. They found no more shotgun pellets with the X-rays, but two of her ribs had hairline fractures. They planned to release her tomorrow.

Ben dropped in late that afternoon. Angel opened her eyes when she heard us talking.

"Be quiet, I've got a massive headache," she moaned.

We were whispering, but I apologized anyway.

"How are you doing, Angel?" Ben asked.

"Head hurts," she answered.

"It's got to be from that big purple bruise on the side of your head. You and Dan look like a matching set," he replied.

She raised her hand to the side of her head and winced when she touched her temple. She looked at me, and I turned to show her the bruises on my head.

"Ouch, do I look like that?"

"Pretty close," Ben answered. "I'll get out of here and let you rest."

"Ben?" she whispered.

"Yes?"

"What do angels look like?"

He moved closer and whispered. "The versions from the Bible give unique descriptions. They don't look like the ones you see on television. They are frightening. One description says the angel was all wings and had lots of eyes on those wings. Another, called a seraphim, has six wings and uses two wings to cover its feet, two to cover its face and two to fly. Other accounts refer to them as looking like normal men or women. But they exist in spirit form only. Why?"

She held up a finger. "Water?"

I handed her a cup with a straw.

She told us about her dream. How real and vivid it appeared. She told us about the cherubs, and we looked up to realize the light was built in and was flush with the ceiling. The room didn't have a window.

"It was a dream," Ben said. "Most likely, the medicine and your subconscious mind played tricks on you after the accident."

Angel stared at Ben. Then she looked at me.

"I'm sorry, Angel. We were lucky we survived the wreck. Do you remember what happened?" I asked.

She shook her head, no. Then the tears started. I assumed she didn't remember, but maybe she did and didn't want to talk about it.

"Hold me, Dan."

I stood and hugged her. It's difficult to hug someone lying on a bed, especially when you're afraid to touch a bruised or injured part of their body, and you have one arm in a sling and your own injuries hurt just from bending over.

Ben came to the bed, put a hand on each of our shoulders, and prayed. When Ben left, she asked me what I thought about angels. I told her the same things Ben had said.

"Angels don't appear to people. When they do, it's usually a single angel. Two cherubs are wrong. That was a dream or a nightmare."

She asked me about the wreck. I told her what I remembered. Then I asked her what she remembered.

"I remember a truck speeding up behind us real fast. Then they passed us and slowed down. The back window had a sliding opening in it. Then a shotgun appeared, and the truck slammed on the brakes. Dad grabbed the steering wheel and pushed it left, steering us into the oncoming lane. I lost control when the jeep went off the shoulder of the road. That's when we started rolling."

She began to cry, but controlled herself. "The windshield on his side exploded, and I lost control of the Jeep."

"Do you remember seeing anyone in the truck?"

She nodded and pulled her legs up to her chest and rocked back and forth.

"Who did you see, Angel?"

I was expecting her to name Donny Ray or Little John. Instead, she identified the guy we had seen on the security camera at the farm with Donny Ray and Little John. We still didn't know his name, but I was going to find out. I stepped outside and asked the deputy to call the sheriff.

Visiting hours were over before Mrs. Cotton returned to the hospital, looking exhausted, like she was going through the motions of doing things. She hugged me and thanked me for staying with Angel.

She didn't know the sheriff and a deputy had been there for an hour interviewing Angel about the wreck. Angel and I were both exhausted from the questions, and she was sleeping again. It wasn't a good time to tell Mrs. Cotton what Angel had told the Sheriff.

I gave Angel a quick kiss and told her goodnight. She stirred and woke up when I left. I felt like I was getting paranoid. Mrs. Cotton did not act like her normal self. Maybe she was emotionally drained to the point of mental exhaustion. That was probably it.

I stopped and searched the parking lot before I opened the hospital door. It was a waste of time. I couldn't see much of the parking lot from the door. There was only one person in the parking lot, and he looked like he was sleeping in his car. I went back inside and told the deputy. He called in a request for a patrol to check the lot and the man in the car.

*****

Angel

I woke up when Dan kissed me goodnight. I didn't want him to leave, but he went home when Mom returned. She was in a foul mood. She didn't ask how I was doing and didn't respond when I asked how she was doing. Mom made her nest in the reclining chair provided by the hospital and went to sleep.

Dan and I had talked a little about the future. He told me Dad had asked him several times to take care of me if something happened to him. Dan promised he would. I wasn't angry with Dan for not telling me that sooner. I wouldn't break a promise to Dad either, and I was glad Dan was there with me.

Exhaustion set in, but I wasn't sleepy, because I had slept for three days, and as much as my body ached; I wanted to get up and move. Running helped me focus, and that's when I did some of my best thinking. It helped me to focus and build determination. I wanted to go home. But home wouldn't be the same without Dad.

Why did he have to die? Why? The shock was hitting me harder now that my brain fog was clearing. Talking to Dan and the sheriff about the wreck, or Dad's murder, made it worse. The sheriff was the first person to refer to it as murder, and my whole body stiffened at the thought. Dan reminded me Dad had said it wouldn't be over until someone died.

"Is it over?" I asked him.

"I don't think so. We witnessed a murder. They'll come after us next."

I shuddered at the thought. I wanted this to be over. Dad should be alive. But my thoughts went back to my birthday. I'll never have another birthday without remembering Dad's murder. They will be sad birthdays. The room felt like it had collapsed on me as I remembered what had happened.

The truck passed us and slammed on the brakes. I saw the man's face through the window until the windshield spider-webbed from the shotgun blast. Then I remembered Dad grabbing the steering wheel and pushing it to keep us from ramming the back of the truck. It happened so fast. The passenger-side window exploded, and glass flew everywhere. I heard Dad scream. The Jeep hit the ditch and began rolling. The door on my side came off, and that's when I hit my head. I remember nothing after that.

Push through the pain.

I had been drinking lots of water since I woke up. I needed to go to the restroom. Mom was asleep in the chair, so I went without help. It hurt to move. My ribs were the worst, but I felt better as the muscles stretched and loosened.

As I left the restroom, I looked at Mom in the chair. Her blanket had slipped off, and her right arm hung beside the chair. I picked up her arm and laid it across her stomach. It felt cold to the touch. I touched her face and bent down to kiss her cheek. She didn't respond. I couldn't tell whether she was breathing. Oh, no. "Mom?" I shook her shoulder. "Mom?"

No response. I grabbed the call button at my bedside and pressed the button. No response from the button. I opened the room door to the hallway and screamed, "Help!"

The deputy was a few steps down the hall talking to a nurse, and they both came running.

The nurse checked her pulse. "Low pulse rate. Is she on any medication?"

"No. I don't know."

"Check her purse for any prescriptions or medication, please."

I grabbed her purse and started searching. The door opened, and another woman came in. She took over from the nurse. The nurse called her doctor, but I missed the last name.

"Did you find anything in her purse?"

Then I found it. A brown prescription bottle with some large pills. I turned the bottle in my hand to see the prescription. I held it up for the nurse to see. The nurse reached for the bottle.

"Hydrocodone," she said to the doctor. She held the bottle out to the doctor. The Doctor reached for the bottle with a gloved hand. "Who is Roger Cross?" she asked me.

"I don't know."

She gave instructions to the nurse and turned to me. "We are going to take care of your mom. She may have taken some medicine she shouldn't have, but she will be okay. Now go wash your hands, because we don't know where this medication came from."

I didn't understand where Mom got some man's prescription or why I needed to wash my hands. But I turned to the sink on the wall and washed my hands with soap and water. The nurse explained that opioid painkillers like hydrocodone sometimes get laced with fentanyl and that is dangerous. Some people have had reactions to the fentanyl, not hydrocodone, just from touching the containers it's in. Better safe than sorry.

When I finished, I turned to find the nurse and the deputy lifting my mom onto a gurney.

"Where are you taking her? I want to go with her?"

"No, stay here. Is there someone you can call to stay with you?"

Without thinking, I said, "I'll call Dan."

"Okay, good," the Doctor answered. "It's too early to tell if your mom took the hydrocodone or how much she took. She could have taken one pill, and it knocked her out, or she may have taken more. I like my patients and their families to know the possibilities up front. I believe she's going to be okay. Call someone to come stay with you, and I'll come back to see you later."

"Okay."

I hadn't seen my phone since before the wreck. Mom's phone was in her purse. I used it to call Dan.

After I called him, I crawled into my bed and pulled my knees up to my chest. Dad was gone. Murdered while protecting me. Mom had overdosed on someone else's medicine. I was in the hospital recovering from a wreck where I was blasted with glass bits and shotgun pellets. What else will go wrong?

I still had Dan. Once, I had questioned his loyalty, but he proved me wrong. He had stayed with me at the hospital. I had pushed him away, but he wouldn't go. Now he had given me a promise ring. I felt for the ring on my finger, but it wasn't there. I remembered the necklace and found it there, hanging from the gold chain.

I wasn't the girly-girl type who needed a guy around all the time. But strong men who knew where they were going in life and what they wanted were attractive to me. Neither Dad nor Dan sat around doing nothing. Dad was continuously reviewing topographical and aerial maps. He cleaned his weapons often or worked on his truck. When he wasn't doing that, he was working out, or teaching me how to fight. We had spent several weeks teaching Dan how to fight. Dan was a farmer, not a fighter, but he was picking up the self-defense parts. I grinned at a memory. Dan said he had to learn to defend himself. He said my punches were leaving bruises all over him. I was so quick, he barely had time to defend himself. I didn't give him time to strike back. If he hit with a strike, he stopped and asked if I was okay. He didn't want to hurt me.

Ben had mentioned that I still had memories of Dad, and no one could take those away. I sat on the bed and choked back tears and refused to have a pity party. I remembered my dad saying, "When you are running and feel the stitch in your side and you can't catch your breath, keep pushing. You'll push through it and reach that euphoric feeling like you're floating on air."

I wiped the tears from my eyes. “I’m going to keep pushing, Dad. But how long will it be before I push through the pain of losing you?”

Chapter 4

Dan

It was two in the morning when my phone rang. Caller ID said Mrs. Cotton. I answered the phone quickly.

"Dan?" It was Angel. "Come back. Mom has overdosed."

"What?" I practically screamed, then remembered Mom and Dad were sleeping.

"They said she's going to be okay. But I don't want to be alone."

"Okay, give me a little time. I'll be there soon."

Mom was already standing in my doorway, listening.

"You don't need to go anywhere at this time of the night, Daniel."

"Mom, I want you and Dad to go with me." My voice quavered for a minute as I thought about Angel possibly losing both of her parents. "Angel says Mrs. Cotton has overdosed."

Mom stared at me and whispered, "Oh, my dear Lord. I'll wake your dad."

I explained what Angel had said as we drove to the hospital. They bombarded me with question after question, and I couldn't answer any of them. I didn't know what she overdosed on, or where she got it. And I didn't know how she was doing, only what Angel had told me.

They asked what Angel remembered about the wreck, and who she believed to be the shooter. I told them.

Dad's next question caught me so off guard, and I didn't have an answer.

"How did they know about the Jeep? How did they know who was in it?" he asked. I shook my head, because Angel didn't even know about the Jeep. How did anyone else know?

We entered Angel's room, and she jumped off the bed and gave me a quick hug. But she hugged Mom the longest.

"Thank you for coming. I'm sorry you had to get up in the middle of the night."

"Hush. Tell us what's going on. What happened?" Mom asked.

Angel got back into the bed and pulled a blanket around her. She had goosebumps from the chill.

She told us the story of finding her mom passed out in the chair. The doctor had left just before we arrived. They woke her, and she explained she had only taken one pill, but it knocked her out. The pills belonged to an old high school boyfriend she had seen that afternoon. They were supposed to help her relax and get some rest.

"The doctor said she will be fine, but they wanted to monitor her for a while."

I knew what hydrocodone was. We had studied the different drugs and what they did to the body in health class. But the EMT class went deeper, and we learned about prescription and non-prescription opioids and the need for first responders to keep Narcan with them. Fentanyl was becoming a popular drug because it was cheaper, easily obtained, and powerful.

"Your poor mom is stressed out. I'll go see her," Mom said.

Dad touched her arm. "Wait. You're correct. She's stressed out, but she is going to be more embarrassed about this. She needs our support, not our pity. Go check on her. She will probably be asleep. Then, you and I are going back home, and we will meet her in the morning like nothing happened. If she tells us, that's fine. If not, then we keep our mouths shut. We don't need to make a big deal out of this. She has enough issues to handle."

Dad rarely chastised Mom, and she rarely pouted. I was seeing a side of my parents they kept hidden from me and Ben.

Mom nodded in agreement and then looked at me. "You understand what he's saying, right?"

"Yes, ma'am," I answered.

"How are you holding up, Angel?" Mom asked.

"I don't know. Everything is a blur. I haven't even accepted the fact that Dad is gone, and now I almost lost Mom." She got the word 'Mom' out and then she broke into tears.

Mom stepped forward and gently pushed me out of the way, and pulled Angel into a motherly hug.

Dad waved at me to get my attention, and I moved toward him. We stepped out into the hallway.

"Your mom and I are going home. I'm going to bring the dually back up to the hospital for you to drive. You shouldn't be driving stick shifts with a broken arm anyway. When Mrs. Cotton returns, you act like you missed Angel and came back early. Don't say anything about this incident. Okay?"

"Yes, sir."

"Do you have your keys, or do I need to bring the keys up to you?"

"I didn't grab any keys at all. I don't even have the house key."

He let out a sigh and put his hand on my shoulder. "Get your head in the game, son. The sheriff is asking questions he can't find answers to. Like with the Jeep, how did they know who was in it? And most importantly, what are they going to do next, and how will you respond?"

I nodded. "Stop worrying, and start planning for all possibilities."

"Right. Your mom and I are always available to talk things out. A second set of eyes and ears can help find loopholes in your plan."

"I haven't reviewed the security cameras since the wreck," I thought aloud. "I need to review those."

"Not only that, but you need a better plan for school. How will you both be safe going different directions each day?"

"I haven't thought about school. You're right."

Mom stepped out of Angel's room and gave me a hug. "Are you okay, Dan?"

I shook my head. "No, but I'm going to be strong for Angel and Mrs. Cotton. They need someone to lean on while they deal with this.

"And we will be there to help you," Dad said.

He told Mom the plan for bringing the truck back for me, and they said goodnight.

*****

Angel

It was a little after four in the morning. Dan fell asleep in the chair. I was wide awake thinking about what Mrs. Brock had told me before she left. "Life is hard. Life is not always fair. You can spend time mourning and crying, or you can spend it living. Your father would want you to be tough, to take care of your mom, and to live your life."

I immediately thought of Dad saying, "Push through the pain." They were saying the same thing in different ways. I eased out of bed and went to the restroom and changed into sweatpants and the shirt Mom had brought for me to wear home that morning.

She was supposed to take me home. It might be me taking her home now. I had barely stepped out of the restroom when the doctor rushed into the room.

"Good. You're awake and dressed. Wake your brother up."

"He's my boyfriend."

"Whatever."

"I'm awake," Dan answered.

She looked at me. "We had to call the deputy downstairs. There was an altercation, and the deputy said you needed to get out of the hospital as soon as possible. Here, please sign this release form."

"Why? I can't leave my mom."

"Don't worry about why, or your mom. She's okay. Now, follow me."

I looked at Dan, and he nodded for me to follow the doctor. She led us down some back stairs, and we were out of the hospital and into the dually in less than five minutes.

We reached the truck, and Dan opened the door and helped me in. He started the diesel engine and let it idle as we searched the parking lot.

"He's gone."

"What?" I asked.

"There has been a guy sitting in that car every time I leave or enter the hospital. The car is there, but he's not."

"You're being paranoid. Let's go home."

He pulled out of the parking lot and down the short drive to the highway. At four in the morning, there was no traffic. Dan looked left, down the hill toward the stoplight. And then he turned right, away from home.

"Something isn't right. This is too rushed." He pulled his phone out of his back pocket.

"Dan, don't call your parents. Let's just go home."

He made the call anyway, holding the steering wheel with his broken arm and the phone with his good arm. "Sheriff, it's Dan. Angel and I just got rushed out of the hospital. Something about the deputy guarding us had to help with a confrontation, and we were in danger and needed to leave. What's going on?"

I couldn't hear what the sheriff said.

"Yes, sir," Dan answered and hung up.

"I wish I had a scanner in here. The sheriff doesn't know what's going on. He's going to find out and call me back. He said, 'Don't go straight home in case it's a trap.'"

I felt goosebumps rise on my arms as I went from being aggravated that Dan was being paranoid to being glad he was, and from being determined to be strong for Mom to being scared for our lives.

We were crossing the dam that divides Greers Ferry Lake from the Little Red River when Dan's phone rang. I grabbed the phone from the console between us. "I'll talk. You drive."

Caller ID showed it was the sheriff. I answered the phone. "Dan's driving with a broken arm, so I'm on phone duty."

"Good. Don't go home. Other than the drunk at the hospital, there's nothing going on. But the deputy said the guy was talking crazy stuff about you and Dan, so he asked the staff to get you out of the hospital. There might be an ambush waiting for you on the way home. So, go for a long drive. I'll call you later."

"Yes, sir," I responded and hung up.

I told Dan what the sheriff had said. Then I turned the phone off. I slumped back into the leather seat. I closed my eyes and squeezed them tight, like that might make everything go away. But it didn't. A large part of me wanted to give up; a tiny piece of me wanted to turn and fight. Then I heard the cherub's voice: "You've been chosen to be a living, avenging angel." Was I going crazy?

"Why did you turn the phone off?"

"Dan, let's run away. Just for a day or two. Let's find a quiet place where we can rest. I'm so tired of this."

"Okay, Cotton Top." Even though it was dark. He looked at me, and I saw his remorseful smile in the dash's light. I waited for him to protest, to argue. He looked at me again.

"We're going to be okay."

Was he trying to convince me, or himself? We didn't talk during the drive. Which was unusual for us. Hours later, we crossed the state line into Missouri and stopped for fuel.

"Do you want to stop in Branson?" I asked Dan when he got back into the truck.

"No, there are too many tourists. Too much activity. I want to find a quiet place."

"Ok."

We reached Springfield almost an hour later. Dan was nodding off. We found a hotel room off the freeway and stopped. We had no luggage and no toiletries. But Dan asked if they had toothbrushes and toothpaste he could buy. Fortunately, they provided some of those things in case you forgot something.

Dan sat on the edge of the bed and fell backwards. I went straight to the bathroom and took a shower. Dan didn't shower. He had no way of keeping the cast from getting wet. I made him switch sides of the bed. I wanted to snuggle with him, not with the cold cast on his broken arm. He took his jeans off and carefully eased under the covers. I watched how slowly he moved and wondered how much pain he was in? My body ached with every movement I made.

I dried my hair and used my fingers as a comb. My hair desperately needed a brush. I dropped the towels and slipped back into my T-shirt. Dan was already asleep. I moved his arm, laid my head on his shoulder, and prayed that this would end soon.

It was nearly four in the afternoon when I stirred. Dan wasn't in bed. The bathroom door was open. He wasn't in the room. I found the note by the sink and grabbed it as I went to the bathroom.

Gone shopping, be back soon. I love you, Dan.

I was slipping my sweatpants on when I heard rustling outside the door. Quickly, I latched the chain. Then I heard the key card in the lock. The door opened, but stopped as the latch caught.

"Angel? It's me, Dan."

I peeked out the peephole and saw Dan and a police officer. "Who's with you?"

"A police officer. Sheriff Tatum put a missing person's BOLO out for us. The officer just wants to make sure you're okay."

I was paranoid, but relaxed when I saw the officer was helping to carry bags for Dan. I opened the door and let them in. Dan was barely in the room before I hugged him.

The officer looked at me, whistled, and said, "I'm glad I wasn't with you two. Are you okay, Miss Cotton?"

As he and Dan put the bags on the bed, I looked at the officer and huffed. "Considering that I lost my dad in this wreck, and my mother almost overdosed last night, and people still want to kill me and Dan, I'm wonderful. Thank you for asking." I was being sarcastic because I was far from okay, and he knew it.

"I'm sorry for your loss. Your father was in law enforcement?"

Without the sarcasm this time, I replied, "Thank you. Yes, he was a game warden."

"This is a welfare check to verify you're okay. I need to see and hear you call home," he said.

Dan shook his head, but reached for his phone and turned it on. "I'll call Sheriff Tatum. There must be forty to fifty messages on here."

Dan hit the call button on his phone for the sheriff.

The officer asked, "You have the sheriff on speed dial?"

"Personal number," I answered for Dan. "He's a family friend."

Dan put the phone on speaker.

"Dan, are y'all okay? Where are you?"

"We're in Missouri. We became overwhelmed and ran away. Give us some time, sir. We've hit rock bottom, and all the talking in the world will not help right now," Dan answered.

"I understand, but you need to come home. Your parents are worried about you.," the sheriff said.

"How's Mom?" I asked.

"She is worried sick about you. Ashamed and embarrassed because of her near-overdose episode last night."

"We're not ready to come home yet." Dan said. "Can you call off the BOLO for us?"

"Not until I hear from a law enforcement officer that you are okay."

"They're okay, Sheriff." The patrolman gave the sheriff his name and badge number with the Springfield Police Department and told him we were alive and as well as we could be, under the circumstances.

"Sheriff, tell our parents we are okay. We will be home in a few days. We will call when we are ready. Until then, I'm turning my phone off, and we aren't taking calls."

"I don't like it, but I understand. The first few weeks after I got shot were the hardest of my life. I can't imagine what Angel is going through. You be careful."

"Yes, sir. Thank you."

Dan hung up and turned the phone off.

I had moved up beside Dan and put my arm around him. The patrolman looked at us and asked, "What did he mean 'when he was shot?'"

We told him an abbreviated version of the long story.

He looked at me just before he left. "Your father was a brave man. He gave his life so that you could live. My thoughts and prayers are with you. Be safe."

I whispered loud enough for Dan to hear. "He gave his life so that I could live. Isn't that a Bible verse?"

Dan hugged me and quoted John 3:16. "For God so loved the world, he gave his only begotten son, that whosoever believeth in him will have everlasting life."

****

Dan

After the officer left, I turned and hugged Angel. We stood there quietly.

I finally relaxed my hug a little. Angel did not. "Are you okay, Cotton Top?"

When she didn't reply, I asked. "Do you want to go home?"

She relaxed a little, wiped her eyes, and finally let go.

"Not yet." She sniffled. "I know I should be there for Mom. But we're the ones in danger. If we stay away, she'll be safe. I don't think they will bother her."

"Okay." I wasn't excited about going home either, but this was about Angel. We were both physically and mentally bruised and injured. But Angel had lost her dad and almost lost her mom. We were frightened now that we knew they had a reason to be after us. They thought we would leave the hospital and run straight home. But we ran away. No one expected that, not even us.

"What do we do now?" she asked me.

"One thing at a time. I picked up some snacks and a couple of bottles of water. There is a brush and a comb. Some medicine and trash bags, so I can cover this cast and take a shower."

Angel looked through the bags at what I had bought. She found the hairbrush and the bottles of water. I watched as she opened the water and drank half the bottle. She brushed her hair in front of the mirror. After a few strokes, she stopped.

"I look horrible," she said.

"You look beautiful." I walked up behind her, and we looked at ourselves in the mirror. "The injuries and bruises will heal, and you won't be able to see them. We need to heal the injuries here." I pointed at her heart. "And here." I pointed at her head.

"The cherubs were back in my dreams last night. Am I going crazy?"

"No," I replied, but I didn't know. "It's just your brain protecting you, keeping you going."

"They didn't say anything," she said. "They were watching over me."

I didn't answer. I took the brush from her hand and brushed her hair. She was strong, but even strong things break. We needed time. Time we didn't seem to have.

She began to cry, and that turned into uncontrollable sobbing.

For hours we lay still and cuddled. The physical pain kept us from moving. Angel had cracked ribs that hurt worse each day. I had enormous bruises across my lower stomach from the seatbelt that broke when the jeep crashed. My broken arm didn't help. We were both fighting headaches, so we stayed in bed, held each other and talked.

Chapter 5

Dan

We returned home two days later. We still hadn't turned the phone on. That ended up being a huge mistake. We missed Officer Cotton's funeral. They didn't postpone the funeral because too many law enforcement officers and former marine buddies were coming to the funeral.

The time we spent recovering from the fear of being chased and killed was gone in an instant. It was replaced by the guilt of missing the funeral and not getting to say goodbye. The messages were there on the phone, telling us the day and time of the funeral. I thought I was being supportive. Instead, I let Angel down.

I expected a stern lecture from Mom and Dad. I didn't expect Mom to yell at the top of her lungs, or for Dad to give me the lecture about being disappointed. Normally, Mom was the most excitable, and Dad was the voice of reason. But not today. I didn't argue or fight back. What do you do when your parents are right and you know they are right? I had let Angel down, and that hurt worse than all the aches and pains I had endured the last few days.

After ten minutes of mostly Mom yelling, and Dad occasionally lecturing. Mom yelled, "Are you listening to us?"

I was sitting in a chair in our living room. I raised my head and whispered, "Yes, Mom."

"What do you have to say for yourself?" Dad asked.

"We are tired, hurting, and scared that any minute will be the last time we take a breath."

"So, you two ran away?" Mom screamed.

I stared at Mom. I was disappointed in myself, and I shook with anger as I stood to face my parents, who had been standing for the whole lecture.

My words came out in a hiss with venom dripping from my tongue, and my mom took a step backwards. I was angry with myself, not her. "We didn't have sex, if that's what you're thinking. We were trying to heal. I held her, and she cried. We talked, and she cried some more. She's nearly had a mental breakdown. And right now, after missing her dad's funeral, she probably has had one. We are both broken. Yelling at me is not helping. Angel and I are adults now. Not because we recently turned eighteen, but because we've survived more murder attempts than any fifty adults will survive in a lifetime." There was a moment of hesitation before I said, "You should be glad that it wasn't our funeral you attended today."

I walked to my bedroom and closed the door, then grabbed a pillow from my bed, which was still unmade from when I left it a few nights before to go comfort Angel.

The corner of my room called to me, so I sat on the floor, then threw the pillow back at the bed in frustration. I did what was right for Angel, and somehow, I failed.

There was a knock on my door, and Dad asked, "Dan? Can I come in?"

When I didn't respond, the door opened, and he looked into my room. When he spotted me sitting on the floor, his eyebrows raised, and he pushed the door open to enter. He walked to where I was and sat on the floor beside me.

"That was quite a speech you gave in there. It put this situation into a whole different perspective for your mom and me."

I said nothing. I sat and waited.

"We thought..."

"I don't care what you thought. I want you to understand why," I replied.

He sighed heavily. "I'm sorry. We are glad you are home. And alive."

He sighed again before he continued. "Your speech reminded us of everything you've been through. We truly are fortunate that we are here."

"How many people have to die? How many threats and attempts does it take for someone to do something?"

Dad stiffened when I said that. Because he Sheriff Tatum tried, he became paralyzed from the waist down. Angel's dad was dead. They tried, but came up short.

"I'm sorry, Dad."

"Don't be sorry. You may be the most level-headed person in this whole mess. Help me up. We need to go check on your mom. She went to check on Mrs. Cotton and Angel."

*****

Angel

I asked Dan to drop me off at my house. I didn't know which version of my mom was waiting. Would she be glad I was home or yell at me for running away? I felt like I had cried in Dan's arms for two days straight. He had talked to me and encouraged me. He built me back up until I thought I was ready to be strong for Mom. I needed to be strong for myself because that was what Dad would want.

Besides, several cars were there that I didn't recognize. I opened the door to the living room and found Mom talking quietly to two ladies I didn't know.

"Mom?"

"Angel." She rushed off the couch and hugged me tight. "Are you okay? Why didn't you call me?"

"We were scared to turn the phone on. We didn't want them finding us."

"You should have called. You missed your father's funeral."

"What?" Every ounce of encouragement Dan had used was gone instantly. I lost what little sanity I had holding me together. How could I have missed Dad's funeral?

Chapter 6

Dan

We found Mom and Mrs. Cotton consoling Angel. She was lying on the floor screaming, and I rushed to her. I put my hand on Mom's shoulder and said, "Angel, I'm here."

Mom stepped back, and Angel grabbed me and buried her face in my chest. She screamed as I picked her up off the floor. That was probably from her bruised ribs. I couldn't stand seeing Angel in pain, but I needed to get her alone, away from other voices and distractions. When people don't understand the root of the problem, their words can be weapons instead of the soothing salve they are intended to be.

"Excuse us," I said, and carried her to her bedroom. There were other people there whom I didn't recognize. I was upset when Dad said we had missed the funeral. I was sure this resulted from Angel learning the same thing.

It took ten long minutes to get her calmed down and stop crying.

"I hate my life," she moaned.

"Does that mean you hate me?" I asked.

"No! You know what I mean." She buried her face against my chest.

"I didn't get to say goodbye," she cried.

"Funerals aren't for loved ones to say goodbye. They are for friends and neighbors. You and your mom will take much longer to say goodbye," I told her, repeating something I'd heard Dad tell a church member once.

"Why don't we start now by going to the cemetery? I'll ask Dad to go with us. Do you want to change? You've been wearing those sweats for three days."

She snorted through the snot in her nose. "I need to go to the bathroom. Then I will change."

"Okay." We had been lying on her bed. We both stood up, and she headed to the bedroom door.

"I'll be right back."

"I'll tell our parents what we plan to do."

The grave had been filled minutes before, and the backhoe operator was leaving when we arrived. Two hours earlier, and we would have made it in time for the funeral.

It ended up being a family visit to the cemetery. Our parents went with us. Dad repeated a brief service. When he was through, I suggested we give Angel a few minutes by herself at the grave. I whispered to her, "I will be close if you need me."

Angel rocked back and forth on her knees at the foot of her father's grave. I almost doubled over from the wave of pain and fear that came over me thinking about losing Angel. How does anyone survive this? Our parents had walked to the Escalade and were waiting for us. No doubt, they were deciding what to do about us.

When Angel stood up and came back to me, she showed no tears, just a look of weariness and determination. She hugged me and said, "Thank you. Let's go home. I'm not running anymore. Dad would want me to be strong and carry on."

"You're right. Let's get our lives back."

She hugged me tightly and didn't let go. Finally, she relaxed and looked up at me until I made eye contact with her.

She said, "It's not our fault we missed Dad's funeral, because it's not our fault that he is dead. We were supposed to be buried beside him. But we are alive. I'm going to get these guys. It may take me years, but I'm going to get them." She hesitated just for a moment and looked back into my eyes. "We are going to get them."

"Okay. Let's get our lives back." I cupped her face in my hand and used my thumb to brush a stubborn tear away. I had waited for this moment since the wreck. It was time for us to get revenge. "I love you, and I will support you. Whatever you decide to do."

"Thank you."

Chapter 7

Angel

As I kneeled and prayed, a breeze blew away the grief and sadness I had been feeling. A calmness came over me, and I knew a plan was being put into place for me. But I had to finish high school, and protect my mother and Dan.

I knew I couldn't do it by myself. The feeling that a path would be shown to me came to me again. I had never been religious, but being around Dan's family made me trust in a higher power. This was the genuine feeling of how God worked, not the cherubs from my dreams. I wasn't sure what the cherubs were — probably a figment of my imagination, like Ben said, or the lingering effects of the anesthesia.

When I hugged Dan, I felt something beyond the feeling of physical desire. I felt his concern, his protectiveness, his desire to spend the rest of his life with me and raise our children. We talked about it many times, but it was verbal communication, not a feeling. Through that hug, I knew Dan loved me. He was my partner. It felt wonderful and frightening at the same time. We had gone through so much together, and he never left my side. I understood what true love was now. I was being allowed to seek vengeance because of love, not hatred. Because I loved my dad, mom, and Dan. It was also frightened, because I couldn't stand the thought of losing Dan, of kneeling by his grave and saying goodbye.

We didn't make it back in time for Dad's funeral because I needed to feel the loss of love. I needed to reach the bottom of that pit, to feel the total loss and understand how a decision could be right and wrong at the same time. We needed space and time to heal, but we missed the funeral because of it. I needed to learn a lesson, and that was to want revenge because I loved Dad, not because I hated his killers. I realized hatred clouds judgement and thinking. Love guides you with clear thinking and great focus. I felt God was giving me permission to seek vengeance through love, not hatred. Hatred is a potent motivator, but love is stronger. There is a fine line between the two, and I had to focus on love.

I knew I could track them down and kill them, but that would be through hatred, and if I died, I would be no better than them. If I followed the letter of the law, and followed God's path, then I might bring them and others down with them. I knew I needed to trust in God, because He had a bigger plan than I imagined.

This was an experience that would stick with me for the rest of my life. Kneeling at the foot of Dad's grave. Would I know what to do and when to do it? The feeling was there. I would know.

I love you, Dad!

Holding Dan helped me process these feelings and thoughts. I didn't tell Dan what I had experienced at the grave. He knew I had experienced something and asked me about it later when we were walking around the farm.

I told him everything. About the breeze, the feeling, the sudden knowledge, and the determination I felt. He smiled at me, leaned down and gently kissed me on the lips. And the realization hit me.

"You knew. How?" I asked.

"I felt a wave of pain, danger, and the fear of losing you come over me while I was watching you. When you stood up, it decreased because I saw a determination in your eyes, and I knew something significant had happened. I didn't know what had happened, but I knew without you telling me you were determined to become the hunter and not the hunted. It was fear that embraced me until I felt your love, not your anger. Feeling your love comforted me."

For the first time since the wreck, I felt focused. My future was determined. I needed to be patient to fill in the pieces and prepare myself. I didn't need to rush. It would come to me at the right time.

When Dan and I walked back to the Escalade to meet our parents, we were holding hands. I don't know what our faces said to them, but there was no yelling, lecturing, or arguing. Only silence. They weren't giving us the silent treatment; they didn't know what to say.

I let go of Dan's hand and walked to Mom. We hugged each other. "I'm sorry I ran away. I was so afraid I didn't know what to do."

"The important thing is you are home now. And you're safe."

I turned my head to see Dan speaking to his parents. I still didn't know how his return home had gone. He expected to get lectured and grounded. I finally saw his mom hug him, and then his dad joined them. Let the healing begin, I thought. Then I thought about Dad. That wound was going to take a while to heal.

We drove back home in the Escalade. I was in the middle of the back seat, between Dan and my mom. The trip was uneventful. We were lost in our own worries. We were back home, and so was the danger.

Dan pulled out his phone and called Sheriff Tatum. "Sheriff, I wanted to let you know Angel and I are back home." He listened to the Sheriff and then said, "Yes, sir. I will." Then he leaned forward in his seat. "Mom. Dad, we need to go back to the Cotton's and wait for the Sheriff."

His mom nodded. I was seeing awkwardness between Dan and his parents I'd never seen before. I didn't know what happened when Dan returned home, but whatever happened, his parents weren't adjusting to it well.

Two women from the church were at our house when we returned. They helped serve us dinner before excusing themselves and leaving us alone.

Sheriff Tatum came by and gave us an update. He said the suspect disappeared. Even Danny Ray and Little John disappeared. They closed their hunting lodge and bar down "for the season" and left town. For me, that was good, because I was tired of looking over my shoulder. I wanted my revenge, but the question was, how do I begin? It needed to be done legally. If Dad were alive, I wanted him to be proud to call me his daughter. I promised him I wouldn't come back to the cemetery until I succeeded.

We ate dinner in our living room with our parents. The dining table was full of food from family and friends. It was a Southern tradition. Mom said that's where the term 'comfort food' came from. People didn't know what to say during these times to comfort the family, so they brought their favorite dishes to comfort them. I don't know if that was true or not, but in this case, I was glad the food was there. Dan and I had not eaten well for the last three days. We'd eaten mostly junk-food and pizza delivery. We didn't leave the motel room. Now we were starving, and we had plenty of food.

It was Dan who started the conversation after we had eaten dessert. My birthday cake had gone stale. It was uncut and stayed that way until we threw it out. Another casualty of my birthday crash and Dad's murder. I had a piece of apple cobbler that was delicious. He made sure I finished eating before he spoke.

"Mom, Dad, Mrs. Cotton, we're sorry we ran away. We didn't plan it. The Doctor rushed us out of the hospital. It didn't feel right, so instead of turning left and coming home, I turned right and called Sheriff Tatum. He told us to drive around until he checked things out. Our first thought was that they planned to ambush us on the way home. We were tired, hurting, and afraid. So, we did what no one expected. We turned the phone off and drove without thinking."

It wasn't our decision. It was my decision. I suggested we run away. Dan wasn't telling the story the way it had happened. He was sharing the responsibility. Or did it happen that way? I spoke the words out loud, but he turned in the opposite direction, and he agreed. I had expected him to disagree, but he didn't. Was he lying? Was he telling his version of the truth? Or did my fear cause me to miss something?

I stayed quiet as he continued our story. "We made it to Springfield, Missouri, before Angel made me stop. I was nodding off. We found a motel and slept most of the day."

He told them about the police officer checking on us. And he surprised me by telling the truth. Mostly. He told them about my breakdown and not leaving the room for three days. He talked about our conversations and how long it took to convince me to come back home.

"We did what we needed to do to protect ourselves, and begin healing. It was wrong not to let you know where we were and what we were doing. But Sheriff Tatum knew, and he chewed us out for our decision. Again, we're sorry for what we did. We'll accept whatever punishment you think we deserve for this."

Punishment? Did we deserve to be punished? Oh! Yes, we did technically run away. Surprisingly, Mom and Mrs. Brock were looking at Mr. Brock. Had they talked about this? They must have.

Mr. Brock looked at us and took a deep breath before he spoke.

"We had a plan to deal with the two of you when you returned home. But your story shows us a different reality than the one we imagined. Dan, you have shown us the depth of your love and commitment to Angel by never leaving her. Your comment earlier this evening about 'even strong things break' shows that commitment. You kept her from breaking down, and when she did break down this afternoon, you stepped in and did what her mom and your mom couldn't do. You put her back together. I'm sorry. We're sorry we didn't see it."

He stopped for a moment and looked at Mom and Mrs. Brock.

He looked at each of us and looked us in the eye. "As Dan said earlier, you are now adults, not because you are eighteen, but because all the things happening around you have pushed into adulthood." He paused before continuing, "Since you are adults, we are going to ask you to continue to act like adults. But from now on, keep us in the loop on your decisions. Your punishment is to put up with our nagging you about where you are. You will have to listen to us say we love you, and hug us more than usual, because we are thankful you're home and not lying in graves beside Jonathan."

That's when Mom and Mrs. Brock burst into tears and came to hug us. We had a good cry. Now I knew what they were talking about before we left the cemetery. I still didn't know what Dan had said to his parents, but whatever he said had changed everything.

When Dan and I went for a walk around the farm, night had fallen and the temperature had dropped into the low forties. I put on my heavy jacket, and we walked to Dan's, and he put on his heavy farm coat.

As we started up the old logging road, I asked Dan, "What did you say to our parents today? I expected us to get grounded for life."

"They lectured me. Dad mentioned the main parts I said tonight. I reminded them we were frightened and that they could have been attending our funerals too."

"People survive wrecks all the time. But how many people can say they survived a murder attempt?" I asked.

"Yeah. Two of them we know about."

"What are we going to do?"

"This isn't over. They will try again."

I shivered when he said it.

We tried getting back into our routine. Walking, not running, in the morning. We weren't healed enough to run yet. Dan needed to check the cattle, so we took the four-wheelers and checked them in the morning.

His mom had picked up our schoolwork and planned to homeschool us until we made up our work. Tomorrow was Friday, and the next week was Thanksgiving. A short week would help us get caught up on schoolwork. Saying goodnight after spending every minute together for the last three days was painful. Now, we needed to spend some time with our parents. They loved and needed us as much as we needed each other.

Chapter 8

Angel

I wish that life returned to normal. But two weeks after the wreck, it still hadn't, and it never would. Mom and I missed Dad.

Dan came to the house one night to check on me and Mom before going home to bed. Mom hadn't been feeling well, so I stayed with her. The sounds he made when he entered the kitchen made Mom look at me and brought us to tears. The creaking of the kitchen door opening, the thud of footsteps on the floor, and the clatter of keys on the kitchen counter sounded just like Dad coming home from work late at night. It was the little things that brought back memories and brought on the tears. The smell of coffee in the morning reminded us of him sitting at the table in the dining room planning his day. Or me thinking of a question and wanting to call or text and then remembering he wouldn't answer. Experiencing that loss is hard, but remembering he will never be there again is the hardest thing in the world.

We worked diligently to get back into a routine. I had relied on Dan so much that I hadn't noticed how the wreck and Dad's murder had affected him. He had been the steady one. I don't think any of us had noticed. But Ben noticed. Mom and I were invited to lunch with the Brocks on Thanksgiving Day, and Ben pulled me aside to ask about Dan.

"How are you holding up, Angel?"

"I'm holding up. Taking it one day at a time. I'm trying to be there for Mom. Dan has been my rock. He's held me together with hugs and prayers," I answered.

"I'm worried about him," Ben said. "He's carried this load since the wreck. He hasn't leaned on me, Mom, or Dad. Has he opened up to you?"

I realized what Ben was saying, and I was surprised I hadn't seen it myself. "He stays busy and never sits down. He must be doing something," I said.

"Yes, I'm glad you see it now. He and I used to have this connection where we sensed when something was wrong with the other. We've lost that connection. I'm asking you to take care of him because you're closer to him now. Can you do that for me?"

"Absolutely. You know I will."

"He's always stayed busy," Ben said. "But the smile is missing. The easygoing, joking banter is not there."

"I don't know if it will return. We've been through a lot. And there are still people who want to kill us. That fear is with us everywhere we go."

"What are you two up to?" Dan asked when he found us standing in the mudroom.

"Talking about you, little brother," Ben answered.

"That conversation won't take long," Dan answered. He was joking, but he didn't have his usual grin.

"I'm worried about you."

Dan didn't answer. He pulled Ben into a hug and held him. When he let him go, he hugged me. I didn't want to let go. I could see it when we let go. The premature lines around his eyes. I felt the tense muscles. And as I held him, I almost relaxed, but then the tension returned.

"Dan, what's going on?" I asked.

"This is not over. It won't be over until someone else dies. It's us or them. The odds are in their favor, and I can't think of any solution."

I pushed away from his hug and stared into his eyes. His revelation wasn't new. We had talked about it. Everyone in families was aware of the lurking danger. But I was speechless because I hadn't realized that's what he was thinking about. Ben said nothing. While I was recovering and helping Mom, Dan had been thinking about the future.

Ben asked, "You really think they are still coming after you?"

"Maybe, maybe not. But we must plan our lives as if they are. That's a chance I don't want to take. We make it easy for them if we aren't prepared."

"What are you thinking, Dan?" Ben asked.

Dan shook his head. "I have found no answers. I don't want to talk about it right now. Let's do something else." He hesitated, but Ben and I waited for him to speak.

"Angel," he spoke softly and put his hand on my shoulder. "I had one more birthday present for you. But the wreck happened, and I never gave it to you. I'd like to give it to you now."

I looked at the ring on my finger, and he slid his hand down my arm to my hand. "It has nothing to do with that," he said.

Ben looked at the ring and said, "Whoa, wait. What is that?"

"A promise ring," Dan and I said together.

"It's not an engagement ring," Dan said. "Not yet."

Ben blew out a breath. Then he looked at the ring again and looked up at Dan. What was he thinking? Promise rings were important only to the two people involved. To everyone else, they meant nothing. But a careful look at the pearl and the two small diamonds told you it was real. Ben knew it was as close to an engagement ring as it got without me saying yes to a proposal.

"Do Mom and Dad know?" Ben asked.

"No. I gave it to her the night before her birthday. We had planned to say something at her birthday party, but... other things happened."

"Mom knows," I added. "I suspect your parents know as well."

"That's a pretty serious step," Ben added.

I saw the flicker in Dan's eye right before he said something he might regret, and I squeezed his hand.

Dan sighed, and I knew he'd changed his tone because he relaxed. "Ben, we've survived two murder attempts and we're barely eighteen. There is a chance we will never see nineteen. We don't plan on rushing things. But we may not wait long after high school to get married either. We plan to enjoy every minute we have together, because it may be our last."

There is a chance we will never see nineteen. That hit me so hard I caught my breath and hugged Dan. Blood rushed to my head, and I felt faint. Then I felt Ben's arm around me as he joined us in a three-way hug. The last time we hugged like this was when Sarah died. What was it with death and hugs?

When we released each other, Dan turned to the hidden gun safe and opened the wall panel, hiding it, and then unlocked the safe. I knew then my present must be a gun.

"I've hesitated giving you this because I'm not exactly a fan of guns right now. You aren't either, I expect," he said.

He was right. But guns were part of our lives. They were supposed to be tools used for hunting game and putting food on the table, not for killing people. He pulled out a long box wrapped in blue paper. There was a red bow with a white envelope taped next to the bow.

"If you don't want to open it... if it's too soon, I understand."

I knew what it was. It was a muzzleloader. That was the only gun we used in our shooting sports competition that I didn't own. But this hadn't been my real birthday present. The promise ring was, and it meant more than any gun.

"A muzzleloader?" I asked. Still not sure how I felt. And I understood his hesitation. But if we were going to protect ourselves, we were going to need our guns.

"Too obvious, huh?"

"Lunch is ready," Mrs. Brock said from the kitchen.

"Can I open it after lunch?"

"Of course, Cotton Top."

Ben, who had quietly watched us, asked, "Are you still calling her Cotton Top? I made up that name months ago."

I smiled then, and for the first time in days, I saw Dan smile. He had agonized over giving me what would have been a wonderful gift two weeks ago. But now, he felt it inappropriate because Dad and I had been shot during the wreck, and he hesitated because he didn't know how I felt about guns now. Well, I didn't like them being used against me, but I wouldn't hesitate to use one on Little John if I had the opportunity.

I forced a smile and said, "Thank you. You were afraid to give it to me now. Weren't you?"

"Yes, let's go eat."

Thanksgiving lunch was delicious. We didn't cause the outburst we thought when Dan announced my promise ring. Instead, our parents seemed happy about it. The only question they asked was, why did we wait so long to tell them? But it was asked in such a way that an answer wasn't expected. Everyone knew the answer.

After I opened my present with Dan and Ben, we decided to go target practicing. I was the one who decided. Something told me I needed to get over this aversion to guns that was developing. So, I suggested we go shoot my new CVS Wolf, .45 caliber muzzleloader. The next day was the beginning of a three-day Thanksgiving deer season. Ben had the day off from work and planned on hunting. Dan had mentioned it to me, but I didn't say anything, so he moved on to a different topic. Remembering that made me realize how much Dan had been reading me and testing my emotions. I needed to go hunting. To get back to doing the things I loved to do.

Ben had put up the tree stands weeks before. I don't know where Dan and I were, but Dan knew the locations by instinct. He told me they put the stands in the same location every year. They put me on a certain stand and said I was almost certain to see a buck there.

They were right. Just after daylight, I spotted him slipping through the trees about fifty yards behind a doe. I raised my rifle and stopped. I couldn't do it. I had killed a deer before. But now, the thought of it being defenseless stopped me. I set the rifle down and pulled my phone out. I zoomed in close and took a picture. "Go on, big guy. It's not your time yet," I said. I sat there for two hours, listening and watching the forest come alive. The birds flying by. Squirrels barked at me, telling me I was invading their space. The sunlight filtered through the pine boughs, thawing the ground below.

It was peaceful. The most peaceful feeling I had felt in days. I thought about Dad and remembered the first time he took me hunting. I couldn't pull the trigger then either. He didn't judge me then, and I didn't judge myself now. What would he say about letting an eight-point buck walk away? I smiled, knowing he would tell me I helped evolution produce a stronger, healthier deer herd.

Voices and the crunching of leaves alerted me, Dan and Ben were coming. I inhaled the earthy smell of the woods one more time. The hunting wasn't productive, but I had healed a little more.

Ben yelled, "Coming to you, Cotton Top."

"No kidding, y'all make more noise than a herd of wild hogs." I climbed down the ladder of the stand and met them on the ground.

"Did you see him?" Dan asked.

I said nothing. I pulled out my phone and showed him the picture I'd taken. He smiled. "I got his picture, too. How many points do you think he has?"

"Eight at least. Let's see your picture. Why didn't you shoot him?"

"Same reason you didn't. I'm not ready yet." It was more because he had trouble holding a rifle steady with a cast on his arm. "I still can't tell how many points he has."

Ben moaned the whole walk back to the farm. “See if I ever let you two have the best stands again.” Just before we entered the mudroom to put our guns up, Ben said, “Just so you two know, he was a ten-pointer. He walked right under my stand. If y’all didn’t shoot him, I wasn’t going to either.”

Chapter 9

Dan

We didn't talk about our hunting expedition much more that day. There is something about sitting in the woods, listening to the sounds of nature, that exposes your soul. It peels back the layers of worry and stress that hinder your thinking and actions.

I did my best thinking when I was working. But lately, I'd spent more time thinking about my next project instead of planning the future. The worry and stress were like radio interference. The ideas and plans were there, but I couldn't hear them clearly until the buck came along.

Angel must have seen him, and didn't shoot. I didn't even raise my rifle, because I had seen enough wounds and injuries for a while. If I needed the meat, it would be a different story. I'd thank God for the opportunity to feed our families, but we had plenty of food. We didn't need the meat.

I said a prayer and asked God to help me understand what His plan was for me. The plan wasn't revealed, but I felt a wave of calmness come over me. I felt the same thing Angel said she felt at her father's grave. I needed to be patient. A plan was being made for us.

Instead of going hunting again that afternoon, we watched the Arkansas/LSU football game with Ben and Dad. Angel snuggled up next to me and said, "What happened to you this morning? You are more relaxed than you've been in days."

"There's something about being in the woods. It brings you closer to nature. Closer to..."

"To God?" Angel asked.

"Exactly."

"Let's enjoy life together while He plans things for us," she said.

Mrs. Cotton said goodbye and went home. She said she was meeting someone.

We watched the rest of the game before Ben left and headed back to his apartment in Searcy. He had to go to work in the morning. That left us sitting with Dad.

He had watched us closely that afternoon and finally spoke. "You two are more relaxed than I've seen you in days."

Angel responded first. "We both had a shot at a ten-point buck this morning. We let him go."

"I think we were too busy having a conversation with God. There is something about sitting alone in the woods that makes you realize you are another small creation. The world doesn't revolve around you. You're just along for the ride," I said.

"Amen," Dad said. "But don't get caught up in expecting God to help. Sometimes he will need your help, and what he asks you to do will sometimes be a tremendous burden. Remember, he wouldn't ask you if you couldn't carry the load." He let us absorb his comment before he continued, "When you need to talk, you can also come to me. You don't have to rely on each other. I think I'll say goodnight to Mom and head to bed."

We said goodnight to my dad, then Angel said, "I need to go spend some time with Mom." She was silent for a moment. "It's been a good day. I finally feel like we are really together. Like we are on the same page."

"I've always been here. What do you mean?"

She bit her bottom lip while she thought about how to word it. "When we met, you were this farm boy who knew exactly who you were and where you were going. I was uprooted from my home and school and didn't know what was going to happen next. I've spent the last few months catching up and fitting in. Sorry, I'm not explaining it well. But I feel like we are seeing the same things now. Like we have the same goals."

"We should. We're practically engaged." She made a fist and hit my chest. Maybe I didn't understand what she was saying. In the first few months after we met, she had watched me chase my dreams. She also had to adjust to a new home, school, and life. That wasn't difficult because we had so much in common. We loved the outdoors, hunting, fishing, and shooting sports. She fit right in. She was a loving person who kicked ass when she needed to. The last few months had their ups and downs. Mostly downs, the up had been my relationship with Angel. I didn't tell her I'd give up everything to help her achieve her dreams. My biggest fear was that neither of us would get the chance to achieve them.

I had done enough thinking since the wreck, reaching no conclusions. I needed a good night's sleep.

"Come on. I'll walk you home." I kissed Angel on the top of her head.

*****

Angel

The moon was bright and made the early frost sparkle on everything in the dark. We heard cars from miles away traveling down unseen highways. It was strange how the sound carried on quiet, frosty nights.

That made the sound of the starting truck and the crunching gravel even louder as it pulled out of our drive and left the farm.

We entered the house through the kitchen. Dan had made it a habit to say goodnight to me and Mom. She was coming down the hallway with her night robe on.

"Who was that, Mom?" I asked.

Mom blushed as if she had been caught doing something wrong. "That was Roger. He's an old high school friend."

Dan squeezed my hand before Mon said anything else.

"I just walked Angel home, and wanted to say goodnight before I went back home," Dan said.

"Goodnight, Dan," she said as she went to the sink to fill a glass of water.

Dan pulled me back outside. After the door closed, we took several steps away from it. He said, "That was Roger Cross, the owner of the pills you found at the hospital."

"He wasn't just a friend; he was Mom's old high school boyfriend," I answered. "Is she getting back with him?"

"Or is he pushing himself onto her?" Dan asked.

"That's got to be it. Mom loved Dad. She wouldn't be looking to replace him so soon." I thought about it a little more before I asked, "Would she?"

"Grief makes people do crazy things."

"No kidding, what do I do?"

"Be there for her. Let her talk about her feelings. Talk about your feelings."

"We've done that."

"Then be there for her. Let her be there for you."

I said, "I feel more comfortable with you, and I don't have to articulate everything I'm saying for you to understand."

"But this is not about you. You're home safe now. Your mom is just now starting to really feel the loss of your dad. Before, she also had to worry about you in the hospital. Those two pains of worry and loss had to share space; now they don't."

"How did you get to be so smart?"

"Listening to Dad. The true job of a preacher is to be more of a counselor than to preach Sunday sermons."

I didn't know that part about preachers, but Dan was right about Mom, and I felt the need to go check on her right then.

"Good night, Dan." I stood on my tiptoes and kissed him. "I need to go check on Mom."

I rushed into the house, feeling a sense of urgency for some reason.

"Mom?"

No response. She wasn't in the kitchen or living room. I found her sitting on her bed. The covers looked like they had been slept on. I had made her bed and mine that morning. She was holding a pill bottle in one hand and a handful of pills in the other.

"Mom?" She didn't look up. I kneeled in front of her and took the bottle from her left hand. She didn't resist me. I held her other hand.

"Mom, put the pills back into the bottle. This is not the answer. I need you, Mom." My voice broke as I tilted her hand to pour the pills into the bottle. Then she broke down and cried, pulling me into a hug.

My cell phone was destroyed in the wreck. I'd had no need of it recently, because the two people I talked to were Dan and my mom. Mom's phone had been there when I needed it, but I kept my conversations and text messages short. I would ask Dan to take me to get another phone tomorrow. My first thought was to text Dan, but I had relied on him too much. I needed to figure this out on my own and to be here for Mom.

Mom finally calmed down, and she began talking. I didn't like what I heard. If she hadn't been so remorseful and suicidal, I would have walked out and gone back to Dan's. But she needed me. And I felt guilty for believing everything was about me this whole time. I didn't see her pain and suffering.

"I've tried to be strong. To move on, but it's so hard. Roger lost his wife to cancer this year. He understood my feelings. We hugged, and then the hug turned into a kiss. The next thing I knew, the hormones took over, and we were in bed."

"Mom! No, you slept with him?"

She slept with the guy. Less than two weeks after Dad died, she slept with another man. I wanted to slap her and call her a crazy bitch. But she was feeling remorse now. Mom needed me.

"I'm sorry, Angel," she said between sobs. "When I realized what we had done, I told him to get out. I didn't want to see him again. I started crying and ran to the bathroom."

She had just showered when Dan and I came home. She was still angry at Roger, she said. But then, when I walked in with Dan, it changed from anger to shame and a sense of betrayal.

"Jonathan and I argued a lot in the last few months. I didn't take any of this seriously. I thought it was a coincidence. When Dan's truck burned up and Lloyd was shot, that's when I took it seriously. Your dad went after them and got suspended. That's when I knew it was real. But it was too late. He was determined to fight back."

I let her talk. If I said out loud the things that were going through my mind, they wouldn't be helpful. Dan had told me to be there for her. So, I held her tight and let her talk. I wanted to scream at her for betraying Dad. For betraying me and being a weak whore.

I understood the hormone part. Dan and I had spent three days in a hotel room. We attempted a few sexual things, but the emotions and the physical pain stopped us. Dan insisted on waiting to have sex. Once we did, there would be no stopping that desire.

I don't know why, but I didn't think adults had those feelings. If they did, it meant Dan and I had lots to look forward to. Then I had a thought.

"Mom, did he rape you?"

"No!" she said, a little too sternly. Then a little milder, "If anything, I raped him." Then she began crying again.

"Really, Mom?" I whispered. I had to get that visual out of my head.

I was angry with her for betraying Dad. But she needed me. We hadn't talked about me and Dan running away, or running for our lives. I felt like she understood. But this? Sleeping with an old boyfriend? I wasn't sure I would ever understand. The pills I understood, and some small part of me wished I hadn't stopped her. That was the angry part of me. The part that loved my mom kept saying, "I understand. I'm sorry. I love you." And I held her until we fell asleep in the bed where she slept with her ex-boyfriend Roger.

Chapter 10

Dan

Angel and I walked around the farm that morning. Her ribs were healing, but hurt when we ran. Walking allowed us to talk, and she told me about her mom. There couldn't say much other than, "I'm sorry."

She decided she needed to spend more time with her mom, which meant less time with me. Unless I spent more time at her house. And that's what I did. I did my chores and went to Angel's. I told my parents that Angel wanted to spend more time with her mother, so we would spend more time at her house. They both agreed it was a good idea.

Sheriff Tatum assured us it was okay for us to go back to school after Thanksgiving. We returned to a familiar routine. It was a modified routine, though. Our Glocks were never far from us. They stayed by our beds at night. We wore shoulder holsters when we ran in the morning. They stayed in their cars during the school day. We didn't tell anyone about that, because it was illegal to carry them onto a school campus. Even if they were kept in our cars. Angel thought we were being paranoid, and I agreed, a little. We started practicing our fight training again as soon as Angel's ribs healed.

Donny Ray and Little John were still missing. Which had the confounding effect of making us feel relieved and look for them everywhere simultaneously.

Mrs. Cotton apologized to Roger, and he showed up more frequently, but never when Angel and I were home. Angel said her mom wasn't the same person after he left. She wasn't sure what was going on, but her mom was changing. She grew more distant when Roger left. We figured it was shame or embarrassment for moving on too quickly after her father's death.

The semester ended, and somehow, we passed. They weren't our normal straight-A grades. We had a couple of B's, but we were happy with the results. And then it was nearly Christmas.

I was in the feed room cleaning and reorganizing everything one morning after our morning run. Angel had gone home to check on her mom. She didn't like being away from her mom for long, and she checked in often.

Dad appeared in the doorway.

"Anything I can help with?"

"Not really, Dad. I'm just cleaning things up. Deciding what to do now that I won't be showing cattle in junior shows anymore."

"I thought you wanted to raise and sell show calves."

"That doesn't feel very important anymore. With college starting and Angel in my life, things have changed."

Dad picked up a bucket and turned it upside down and used it for a stool. That was a sign he wanted to talk about something, and I was finally ready. There were things bothering me I hadn't brought up to Angel.

I grabbed another bucket and did the same thing.

"How are you and Angel doing? Y'all have spent so much time at her house that your mom and I feel you are avoiding us."

"I'm sorry, Dad. We're not avoiding you. I promise. Angel and I are doing okay. It's Mrs. Cotton we are worried about. She's seeing her old high school boyfriend more, and every time he leaves, Mrs. Cotton's mood changes. Angel is really worried about her."

"Your mom and I have noticed the changes too. But she is a grown woman, so she will be okay. How's your relationship with Angel?"

"We are good. We love each other, and we want to build a life together. But this threat to our lives makes it difficult to see or plan a future."

"That's what I wanted to talk to you about. What are your plans now?"

"My school and college plans haven't changed. I'm not sure about my farm plans. I plan to keep raising cattle, but I'm just not sure about raising show calves anymore."

"Good. You haven't talked about college much lately, and your mom and I were getting a little worried."

It was time to tell Dad about my other plans. He wouldn't yell at me the way Mom did. He would ask pointed questions and make me look at the positives and negatives of a decision.

"Dad, I'm going to ask Angel to marry me. I know it's pushing things. We're still in high school, and it's early. But we've already made that commitment to each other."

I couldn't tell from his lack of response whether he had expected this. He was silent longer than normal. He often had another question ready to ask.

"Your mom found the rings. We knew you had something planned. We just don't want you to do anything rash. What are your plans?"

I hadn't hidden the rings. They were in one of my top dresser drawers.

"When did she find the rings?"

"A few days ago."

"I can't believe it took this long for us to have this conversation," I said.

"We wanted to have it sooner, but you have been busy with school and spending time with Angel and Mrs. Cotton."

"Is Mom angry?"

"Yes, and no. We love Angel. She is a perfect fit for you."

"But you think I am rushing things?"

"Yes, we do."

"I plan to propose on Christmas," I said. "But there is no date set. I don't want to set a date yet." I took a deep breath, because what I planned to say was not a conversation I wanted to have with Dad, and I certainly didn't want to have it with Mom. She had already told me she didn't want grandkids yet.

"We haven't had sex yet. But with the feelings and emotions we have, it's inevitable. And while we plan to wait until we're married, it may not happen. I want my commitment known to God, and you and Mom, in case we can't control ourselves."

It was Dad's turn to take a deep breath. "I take it y'all have talked about sex and marriage?"

"Angel and I want our first time to be with someone we love. We keep very little from each other. She loves the farm. And we both want half a dozen kids running around this place."

He shook his head. "I don't know whether to laugh or cry right now." He rubbed his eyes. Was that a tear? "Son, you have a way of saying things that disrupts my entire thought process. You have obviously talked about things at a much deeper level than we expected. Teenagers normally give in to the temptation so easily that we expected you already had sex. Most teens don't talk about it; they just do it."

He shook his head again. "You make me proud, Daniel. You've grown into a man these last few months. I give you my and your mom's blessing to ask Angel to marry you. But hold off setting the wedding date until after college."

He stood up and then walked out of the feed room. I sat on the feed bucket for a few more minutes sorting through that conversation. I wasn't prepared to be given permission to ask Angel to marry me. That should have been Mr. Cotton's responsibility. But he had told me once that it was Angel's decision, not her parents.

For Dad not to give me the lecture about moral values meant he either didn't believe me or he had a lot more faith in me than I had in myself. It had to be the latter. If he hadn't believed me, he would have lectured me. The timing of sex was wrong when we ran away. The emotional pain and physical pain combined did a number on us both. We were afraid for our lives and felt guilty for running away. We felt guilty for sleeping practically naked with each other, and I didn't want that guilty feeling hanging over our heads. We were so open with our parents; we didn't want to betray their trust more than we already had by running away.

I wasn't sure Mom was going to be okay with this, but if she hadn't already lectured me about the rings, then Dad had intervened. Maybe the danger that hung over us had everyone worried. That had to be it. They would rather us make mistakes and be home safe than push us away and let us make mistakes where we were in danger of being murdered. Angel and I were walking a tightrope. I think Dad wanted me to know they were right there with us.

Chapter 11

Dan

When I walked into the Cotton's, they were putting up their Christmas tree. It was the week before Christmas, and Angel had been asking her mom about the tree. She knew her mom wasn't feeling up to doing Christmas, but Angel was pushing her to stay busy and continue the normal routine.

Angel was becoming a workaholic. She was always busy and encouraged her mother to do things with her. She was seeing her mother change into something she didn't like. A dark, sullen, unhappy woman. If you worry about your problems and feel sorry for yourself, then worry becomes a little worm that burrows itself into your head and begins to eat. Soon it becomes so big you can't stand up or move or even see around it. It consumes you, and it slowly kills you. Activity is the best medicine. Walking, doing small chores, and celebrating each tiny accomplishment. Dad had taught me that, and I told Angel. We had talked about running and how much it helped us mentally to begin each day. Staying active didn't give you less time to think, but it kept you productive, and that was one less thing to worry about.

I stood in the doorway between the kitchen and the living room, watching them decorate the tree. The radio was playing, so they hadn't heard me come in. 'Mary, Did You Know' came on the radio and I started singing along with it. They jerked around in surprise and stared at me until I stopped after the first verse.

"I didn't know you could sing," Angel said.

"You have a beautiful baritone voice," Mrs. Cotton said.

Angel stood up and came to give me a hug. "Where did you learn to sing?"

"Church."

"Of course," she answered.

I helped finish decorating the tree and told as many corny 'dad' jokes as I could remember. It was something Dad used to do when Ben and I helped decorate the tree. It lightened the mood, and we would end up laughing hysterically at one of his jokes. And it worked today. Angel and her mom tried not to laugh, which made it worse, because they ended up laughing at each other.

Angel wanted to go Christmas shopping afterwards, so we went to Searcy. I texted Ben to invite him, but he was at work. He said he would see us on Christmas morning at home and that he might bring a friend.

We hadn't left the farm in days. We shared our shopping lists for the family and discussed options if we couldn't find the things we wanted. Then we told Mom and Dad and Mrs. Cotton where we were going shopping and how long we planned to be gone.

The traffic and stores were crazy. Driving the green machine, I set up higher, and I could see traffic easier. It helped me to avoid a collision at a red light because I could see that a car wasn't slowing down and ran the light. He was on his phone.

"I wish we could wrap these presents before we go home," Angel said.

"I have an idea. Let's go see Ben. I'll see if I can borrow his key so we can use his apartment."

"I haven't seen his apartment," she said.

"Neither have I." And I found it unsettling that I hadn't visited my brother at his new place in four months. Never mind that we had been busy and distracted.

Ben was scheduled to get off work in an hour. He said he was working more hours than he wanted because it was impossible to keep employees at a dollar store. He gave me his apartment key and said he would be there soon. We bought wrapping paper, tape, bows, and name tags while we were there.

We worked as a team. The presents were for our parents and Ben. We hadn't shopped for each other. We hadn't even discussed what we wanted.

Ben's presents were wrapped first. Just in case he came home early. Two presents were all Angel allowed me to wrap. She said I was too sloppy. So, she wrapped, and I put on bows and name tags.

We were wrapping up the last one when Ben got home. "Have you wrapped them all? What did you get me?" he asked teasingly.

"They're already wrapped, and you will have to wait," Angel told him.

"We should have bought him some groceries," I said. "Ben, your cabinets, and fridge are bare."

"Grocery shopping is on tomorrow's agenda," he answered. Pointing at the calendar on the fridge and the list beside it.

"I'm going out to eat tonight," Ben said. "Do you want to join us?"

"Us?" I answered. "We don't want to interrupt a date."

"It's not a date. I'm having dinner with some school friends. Come on, you decide while I change, or we will be late."

"Why not?" Angel answered, looking at me. "We have done nothing like this since your birthday."

I saw her flinch when she said it. It must have reminded her of her birthday.

Ben said, "I need to change clothes. I'll be right back."

"How will we fit in with actual college students?" I yelled after Ben.

"You'll fit in just fine. You're both taking AP classes and college classes half a day. Besides, y'all are more mature than some of my friends."

We went after texting our parents and letting them know what we were doing. Being impulsive was not something we had been able to do. We were going to a public place with a group of people. But we would still be cautious and on the lookout for our enemies. I hadn't thought of them as enemies before, but that is what they were.

There were eight of us around the table at the pizza place. Ben was right; we were more mature than his friends. There were three girls and two more guys. The conversations ranged from Harding's football team, professors, class assignments, to politics. Angel and I listened and answered a few questions. It was obvious Ben was a leader and well liked. He took charge of ordering and splitting the bill when it came time to leave. He even made sure they left a good tip. I was feeling a little melancholy. Ben had a new life, with a lot of friends, and it took me five months to discover it. We weren't best friends anymore; he had moved on and was growing into a different person than my older brother used to be. I missed his being around home, but I was proud of the man he was becoming.

I told Ben I was proud of him as he drove us back to his apartment in his car. He brushed it off as he was just being himself. Angel had a different view, though.

"That should be us, Dan. Instead, we are hiding and looking over our shoulders. It makes me, ugh, so angry that we can't live a normal life."

"I didn't mean to upset you, Angel. I've missed you and Dan, and I wanted to include you."

"It's not your fault, Ben. I mean, I'm happy you pulled out of the depression you were feeling this summer. It's just that I'm a little jealous."

I reached over the seat to grab Angel's hand.

Ben said, "I admire you, Angel. I respect both of you. I fell apart over Sarah's death, and she was Dan's ex-girlfriend, not mine. You and Dan have handled that plus more. If I had run away when y'all did, I don't know if I would have come home. I think I would have lost my faith in God. But according to Dad, you seem to have gained or renewed your faith. How?"

It wasn't a question that Angel or I expected. It was a surprise that Dad had noticed, because we hadn't told Dad about Angel's experience at the cemetery. We weren't the only ones who felt it that day.

After Angel went to the bathroom at Ben's, we sat and told him about the day we came home from running away. I told him about my argument with Mom and Dad. Angel told him about her breakdown after learning she had missed the funeral. We told him about going to the cemetery and the feeling that washed over us while we were there.

We sat quietly for a few minutes, letting Ben take in the story.

"Dad felt it," Ben said. "He said he knew he should let you be; that God had a plan and that everything you were going through was preparing you for something bigger. He felt God was testing your love and your resolve and testing him as well. Whatever you two do, He will support you, because he believes God has a plan for you."

"That explains a lot about Dad's behavior," I said. "Whenever I've expected him to lecture me, he hasn't. He told me he was proud of me. That I've become a man in the last few months."

"You're not the same happy-go-lucky brother I used to know," Ben said. "But looking over your shoulder all the time will do that to you."

Chapter 12

Angel

We were quiet on the way home. I was feeling overwhelmed by Ben's revelation about his dad.

Dan finally said, "Dad found me in the barn this morning and we had another conversation."

"What did he say?" We had expected to be lectured and grounded for life after running away. But they didn't. We waited for it even after they said they wouldn't.

"Basically, he said he supports us, and he is proud of the adults we are becoming."

"Is that everything?"

"No. But I can't tell you the rest without giving away a Christmas surprise," he said.

"A surprise for me?"

"It's a present for you. But it will surprise everyone."

"Oh. You can't leave me in suspense like this. Give me a hint."

"Nope. You'll have to wait."

We pulled onto the farm road, and before I could think of a comeback. He asked, "Where do the presents go? Your house? My house, or split in between?"

"You're mean. You can't change topics like that." I hit him lightly on the shoulder, and he smiled at me.

"Where do we go, Cotton Top?"

"Both, I guess. I don't look forward to Christmas without Dad. But we are having lunch at your house. I think it is good for Mom and me to have a few presents to open together, or with you there," I said hopefully.

"I'll be there if you want me there. My whole family will be if you want them."

"Just you," I said. "Mom and I both depend on you more than you realize."

"Okay, so let's take the presents to my house, then we will say goodnight at your house."

Even as an eighteen-year-old who no longer believed in Santa Claus, I still looked forward to Christmas morning.

This year was going to be tough without Dad, though. That's why I wanted Dan there. I loved him more than I could have imagined and hoped he liked the simple presents I bought for him. What do you get a guy who doesn't want or need anything?

Whenever I asked him what he wanted for Christmas, he began singing *All I want for Christmas is you!*

His teasing and singing thrilled me, but frustrated me at the same time. I finally asked his mom, and she gave me several practical ideas. The best idea was a new farm jacket. The one he used was stained with oil, grease, and paint, and one arm was ripped and the iron-on patch was peeling off. So, I ordered him a new Carhartt work coat online, wrapped it and put it under our tree. It wasn't enough, and it didn't express what I wanted to say to him.

We didn't run on Christmas morning, but we walked our usual path. Another Christmas without snow. I had never seen a white Christmas anyway, so that was normal. I woke up that morning very anxious, and I mentioned it to Dan.

He stopped and cupped my face with his hand. I leaned my head into his hand, and he leaned over and kissed me.

"There's nothing to be anxious about," he said after kissing me. "Everyone is here and safe. Ben and one of his college friends who couldn't go home for Christmas will be here later. And according to Sheriff Tatum, our enemies are still out of state."

"I know," I said, and grabbed his hand and started walking again.

"It's cold when we stop walking," I explained.

"I should have grabbed something besides my old work coat. It's got more holes than Mom's spaghetti strainer."

I laughed and smiled, knowing he wouldn't have to wear it much longer.

Mom was up and had coffee made when we came in. She also had biscuits in the oven and was making gravy. Biscuits and gravy was our Christmas morning tradition and one of Dad's favorite breakfast foods.

We both hugged Mom, and she said, for Dan's benefit, "I hope you like biscuits and gravy. It's our Christmas morning tradition."

I added quietly, "It was Dad's favorite breakfast, too."

He smiled at me and hugged me. One thing I loved about Dan was his ability to show love and support without saying a word. It was only right that I thought about Dad on Christmas morning. When Dan let me go, I turned and hugged Mom again, and we cried. Mom was holding a spoon out away from us, and Dan gently took it out of her hand and stirred the gravy.

"It's getting thick. I think it's almost done," he said.

She kissed me as she pulled away. Then she rubbed Dan on the back and said, "Thank you for looking after the gravy while Angel and I had a moment."

"You're welcome."

"Dan?" I asked, and batted my eyes at him.

"Yes?" He drew his reply out.

"Will you help me start a fire in the fireplace? That will make it feel a little more like Christmas."

We got the fire started and had breakfast around the fireplace. The house had central heat and air, so the fireplace was more for decoration. Mom told stories about our Christmases when I was younger. Then it was time to open the presents.

We opened presents at my house, then we walked to Dan's. Mom stopped in the kitchen to help Mrs. Brock, who was already preparing Christmas lunch. Dan and I went to the living room to say good morning to Mr. Brock. He was putting some last-minute presents under the tree.

Dan and I returned to the dining room and, without being asked, we set the dining table.

We put out plates, glasses, and silverware from the china cabinet. When we were finished, Dan reached into the pantry and pulled out a trash bag and handed it to me. He said, "I'll take out the trash if you put a new bag in."

It was a good morning. It was the happiest we had felt in a long time. I missed Dad, but Dan and his family made it fun. His dad was singing Christmas carols, and we would join in. Cookies and desserts were already made, but taking up room on the kitchen counters. Dan grabbed a folding table and set it up in a corner of the dining room. We moved the desserts out of the way.

Mrs. Brock asked Dan to take the turkey out of the oven and put the ham in. Everything was ready except for the ham.

Ben arrived with more presents and his friend. Her name was Lily, short for Liliia, and she told us she was from Ukraine. Which explained why she didn't go home for Christmas. She said the flight home was too expensive.

It was time to open presents. Dan and Ben took turns passing out presents. That was a tradition they had followed for as long as they could remember. When the presents were opened, I looked around and realized the only thing Dan had given me was a t-shirt with a female runner on it that said *Catch me if you can.* My breath just left me. Was that all he was getting me? I was disappointed until I looked up at him. He was looking at me and smiling. Everyone was looking at me, including Lily.

"I have one more gift for you, Angel."

He kneeled in front of me and took my right hand with his left hand.

"Dan, what are you doing?" This couldn't be what it looked like. I went cold and then hot.

He opened his right hand and held up a diamond ring. I'm not ready for this. And yet, I want this so badly. Do I say yes like I want to? Everyone disappeared except for me and Dan.

"Angelina Michelle Cotton, will you marry me?"

I slid off the couch into his arms. I kissed him hard until he finally pushed us apart.

"Is that a yes?"

I nodded. "Yes. But not anytime soon." I heard clapping then. Did everyone know except me?

"Of course," he said, smiling. "After college?"

"Yes," I said, letting go and looking at the ring.

"Let me put it on," he said.

I held out my shaking hand and saw the promise ring. "Let me take the promise ring off."

"It's okay. They are part of a set." He slid the ring on, and it fit together perfectly.

"A set?" I asked.

"I have the wedding band, too."

"Is this the conversation you had with your dad?"

"Probably so," Mr. Brock said, reminding me there were others present besides me and Dan.

I looked around the room. Dan's parents were smiling. Mom had her hands to her face. I couldn't tell if she was smiling, crying, or both. Ben was grinning from ear to ear. And Lily was staring at us. She didn't know what to think. Ben would have to do some explaining.

I kissed and hugged Dan again. Then I went to Mom. "I'm not ready for you to grow up," she said between sobs.

Chapter 13

Dan

It appeared that happiness in our lives is short-lived. Angel's mom left right after lunch to go home and meet Roger. We went for a ride on the four-wheeler through the woods. Mrs. Cotton called Angel an hour later and asked her to come home. She wanted to introduce her to Roger. He had visited at least once a week since Officer Cotton's funeral. We had a good idea of what they were doing when Angel wasn't there, so she stayed away until he left.

Neither of us wanted to meet the guy. He hadn't made a good first impression by providing Mrs. Cotton with painkillers. I dropped her off and went home to visit with Ben before he went back to Searcy.

I had been talking to Ben and Lily for ten minutes when we heard a commotion from the garage and a scream. Ben and I both jumped up and met Angel running through the mudroom, screaming.

"What's wrong, Cotton Top?" I asked as I caught her in my arms.

"She's moving to Clarendon to live with Roger." She mumbled into my chest.

"What?" My heart dropped.

I heard Mom ask, "Ben? What's going on?"

"Her mom is moving to Clarendon with Roger."

"Oh no. Lloyd?"

Dad walked in and said, "Come into the living room and sit down. Let's talk this out."

Did Mrs. Cotton have this planned? Just as Angel and I had become engaged, was she ripping us apart? My mind raced, looking for solutions to our newest obstacle as we moved to the living room.

Dad had a calming voice in frantic situations. I prayed he had a solution now. "Now tell us what happened?"

"Mom introduced me to Roger. Then she told me she was moving to Clarendon to be with him. I can either go or stay here." We were sitting on the couch. Dad sat in his favorite chair. I had my arm around Angel, and she was leaning her head against my chest. Mom was sitting on the other side of me and had her hand on my back.

Angel looked up at me and asked, "Is God testing us?"

"No." Mom, Dad, and Ben all chorused.

"God doesn't test people. He prepares. He gives you obstacles to strengthen you and prepare you for what is coming," Dad said.

Angel and I never stopped looking at each other. "I have to go with Mom, don't I?"

I nodded. "To protect her from herself and those pills, which Roger has an abundance of."

"I can't believe we just got engaged, and a few hours later, I'm leaving you." She was crying again.

"We'll figure it out. You take the Mustang, and we'll alternate weekends visiting each other. We're a phone call or a text away."

Angel squeezed me in a hug and buried her face in my chest. She took a deep, shuddering breath and said, "I don't know what God is preparing us for, but if it hurts worse than this, I don't know if I can handle it."

I looked up at Dad. He was wiping a tear from his eye. "I'm proud of you two. You didn't hesitate to make the right decision."

"There wasn't another decision to be made, Dad," I said. Without Angel, there would be a deep hole in my heart when we were separated. It would only be filled when we were together.

Chapter 14

Angel

Dan finally met Roger. We walked to my house, my former home, after my meltdown. Logically, I knew I needed to move with Mom, but my heart wanted to stay with Dan. I knew Mom was still grieving for Dad. We talked about it regularly. I knew she liked Roger because she talked about their high school days and how close they had been.

I'm not sure I understood her decision to move in with Roger. Nothing was said about marriage, and I didn't ask. I was still in shock.

I looked at my ring finger. It took me a while to get used to wearing a promise ring. It will take a while longer to get used to wearing an engagement ring. I still can't believe our parents let us get engaged. There was something at work here that I didn't understand. Is this how God works? The decision to accept Dan's proposal was easy and joyful. The decision to move with Mom had been right. But it was painful.

Dan and I decided Roger wasn't the beast we thought him to be. He was gentle and supportive of Mom. He was tall, with graying hair and gray eyes. I tried to stare him down, but he looked at me with kindness and patted my shoulder.

He said we just needed to bring some clothes. This would be a test run, to make sure we could get along. If something didn't work out, we could always move back. I knew that. This was the first house that felt like home, and I wanted to live here with Dan.

"There's a spare bedroom you will use, Angel. I'll call Robby and have him clean it up a little."

"Who's Robby?"

"He's my son. He's about your age." I remembered Mom telling me about her breakup with Roger after high school. His previous girlfriend before Mom discovered she was pregnant. He broke up with Mom and married the pregnant one. Robby must be that child. Well, he wouldn't be a child if he were my age.

Dan was being quiet, and it bothered me. I wanted him to talk to me, to tell me I was doing the wrong thing. I wanted to run away again, but

I couldn't. Losing another parent was not an option. I had to be there for Mom.

*****

My first impression of the Cross home was that it was stuck in time. The furniture and pictures were older than I was. The curtains and shades were closed, and the house felt dreary.

Moving to Clarendon felt like a huge mistake to me. Our farmhouse was open and bright. There were beautiful views out every window. But the Clarendon neighborhood was small and closed in. It was depressing. I could almost reach out the window of my room and touch the house next door. It wasn't really that close, but compared to the farm, it was. We drove for two hours, and I had to remind myself the whole way that I was doing this to protect Mom.

The only bright thing in the entire house turned out to be Robby. His bright smile, good looks, and cheerful attitude made him easy to like.

I had dropped my gym bag on the bed and looked around the sparse room. It had a bed, a small chest, and a tiny closet. I turned to find Robby in the doorway, leaning against the frame, smiling at me.

"Welcome to Clarendon. It's not the end of the world, but I'm sure it's somewhere near here." He smiled at his joke, stood up straight, and stuck out his left hand. "I'm Robert, but everyone calls me Robby. You must be Angel."

I smiled. "Hi Robby. Yes, I'm Angel." I held out my left hand, and he shook it and then stopped. He turned my hand over to look at the engagement ring. "I got engaged this morning. Then Mom announced she was moving in with your dad."

"And now you're here." He finished for me. "I imagine it's the last place you want to be. Do you have a picture of your fiancée?" he asked.

I showed him a picture of Dan that I had taken at the fair while he was showing one of his calves. It was a side profile shot, and the intensity of his look made him look handsome. I had cropped and enlarged the picture until I got it right. Then I remembered we hadn't taken engagement pictures. It was Christmas, and I was still shocked our parents had allowed it to happen.

"Damn girl. I'm jealous," Robby said.

"Wait. Are you jealous of him? Or me?"

"I'm jealous that you have each other. It must be nice to have someone to talk to."

I sat down on the bed. "We've been through a lot together. He rarely left my bedside when I was in the hospital," I said. He was tall, ruggedly handsome, wearing old jeans, worn-out boots, and a camo Henley shirt. "You'll find someone, but you have to get out into the world to find them."

"I only seem to attract guys. Please keep it a secret. You can't be a redneck and be gay. You are the only person in Clarendon I've told."

He became extremely nervous. "Come on. There's nothing to do here. Let's go for a ride in your beautiful Mustang, and I'll show you around town."

I didn't move. "Why are you telling me your deepest secret? We've just met," I asked.

His smile disappeared. "Because I'm tired of keeping secrets. And if you're going to live here, there can be no secrets between us. I'm going to need your help. Let's go for that ride, and I'll tell you everything."

Clarendon appeared to be a town made up of people who couldn't afford to escape, or lacked the motivation to escape. I missed the farm already, and I'd only been gone a few hours.

Robby showed me the dollar stores and the Mad Butcher. That's where they bought most of their groceries and supplies. Everything in town was closed for Christmas. Occasionally, he could go to Stuttgart, to Walmart, and do some real shopping.

"That's not real shopping," I said.

"It is for me. The school and the sawmill are the largest employers in town. Dad used to work at the sawmill until his wreck and he became disabled."

"He doesn't look disabled."

"He is. Broke his back in four places. He says he is in constant pain. Some days are better than others. That's why there is a miniature pharmacy on the table beside his recliner."

I scowled at the memory. "Mom almost overdosed on one of his pills when I was in the hospital recovering from the wreck where Dad was murdered."

He didn't speak for a minute. "That's what we need to talk about. Turn here. You'll get up onto the levee and follow it until you see the launch ramp for the river. It's my favorite place to park when I get to use the truck."

It was getting dark. I couldn't believe that I started Christmas morning living in a house where I could see the Little Red River, and I ended it by watching the muddy water of the White River from a launch ramp. Besides us, there was one truck and boat trailer in the parking area.

"Who goes fishing on Christmas Day?"

"Who knows? It's not Christmas without Mom," Robby said. "Neither of us felt like celebrating this year. No tree and no presents. We just ignored it."

"I'm sorry about your mom. What happened?" I asked.

"Cancer. She fought it for four years. The bills are horrendous. Dad pays a few hundred dollars a month toward them. Even if he lives to be a hundred and fifty, he will never pay them off. He's thinking about filing for medical bankruptcy. But we don't know if that will help. He can't afford an attorney to get the process started."

"I'm sorry. That's something we have in common. We've both lost a parent this year."

"How did you lose your dad?"

It took me half an hour to tell the story. Robby never interrupted me and listened intently. I decided I liked him.

When I finished my horror story about Donny Ray and Little John, he said, "They are from Des Arc. That's not far from here."

"I was nervous when we drove through there. I was afraid someone would recognize me. Dan has been the one thing that has held me together. How have you handled losing your mom?"

"I've had four years to prepare for it. It was almost a relief when she died. She didn't have to hurt and suffer anymore. And I don't have to watch her get weaker and weaker. But I don't think Dad is going to last much longer. He takes his oxycodone as if it's candy. Then he buys the illegal stuff to make it through the month until he gets his prescription again. I've had to drive him to the emergency room twice because he took too much. Every day, I come home from school at lunch to check on him, just to make sure he's alive."

"I'm sorry," I said.

"That's where I need your help. To watch him. To keep him from overdosing."

"Isn't it supposed to be the other way around? Shouldn't our parents be worrying about us doing drugs?" I asked. "That's why I came with Mom. Your dad gave her some pills, and she almost overdosed on one pill. I have to watch my mother, and you want me to watch your dad too?" The more I thought about it, the angrier I became.

"I'm not asking you to do my job for me. I'll watch your mom too, but I need help. Sleep is not something I do much, and I wake up every two to three hours at night just to make sure he's breathing. One morning, I'm afraid I'll wake up and find him dead in bed."

I relaxed and calmed down. "I'm sorry. It's like we both have been living with own fears. I was afraid Dan and I were going to be murdered, and we are still looking over our shoulders, and you were afraid your dad was going to accidentally off himself and you're still watching him. They'll be together most of the time, and we can take turns watching."

"Dad has his good days and his bad days, but lately, he's had more bad than good."

Chapter 15

Angel

It was dark by the time we stopped talking. Was it odd that I felt like I had known him my whole life? Maybe it was because we experienced similar circumstances of losing a parent. We had reached an agreement when we left the river, though. We would help each other watch our parents. Losing another parent was not an option.

I missed Dan and drove back to the farm the next day. I kept thinking of him as my boyfriend, but he was my fiancé now. It will take time to get used to the diamond engagement ring and calling him my fiancé. I may have moved away, but my love and my life were on the farm. The farm had become and would always be my home. I didn't know anyone at this school besides Robby. I took my promise ring and engagement ring off and put them on my necklace. It was easier than answering why I was wearing a two-carat diamond ring, or worse, having people think it was fake. I wasn't looking for a guy. Dan was all I wanted.

I started the spring semester of my senior year at yet another school. Robby and I took a selfie together that morning to remember the day. I looked at it and said, "That's a good one."

"Do you notice anything odd about this picture?"

"It's a good picture," I repeated. "Come on, I have to go to the office and pick up my schedule."

He didn't move. He was staring at his phone. "We could be brother and sister," he said.

"For all practical purposes, we are stepbrother and stepsister." He grabbed his backpack, and we headed out the door. Mom and I had gone to the school the week before to sign me up for classes.

I picked up my schedule at the front office and was told the principal would like to meet me. The secretary told me to go on into the office. There were two men in the office.

"Excuse me. Good morning. I'm Angelina Cotton. I was told you wanted to meet me?"

They both stood, and the man behind the desk said, “Good morning, Angelina. I’m Principal Martin, and this is Coach Pugh.” I sensed someone behind me and turned to find a tall, black girl there.

Coach Pugh said, “And this young lady behind you is Tricia. We understand you are interested in running track. Is that right?” I moved over to let Tricia in.

“Yes, sir,” I said and was echoed by Tricia. I looked at her and smiled.

“We don’t have a track, as you may have noticed. We have a few football guys who would benefit from running track. But we don’t have many young ladies interested. Are you any good?” asked the principal.

Tricia spoke first. “I won a couple of two-hundred-meter races my sophomore year. Placed well in the four hundred, but I couldn’t beat the seniors.”

“And you’re a junior,” Coach Pugh said.

“Yes, sir.”

“What about you, Angelina?”

“Please call me Angel. I won the district meet in the 800 meters for Wynne last year and placed third at state. I won the state cross country championship for Heber Springs last fall.”

Coach Pugh and the principal looked at each other. Principal Martin said, “I was prepared to tell you both that we didn’t offer track. But your talent level says we would be missing an opportunity not to work something out. Coach Pugh, you know we don’t have a budget for track. What do you think?”

“I’ll call a few boosters to see if I can raise some money for uniforms and gas to go to a few meets.”

“If you can raise the money, I’ll talk to the superintendent.”

“Thank you,” I said.

Tricia said, “Thank you, Mr. Martin. Thank you, Daddy.”

As we stepped out into the hallway, Tricia turned to me and said, “And thank you, Angel. Without you, I wouldn’t be running track.”

“Is Coach Pugh your dad?”

“Yes, and the school can’t say no to the two of us. They need another girl’s sport to balance the athletic program. I am so glad you are here.”

We started running together the next morning. I was going to run my normal five miles, but Tricia was a sprinter and wanted to do sprints on the football field. We alternated days. I knew sprinting would help me in my races. The best eight-hundred-meter runners sprinted from the start to the finish line.

The time I spent with Dan passed too quickly, and the time I spent in Clarendon passed too slowly. Robby stared at our selfie every morning when we drove to school. It took less than five minutes to drive there, but it bothered me he stared at it.

"Why do you stare at our picture?"

He glanced at me and then turned his phone off. "What if we were really brother and sister?"

"There's no way. You know who your parents are, and I know who mine are. What makes you think there's even a chance?"

He got a little antsy and turned to face me. "When's your birthday?" I told him, and he replied, "I was born two months before you. My mom and dad broke up, and Dad dated your mom until he found out my mom was pregnant. Then, he went back to her and got married. What if you had been conceived during that time?"

"Impossible," but I was remembering a conversation I had with Mom. It wasn't impossible. I didn't want it to be possible. "It can't be. Mom dated Dad while he was home on furlough for two weeks. She discovered she was pregnant several weeks later."

I was starting to like Robby like a brother. Was it possible that we were actually half-brother and sister? I loved Dad so much, and I know he loved me. Could this be possible?

"Let's do one of those Ancestry DNA tests. And we will see if it's possible," Robby said, a little subdued now. I could see he wanted this. He had no one left in his life except his dad. He didn't have any aunts, or uncles or grandparents. I think he desperately wanted it to be true.

"Okay, you get the test. I think it's a waste of time. Either way, I'll always be your stepsister, in a way."

I'd hurt his feelings. I could tell by the look on his face. "It's not that I don't want to be your sister. But I loved my dad. He was my hero. How would you feel if I told you that your father wasn't the one who conceived you?"

I pulled into a parking spot at school and parked the Mustang. My comment got through to him. He leaned back in the seat and sighed. "I'm sorry. The idea of you being my sister has consumed me so much I didn't think about your dad. I didn't mean to put your dad down."

"You order the test and I'll take it. Just to prove to you we aren't related."

Coach Pugh and Mr. Martin called a short meeting with the boys and girls track team that morning. There were four boys, Tricia, and me on the track team. Coach had found three track meets we could take part in. He looked at me and Tricia when he said, "If you're good enough to go to district and state meets, then we will see what we can do."

*****

Dan

Telling Angel that she needed to go with her mom was easy. Letting her go was the most difficult thing I think I've ever done. The void that was normally filled by Angel grew larger each day she wasn't with me. The weekends we spent together didn't fill it.

She had a responsibility to be with her mother. I thought I understood responsibility, because I'd been responsible for the farm and raising show cattle for several years. I accepted that responsibility with love and pride. Angel's responsibility wasn't the same. I could sell the cattle and rent out the farm. You don't walk away from your parents when they need you. They wouldn't do that to you. But it was hard not to despise the reason for Angel's responsibility. I didn't despise her mom; it was Mr. Cross that I despised.

Then Angel explained the situation to me. She explained why he needed the drugs. Robby had explained it to Angel the day they met. He was open and honest about losing his mom to cancer, and about being frightened about losing his dad.

I felt like an idiot for despising a man who wasn't being properly cared for by the same medical system I wanted to join. Did that make me a hypocrite? A hypocrite wouldn't change their mind based on evidence to the contrary, so I became determined to learn everything I could to make a difference with my medical training.

I was disappointed in myself. I was pouting like a child because I missed my girlfriend. My fiancée. Dad used to tell me as a kid to "suck it up, buttercup." Then he would tell me and Ben to look around. "You'll find at least five more people you know with worse situations than you - feel sorry for them, not yourself. Then when you're through feeling sorry for them, offer to help them."

Dad was right. Four of those people were living in one house, and the most important one who needed my help, and not my pity, was Angel. The second was Robby. They needed my support and understanding, not me feeling sorry for myself or them.

It turned out that I was going to have a major distraction. The paramedic coursework was going to require an additional three hundred hours of clinical and internship work to get done during the spring semester. I would go to classes all day and work an additional twenty or more hours per week at night and on the weekends. There was no time for a pity party. I was going to need it for sleep.

Chapter 16

Angel

Instead of alternating weekends like we had planned, I ended up driving to the farm on most weekends. Dan's schedule had become overwhelming for him. He had high school classes in the morning, EMT classes in the afternoon, and lab and internship work in the evenings and every other weekend. Plus the farm work, which I helped him with when I was there. I didn't care what we did as long as we were together.

Robby and I worked out a plan where I would check on our parents during the week, and he would hang around on the weekends when I was gone. It wasn't fair. But he said it allowed him to relax more, now that someone else was helping to watch.

I didn't mind the one-way visitation. It got me away from a house where the feeling in the air was one of 'we're sitting here waiting to die.' Robby and I both hated that feeling. We suggested getting out and going to dinner or even for a walk, and they declined. I couldn't talk to Mom about how worried I was because Roger was always there. He was too kind to make a fuss or argue. But he refused to see that sitting in one place all day was killing him.

The first track meet of the year was at Brinkley, a school in a nearby town, which we had gone to practice a few times so we could get the feel of a proper track. The boys' team members weren't into the practice or the competition. There were two running backs, a quarterback, and a receiver from the football team. They focused on the 100-and 200-meter races. Tricia and I ran the two hundred, four hundred, and eight-hundred-meter races.

The boys' team had one member place second in the one-hundred-meter race. The rest did not place in either race. They weren't prepared for the competition. Tricia placed second in the two-hundred meters and 400-meter races. I was fifth and third. But eight-hundred meters is where we shined. I won by ten meters, and Tricia, who was tired from the other races, struggled for another second-place finish.

Coach Pugh was not happy with his football players turned track team. He made them watch and cheer for Tricia and me. Our girls' team, with just two members, placed second out of five teams. The boys' team placed last.

I was often aggravated with Dan. I was always the one who started the conversations between us. It was me who texted or called. But I also knew his schedule. More importantly, I knew the breaks in his schedule. So, I was surprised when I got a text from him.

Hey gorgeous. How did the track meet go? I'm on a bathroom break.

I texted him back with my results.

Great job! I love you. Got to go.

It made me feel better. I knew he was thinking about me. Tricia and I gathered our stuff and found Coach Pugh and the boys. He was lecturing them again. When he saw us coming, he stopped and asked me, "Angel, what does it take to be a champion? She knows because she won the state cross country championship last fall."

"Hard work," I answered. "My fiancée and I ran five miles every morning at five a.m. The cross-country race is only three miles. Three miles is easy when you know you can do five. You can't sprint ninety of the one hundred meters and expect to win. Sprint for one hundred and ten meters. You don't finish at the finish line; you finish after the finish line."

"That's it, guys. You get into shape. You practice and then execute." Coach Pugh said. "It's the same thing in football. You push past the goal line. Got it?"

"Yes, sir."

I was not a two hundred meter or a four-hundred-meter runner, but Tricia was. She placed second at the district track meet in the two-hundred meters and won the four-hundred-meter race. She placed second behind me in the eight-hundred. We were sitting in the bleachers waiting for the guys to run the four-hundred-meter relay when Tricia stood up and yelled, "Jerome! Up here."

A young black man waved back and lifted a McDonald's bag up. She looked at me and said, "Jerome is my cousin. I texted him and asked him to bring us some cheeseburgers. I'm starving."

"Good thinking," I said. "Did you get a couple for me?"

"Of course I did."

She hugged Jerome, and he said, "Long time, no see, cousin."

"Six months. That's not very long. Ask me how I did today?"

"How did you do?"

She told him and finished by adding, "And my teammate beat me in the eight hundred."

"You don't sound upset that she beat you."

"I'm not. Without her, we wouldn't have a track team. She's helped me get better at the sprints."

She introduced me, and then we sat and ate our cheeseburgers. When we finished, Jerome looked at me and asked, "Aren't you staying with Roger Cross?"

"Yeah." I was suspicious. "How did you know?"

"Don't worry about that." He handed me the McDonald's bag and said, "Just take this to him and tell him Jerome sent it."

"What's in here?"

"Just a couple more cheeseburgers, that's all." He turned to his cousin. "Tricia, I've got to go. It was good to see you. Keep up the good work."

As he walked away, I started to open the bag, but Tricia put her hand over mine. "Don't open that bag. Put it in your backpack, give it to your stepdad, and pretend you know nothing about it."

I realized then what was in the bag. I had become a drug courier for Roger. These were the street drugs Robby had mentioned.

"Dammit, Tricia, did you know this was going to happen?"

"No, I promise I did not know. I just thought I could get him to bring us some lunch."

I threw the bag into my backpack, leaned back, and stared at the track.

"Angel, I'm sorry. I didn't know. Please believe me."

"I believe you. I'm just mad about the whole situation Roger is in. Our whole medical system sucks."

I was angry throughout the bus trip back to Clarendon. I couldn't call it home, because I had decided to move back to the farm after graduation, whether Mom moved with me or not. How did I end up becoming a drug courier for Roger? I wanted to throw them away, but I had seen for myself how much he needed them. On the one hand, I blamed Roger for this. On the other hand, I understood Dan's view that it was our broken medical system that caused it. Even after rationalizing this, I was still angry, and the worst part was I didn't know who to be angry at.

Tricia even suggested that I call the cops on her cousin. But I explained Roger needed the pills. I couldn't do that.

"How did Jerome know who you were and that you would be with me?"

"Roger, probably," I said. "There's only us two of us on the team. We train together. It's a reasonable guess."

"Yeah, but how did he know?"

"I tell Mom everything about our meets, and since she's always with Roger. He hears everything I tell her," I said.

"Okay. That makes sense."

The house was quiet and dark when I pulled into the drive, even though the sun was setting. I unzipped my backpack and took the bag with the pills out. I could have called them drugs, but I preferred to think of them as pills because it sounded more like medicine. But no amount of justification changed the fact that they were illegal.

I entered the house, and Mom and Roger both looked up from their permanent perches on the recliners in front of the television. They never moved.

"How was your track meet?" Mom asked.

"I won," I replied and tossed the bag on Roger's table. "Jerome sent you some cheeseburgers. Don't ever use me as your courier again."

To Mom's credit, she said, "Roger? Do you know how much trouble she could get into having those on school property?"

"I'm sorry," he said. "I ran out this morning, and it was going to be two days before I could get any delivered here. Forgive me Angel. I didn't mean to put you at risk. But thank you for bringing them."

"I'm going to take a shower," I said and went to my room. Robby had been listening from the hallway and turned and walked to my room.

"I'm sorry he did that to you," he said sheepishly, looking down at his hands. That's when I noticed he was holding a piece of paper. "I got an email today and printed this off." He held it out to me.

"What is it?" I asked.

"DNA results."

"Really? Today is not the day for this. Just tell me the results." I hadn't intended to raise my voice. "Sorry, I didn't mean to raise my voice."

"Yes, you did, and I don't blame you."

I just stared at him. He understood. "Has he used you like that?"

"All the time," Robby replied.

I sat on my bed and patted the spot beside me. "I guess it's my turn to say I'm sorry."

He sat beside me.

"What's the printout say?"

"Read it," he said.

"What did yours say?" I was nervous about what his answer was going to be. I liked Robby, and wouldn't mind having him for a brother, but that meant my dad wasn't my real dad.

"Are you sure you want to know?"

"Let's get this over with," I responded.

"It said I have a biological half-sister. If yours says you have a half-brother, then we know my guess was right."

I opened the letter and read it until I found its listing of siblings. One biological half-brother. My life was a lie. Robby was right.

He grabbed the printout and read it. "Hi, sis," he said hesitantly. He already knew how I felt about it.

I grabbed the letter from him and stomped into the living room. I felt my face getting hot. "Mom, I can't believe you have lied to me my whole life." I threw the letter at her. "Robby and I did a DNA test. We're half brother and sister."

That's when I started bawling. I ran back to my room and started packing clothes. I was going to Dan's.

Mom was knocking on my door. "Angel, let's talk about this."

I could tell from her voice that she was upset now. I zipped up the gym bag, and opened the door and let her in, but I slipped under her arms when she tried to hug me and ran down the hall.

Roger and Robby both called after me as I ran out the door. I started the Mustang, backed into the street, and squalled the tires as I left. The Mustang fishtailed as I rounded a corner and almost hit a mailbox. That caused my body to tingle with the adrenaline rush of fear. I slowed down. I realized a wreck was the last thing I needed. It did not stop me from driving into the sunset and bawling my eyes out at the same time.

My phone started ringing. Mom was calling. I turned the phone off, not wanting to talk to any of them right now. I wanted to be with Dan. I turned my phone back on to call him. But it started ringing before I could call him. This time, it was Robby.

I turned it off again and threw it on the passenger floorboard. I would have to surprise Dan.

Chapter 17

Angel

Dan was waiting for me when I reached the farm. Mom and Robby had both called him.

"Why didn't you call me?" He asked.

"I tried. But Mom and Robby wouldn't stop calling, so I turned the phone off."

"And threw it on the floor," he said as he grabbed my gym bag, backpack, and phone from the car. "How are you doing? It looks like you've had time to calm down."

"Everything hit me at once today," I told him as I hugged him.

"Tell me about it before we go in and talk to Mom and Dad."

I told him about Jerome and the pills, about my conflicting feelings of throwing away the pills or delivering them to Roger. Then Robby shared the DNA information, and I fell apart.

"Thinking about you and your parents helped me settle down," I told him. "You and Ben are adopted, but you still love your parents."

"Officer Cotton loved you. He was your father. Forgive me for saying this, but Roger was just a sperm donor." Dan took a deep breath. "Your dad died protecting you. There is no greater love than that."

Dan was right. Dad died protecting me. I was so tired from crying, I couldn't find the strength to cry anymore.

"I know. But the shock of finding out. Everything hit me the wrong way. I knew you would understand, and I missed you."

"I missed you too, Cotton Top. Come on. Mom saved you some dinner. And I need to let your mom and Robby know you made it safely."

When I came back to the farm on the weekends, I stayed in Ben's room. If Ben was home, which was rare, I stayed in Dan's room and he slept on the couch. I had thought about sleeping in my old house, but Dan's mom reminded me I was still be in danger and would be safer in their house. I'm sure the real reason was to eliminate the temptation of Dan and me sleeping together because we all knew Dan wouldn't let me stay there by myself.

Mrs. Brock hugged me as soon as I entered the kitchen. She didn't jump in asking me questions about why I was here on a Thursday night instead of Friday. She asked whether I was hungry. I answered yes, of course. The last thing I ate was the two little cheeseburgers Jerome gave me. Dan took my bags to Ben's room and returned to the dining room to sit with me while I ate.

We talked very little while I ate pot roast and mashed potatoes smothered in brown gravy. I hadn't realized how hungry I was until I took the first bite.

After I ate, Dan took my dishes to the kitchen while I used the toilet in the mudroom. I had spent enough time with Dan's parents to know I was going to be asked about what had happened today. Mr. Brock had told me that most of his job as a minister was being a counselor. The type of counselor varied from a grief counselor to a relationship counselor.

They were gentle with their questions and made it feel more like a conversation than an interrogation. I'd had time to think on the drive to the farm after exploding in anger. I was sure they had already talked to my mom. They knew the story, but wanted to make sure I was okay.

Mr. Brock stood as Dan and I entered the room. He motioned for me to give him a hug. "Angel, how are you feeling?"

"I've had time to calm down. I think I overreacted. It's just that today has been very... emotional."

"I'm not sure you overreacted," he said as we sat down. "You learned a moral code from your dad. You learned what was right and what was wrong. Transporting illegal drugs under any situation is wrong, but you already knew that, and you had a right to be angry for being put into that position. I won't tell you that you were right or wrong for taking the drugs to Roger. But it's certainly a moral conflict anyone would have, or should have. Finding out he was your biological father after putting you through that moral conflict caused you to be angry. The dad that raised you taught you a moral code, and now the dad that contributed to your creation forced you to break that code without even asking. I'm afraid I wasn't very polite to your mom when she told us what happened. You had every right to be angry. I know you're eighteen and legally an adult, but parents shouldn't use their children that way without asking politely."

I was shocked. He took my side and expressed my feelings in such a way that it was clear why I had reacted the way I did. "Thank you," I said.

Normally, he was quiet and unemotional. But, he was angry for me. And I could see his emotions. His face was red, and his lips were tight.

"Jonathan was your dad. He loved you and raised you and was there when you needed him. Roger hasn't contributed to your upbringing. I'm not a fan of people with weak moral character," he said.

"Lloyd," Mrs. Brock cautioned him.

Mr. Brock sighed. "I'm sorry for preaching. You were put into a difficult situation, and that made me angry. He shouldn't have done that. Now. If you will excuse me, I think it's time for me to retire and read my Bible and ask the Good Lord for forgiveness."

I stood and gave him another hug before he left. I felt better than I had all evening, but I was also exhausted. After he left the room, I said, "I wasn't expecting that."

Mrs. Brock said, "You heard the mild Cliff Notes version."

Dan added, "I'm afraid your mom and Roger heard the hellfire and brimstone version."

I leaned into Dan and said, "At least I know I'm loved here."

He kissed me on the top of my head and wrapped his arm around me. "I love you, Cotton Top."

Chapter 18

Dan

My phone, lying on my nightstand, rang a little after three a.m. in the morning. I hadn't turned it off since Angel moved to Clarendon. I looked at the caller ID. Why was Robby calling me? I remembered Angel hadn't turned her phone back on.

"Why are you calling me in the middle of the night?"

"I need to talk to Angel."

It sounded as if he was upset. "She doesn't want to talk to you right now, Robby. What's going on?"

"Dad's dead. He overdosed. They've taken her mom to the hospital. There was something wrong with the pills," he said. His voice was shaking.

"Oh no. Robby, I'm so sorry. Let me go wake her. Hold on." I put the phone against my chest and went to Ben's room. I flipped the light switch on.

"Angel?" She sat up immediately.

"What's going on?"

"It's Robby. You need to talk to him." I handed her my phone.

"I'll call him in the morning."

"This can't wait. Talk to him. I'm waking Mom and Dad."

The look on her face expressed fear as I turned to go. "Robby?"

I stepped into the hallway when she screamed. Mom was already in the hallway. "Roger overdosed, and they've taken Angel's mom to the hospital."

"I'll wake your dad. You calm Angel down." She was still screaming. My phone was lying on the bed. I picked it up. "Robby, are you still there?"

"Yeah." He was crying now.

"I'll call you back. I've got to calm Angel down." Not waiting for a response, I hung up and focused on Angel.

She had rolled onto her side and was crying into a pillow. She stopped screaming. I lay down and put my arm over her and started talking to her.

"I'm here for you, Angel. Calm down. Your mom is going to be okay. We need to find out where they took her, so we can be there for her. Pull yourself together? Crying is not helping her or you."

Dad stepped into the room. He was dressed in dress slacks and a matching suit jacket, but no tie. "Where are they taking her?" He asked.

"I don't know. I told Robby I'd call him back after Angel calmed down." Angel was still crying, but rolled over and sat up.

"Angel, pull yourself together. Dan, call Robby back and find out where they took her. Then, you both need to get dressed. We need to be on the road in ten minutes."

Angel had stopped crying. "Okay." She sniffled, and then asked, "Dan, where's my phone?"

I had put it on the nightstand and plugged it in to charge when I brought her bags into the room last night. But I hadn't turned it back on. It was a good thing I had.

"On the nightstand. It should be fully charged."

"I'll call Robby," she said.

Dad left the room, and I followed him to get dressed. It took a whole ten minutes for us to get ready and get into the Escalade. Mom was driving.

Robby said they were taking her to Baptist Hospital. He stayed in Clarendon, waiting for the coroner to come and take his dad's body.

I called our local dispatch on the non-emergency number, and they helped me find where the ambulance was going. Baptist had a main hospital in Little Rock and a smaller hospital in North Little Rock. They were going to North Little Rock.

Angel was quiet. She was looking straight ahead, but she wasn't crying. I reached for her hand, and we wrapped our fingers together.

"I keep telling myself it's not my fault, even though I brought him the pills," she said. "That was Robby's fear the first day we met. That he was going to overdose. So, it was probably inevitable."

She hadn't changed the direction she was looking. Dad had turned in the front seat and was listening. We didn't say anything. There was only the sound of the blinker as Mom turned off Hiram Road onto Highway 110.

"Robby said Roger took two pills and Mom took one. That was nothing unusual. It was almost routine. The only difference was the pills."

"Fentanyl," I answered. "It's cheaper and much stronger than oxycodone." That had been pounded into my head in my EMT class. Many drugs were being laced with fentanyl to give them an extra kick. It's one of the many reasons it was important for emergency workers to wear latex gloves when working with patients. HIV started the glove requirement, but it wasn't the only reason anymore. Fentanyl was often shipped in powder form, and the dust got onto everything. You still had to be careful, because it was human instinct to touch your glasses, mouth, or nose and possibly ingest the drug yourself.

Angel finally looked at me. "Is she going to be okay?"

"I'm sure she is in excellent hands. Remember what happened at the hospital here? If she was unresponsive, they used Narcan. That will stop the drug from reacting with the body. The important thing is for her to stop using the drug. There are going to be long-term effects she will have to overcome." My classroom training was coming in handy. But I didn't enjoy needing it for people I considered family.

Dad added, "We will have to wait and see how she is doing when we get there."

"Robby used the Narcan nasal spray on Mom. He said it was too late for Roger. It was supposed to be my job to check on them during the week."

"He's not blaming you, is he?" Dad asked.

"No, he feels guilty for upsetting me with the DNA test results. He said he checked on them once an hour, like I usually did. But he woke up when he didn't hear his dad snoring. It was the quiet that woke him."

We sat in silence as the Escalade rolled down the road. The passing streetlights created an alternating light and dark montage of a horror movie showing the monster getting closer. Only Angel had already met the monster. She had delivered it to Roger herself.

Her mom was already at the hospital when we arrived. She was in a room and sedated. Angel was the only person allowed to see her. We had to stay in the waiting room. I wanted to talk to the EMTs, but they had already left. After half an hour, Angel found us in the waiting room. I stood as Angel came to me and hugged me.

Dad asked. "Can you give us an update?"

She nodded. "They have her sedated and resting. She will be okay." Then she looked at me. "The pills tested positive for fentanyl. One of the EMTs used a test strip to test them."

"Those are illegal in Arkansas, but no one enforces the stupid law. They save lives."

"They can release her in a few hours. But they prefer her not to go home. They want her to go through a three-day detox program here. Then they said she should go to a rehab facility. But we don't have the money for that. They want me to pay upfront right now. I don't know how we are going to pay for this."

"Don't worry. I'll pay for it," I said and looked at Mom and Dad. Dad nodded at me. Ben and I didn't consider ourselves rich, but our biological parents left us trust funds from their life insurance policies. Ben was using part of his to pay for college and living expenses. I was using some of mine for college expenses as well. But we had to access the funds through Mom and Dad. We couldn't use it to travel, or party and buy fancy toys.

"How are you going to pay for it?" Angel asked.

"I'll sell some of my cows. The herd needs to be reduced anyway. And I'll borrow from my trust fund."

"Wait. You really have a trust fund? I thought you and Ben were joking."

*****

The next few days were a blur. I felt sorry for Angel and Robby, but I was also proud of them. They worked together to plan Roger's funeral. Angel's mom went back to Clarendon for Roger's funeral. Then she went to rehab. I was with Angel as much as my free time allowed. I couldn't fall behind in my classes, so I was on the road a lot.

"Will my life ever be normal?" Angel asked after Roger's funeral. "I feel like I'm living in a psychological thriller book."

Taking her hand, I smiled, because I couldn't laugh. Too much had happened since I'd known her to disagree. "Yes, it will be normal," I said. "Starting today, okay?"

She smiled back at me and squeezed my hand. "Okay."

I had no idea what I was talking about. I couldn't predict the future, but it sounded good.

Chapter 19

Angel

We were at the Meet of Champions, an invitation-only meet for state track champions from every classification.

I recognized the tall black woman, but didn't understand why she was wearing civilian clothing.

"Sergeant Johnson? Why are you here?" I asked.

The woman smiled. "I'm here to express my condolences. It's not often a young lady loses two fathers in one year."

I said, "I don't believe you. You're here for another reason."

Sergeant Johnson smiled. "Beautiful and smart. You're right. Let's find somewhere quiet where we can talk."

We found some seats at the top of the bleachers and sat down. Sergeant Johnson asked, "How are you doing, Angel?"

What an odd question, I thought to myself. "I'm surviving. Like you said, I've lost two dads. How did you know that?"

"It's my job to know things," she said. "How I know is not important. How is your mom?"

"Recovering in rehab. Thankfully, Dan is paying for that."

"Why would he do that?" She asked.

I pulled the chain out of my shirt that held my promise ring and my engagement ring. "We're engaged," I said. "But I guess you already knew that, too."

"Actually, I didn't. I suppose congratulations are in order."

She appeared to be disappointed. She looked as if she were deciding something.

"Why are you here, Sergeant Johnson?"

She smiled again, and I noticed for the first time that she was beautiful when she smiled. "You know, I ran track in high school and college, too. I was pretty good, but not as good as you. I like to come to the state meets because that's where the best high school athletes are. You should be getting college scholarship offers by now."

"I've talked to some coaches, but the offers have been partial scholarships from schools too far from home.

I asked my next question before she changed the topic. "What can you tell me about my dad's case?"

"Which dad?"

"You know which one. The one Donny Ray, Little John, and that asshole former marine killed. The father who raised me." And I stopped talking and wiped the tear from my left eye that was forming there.

"I can tell you that Donny Ray and Little John are supposedly back in Arkansas."

"Is there anything I can do to help?" I asked.

"For starters, watch your back. Tell Dan and your mother to watch theirs too."

I asked her again, "What can I do? How can I help?"

The sergeant sighed and asked, "How far are you willing to go, Angel? Are you willing to give up your life as you know it? Give up your mother and Dan?"

"What do you mean?" Giving up my family was not an option.

"I'm looking for young women who will go undercover."

"I'm in," I said before she explained anything else and before I changed my mind.

This was the chance I'd been waiting for. My chance for revenge. God's plan for me.

"I didn't ask you, Angel. They could easily recognize you."

"I doubt it. How many girls did they mistake for me? They look at hair color, boobs, and to see if we pee sitting down. I'll cut my hair into a pixie cut and dye it blond. Besides, they haven't bothered me or Dan since they murdered Dad. But I don't expect that to last."

Sergeant Johnson winced, but she never broke eye contact with me. "You really want these guys, don't you?"

"They killed my dad. Most likely, both of them. They've attempted to kill me and Dan twice. But I don't want just them; I want the people who allow them to do these things and get away with it. I want to bring them all down."

She sighed before saying, "Alright. You convinced me. I can't promise that my plan will work, though. It's a long shot."

"What do I need to do?"

She briefly laid out her idea. I needed to be a full-fledged law enforcement officer and attend the academy. I was too young to become a state trooper, but I could become a deputy sheriff under certain guidelines. Sheriff Tatum would hire me as a deputy and assign me to a statewide task force. The first step was the application process and psychological evaluations. We exchanged phone numbers and email addresses, and I left.

She had cautioned me to keep this a secret, even from Dan and Mom. Leaks came from the people we loved. Not because they meant to hurt us, but because they loved us and were proud of us. They wanted to brag about our important jobs, and that was the reason we had to keep secrets.

It wasn't a coincidence that she came to talk to me. She came to recruit me to go undercover. She knew that, out of all the teenage girls in Arkansas; I was one of the few who would put myself in danger.

What did I do? I wasn't changing my mind, but I had second thoughts when I thought about Dan. I wanted to be with him. But I had kneeled at Dad's grave and promised I wouldn't be back until I brought them to justice. I remember the feeling that a plan was being put into place, and I felt like this was it. This had to be it. But I questioned myself aloud, "Am I ready for this? I didn't start this fight, but I sure want to finish it."

Chapter 20

Angel

I rejoined my teammate on the field. Sergeant Johnson was still in the stands, sitting where we had talked. My race was coming up soon.

I stretched a little and jogged from one end of the infield to the other. Normally I was a little nervous, but I was thinking about what I had committed to. My teammate Tricia warmed up with me.

"Hey, who's the recruiter? You didn't want to include me?"

"She's a recruiter. Just not the college track kind," I answered.

"Shit. Don't they normally wear uniforms everywhere?"

"Normally," I replied and grinned.

"I want nothing to do with the military."

She was thinking about military recruiters. I didn't tell her the difference and that the uniform would be a police uniform. This was a secret I could only tell Dan. I didn't care what Sergeant Johnson said. He was the one who stayed with me and put me back together after everything I went through this past year. If there were such a thing as a soulmate, he was mine.

Our coach yelled at us. It was time for our race. Tricia and I walked to the starting line silently. We had become fast friends, training partners, and fierce competitors on the track. We'd agreed that one of us would always win the race we were in. And we had tried. We had worked together during races to get the lead. When it came to sprint speed, we were equal. In the short races, Tricia was better. But in the distance races, I had the edge.

This was the last meet of the year. The Meet of Champions was where the best competitors from every high school classification came together to compete. Tricia and I had already placed first and second at the 3A state meet. This was just for bragging rights, the trophies, and recruiting. Whoever won this was going to get recruited. One of our competitors from the 6A division had already committed to the University of Arkansas, which has one of the most elite college track programs in the country. The men's indoor and outdoor track program had won nearly thirty national championships over the years and produced many Olympians. The women's program was on the rise now.

We stepped onto the track and got into our lanes. We fist bumped. "Time to shine," Tricia said.

"Time to shine," I repeated.

It wasn't our race to win that day. We placed second and third with our best times of the year. We learned what elite was because that Arkansas signee sprinted the entire two laps and finished a good ten yards ahead of us.

"Shit," Tricia huffed. "I thought we were good." We were walking on the infield, relaxing our muscles and getting our breath back.

"We are," I said. "Bet we see her in the Olympics someday."

"Did they say she set a state and meet record today?"

"Yea. One day, we can say we raced against her before she became famous."

Tricia laughed. "I hope so, because I don't like getting my ass beat like that."

Coach Pugh told us, "Y'all did great. I almost chewed you out for not trying hard enough. Then I saw your times. You both beat your personal best times." Apparently, he was stunned as well.

I sent Dan a text when I got into the coach's car to head home. It was just the three of us.

We have a lot of planning to do when I see you tonight. I texted him.

Hey gorgeous! How was the meet?

I smiled. We always talked a lot when we got together on the weekends.

Tricia and I placed second and third. That Arkansas signee set meet and state records. Beat us by ten yards.

Ouch! What time will you be in? Your mom is here.

I had lots of questions now. Mom had been in rehab. I thought she would come back to Clarendon. But she went there instead. We both felt like the farm was home, but why didn't she come back to Clarendon?

When I didn't reply. He texted, *She is here for the weekend. She knew you would be here, and she wanted to see you.*

That made sense. *Okay, I'll let you know when I'm leaving Clarendon. Love you.*

I love you, too.

There was plenty of time to think on the ride back and the drive from Clarendon to the farm. I didn't regret my decision to join the state police. I had grown up wanting to be a game warden like my dad. Fighting Little John on the boat ramp and his pulling a gun on me had changed my mind. Having someone point a gun at me was an emotional moment. I didn't want to be in law enforcement after that.

When they killed Dad and attempted to kill me and Dan, I changed my mind again. I don't know why I thought I could bring them down when other law enforcement officers hadn't been able to. My Dad included. But there was that feeling I had kneeling at Dad's grave. This had to be the plan.

Four hours later, I pulled the Mustang into the driveway of the house I would always consider home. I had only lived here a few months, but inside and out, the house and the farm felt like home. There were memories here. Good ones, and sad ones. And I planned to marry the man who owned it. Dan was standing on the front porch with my mom, waiting for me.

It had been two weeks since I'd seen Mom, but it felt like forever. Every night, I phoned her before I called Dan, but it wasn't the same. I missed her, and I missed Dan. I got out of the Mustang and ran to hug them both.

Chapter 21

Dan

We always had a lot to talk about during our weekends. But this weekend, Mrs. Cotton had come home from rehab, and Angel brought news of her own. Mrs. Cotton had asked Mom and Dad if she could move back to the farm. Mom and Dad deferred, saying it was my decision. I said yes, of course, even though I knew Angel didn't want to leave Clarendon in the middle of the semester. But my decision wasn't about getting Angel back. It was about giving Mrs. Cotton a safe place to live away from terrible memories and a source of painkillers.

Then Angel came home. She was thrilled to see the two of us. She often said my grandparent's house felt like home because she was at peace here. On weekends, we would sit on the swing on the back porch and listen to the sound of the river. She would fill her mother's bird feeders, and we'd watch the birds. It was peaceful, but my peace came from Angel's smile and having her by my side. But tonight, she kept her distance from me, but she kept looking at me. I couldn't read her expression. She still smiled and said all the right things. Her earlier text said we needed to talk. We always talked, so I dismissed it. That she had said nothing to her mom meant she only wanted to talk to me about it.

Mrs. Cotton had gone grocery shopping and bought enough supplies for the weekend. We made a simple dinner with salad, spaghetti, and garlic bread. Mrs. Cotton talked about the rehab program. She explained the methadone treatment she had undergone. It helped in gradually reducing the need for opioids. The therapy sessions helped her understand the symptoms and the cravings. She explained the need to change habits and environment so you can break the mental association with the need for the drug.

"Angel, I want to come home," she finally said.

"Mom, you can come home at any time. Are you sure you're ready?"

"Sweetheart, I want to move back here to the farm. You, me, Jonathan, we felt like this was the first home we ever really had. Going back to Clarendon will not be good for me. There are too many memories of drug use and the need for it to get through the day. I don't want to go back."

Angel reached for her mother's hand and smiled. "Okay, Mom. We will work it out." Then she turned to me. "Dan?"

"We've already talked about it. I told her, it was okay with me."

"Mom, I have seven to eight weeks of high school left before I graduate. As much as I want to be with you and Dan, I can't leave with that little time left," Angel said.

"I know, and I'm not asking you. I will be okay without you. Dan and his parents will be here. And you will be okay without me. You and Robby get along well. I think he will be okay with your staying until the end of school."

I was sure Robby would be okay with it. He was the one who figured out Angel was his half-sister, and he was the only one excited about it. Robby was a good guy. He would do anything in the world for Angel.

We talked a little longer as we cleaned up the kitchen. Angel encouraged her mom to go sit on the porch and watch the birds, and told her we were going to take a walk around the farm.

As we stepped out the front door, Angel stopped and hugged me. "I love you."

"I love you, too. Now, what's bothering you?"

She released her hug and glanced at the door. "Let's walk."

A feeling of dread hit me. I would not like what she was going to tell me. Exhaustion washed over me. I had studied and traded shifts to get my clinical and lab time in before the weekend.

"Is life ever going to get easier for us?"

"Yes, Cotton Top. It will someday." I wasn't sure I believed it myself, but positive thoughts were supposed to bring positive outcomes. "It won't slow down, but it will get easier as we learn from experience."

She squeezed my hand. "I hope so, because I had a visitor at the track meet today."

"A coach? Did you get a scholarship offer?" This was something I could live with.

"No. It was Sergeant Johnson with the State Police."

I stopped walking. "They're back, aren't they?" Now I knew the source of my dread.

"Yes. And she told me to warn you and Mom to watch your backs."

"Shit," I said.

She hit me on the shoulder. "Hey. Watch your mouth. You never cuss. I don't want the future father of my children cussing."

"Sorry," I said, fully chastised. We started walking again.

"I'm joking."

"I know. But that's not all, is it?"

"No. I agreed to be part of an undercover operation."

I stopped again. There it was. She just blurted it out. That sinking feeling of dread and fear cut my knees out from under me. I had to stop a big sob, and I knelt on my knees. The sheer exhaustion wasn't helping my emotions.

"When you said we needed to talk, I did not know this was the conversation we would have," I said.

"Dan, this feels right to me." We were still holding hands, and she kneeled facing me. "This is the plan God has made for me. I've thought of little else since I talked to her today. I even prayed about it. This is the path I'm supposed to take."

I said, "That day we went to the cemetery. When you felt God was preparing a plan for you. I felt pain, fear, and danger, and I'm feeling it again. I don't want to lose you, Angel. We just found each other."

We kneeled in the middle of the road, and she hugged me. Strangely, I felt she was right. I was still frightened, but she was right. I had to man up and support her, but it wasn't easy, because I wanted to take revenge for her. It was my job to protect her. I'd had daydreams about blowing up their cars and beating them up.

She leaned back, and she caressed my face. "I'm not doing this out of a sense of anger or revenge. I'm doing this because I loved Dad. Losing him has made me stronger. Being separated from you has made me independent. Mom's drug issues made me accept more responsibility. Roger and Robby taught me how to be supportive and how to keep a secret."

Robby was gay, and his dad died not knowing it.

Angel continued, "Do you remember Christmas day when I ran to your house and told you Mom was moving to Clarendon?"

"Yes," I said barely above a whisper.

"I asked if God was testing us. And you and your whole family said no."

I answered, "God doesn't test us; he prepares us."

"Yes, he has prepared me for this. I believe this is the path I'm supposed to take. I have lost so much this past year, but I also found you, and I found the confidence to take care of Mom and Roger, and to live by myself." She searched my eyes. "I have you, don't I?"

I pulled her to me. "Always." She was right. She had grown stronger these last few months. The Angel I met and fell in love with was confident, but reserved. The Angel in front of me was confident and focused. She was reassuring me, and it was usually the other way around.

She stood up. "Come on. We have a lot of talking to do. And I think better when I'm moving."

She told me I had to keep this a secret. Sergeant Johnson had told her that families were often the ones who, unintentionally, revealed the undercover officers' identities.

"I won't tell anyone," I said.

"I know. And I won't keep any secrets from you. I need your help to prepare for this."

"How can I help?"

"You're the best person I know for looking ahead and preparing for all possibilities."

"When do you start? Do you go through any training?"

"Right after I graduate. I go to the police academy so that I can become a police officer. After that, I'm not sure. Sergeant Johnson said that she was recruiting several young women. She wasn't sure her plan would work. If it does, it could be very dangerous."

"No kidding. Look at what they have done to our friends and family. To us," I said. I stopped again and faced her. "Angel, I want to support you, but this is a potential suicide mission. I don't want to lose you before we even begin our life together."

My voice quavered. She was talking about this as if it were nothing more than another track meet. I remembered Sarah and Angel's dad. Both dead and buried. Nothing but memories in our hearts and minds.

She placed her hand on my chest and stood on her toes and kissed me. It calmed me some. "I've had several hours to think about this," she said. "It's a long shot that I will get close to them. Maybe I'll get to be on the sidelines when they're brought down."

"They will recognize you," I protested.

She huffed, "I'll cut my hair into a pixie cut and dye it blonde. I'll change my name, and they'll probably only look at my ass and tits."

"It's my job," I mumbled. I knew I would not change her mind. I might as well make a joke and try to lighten my mood. It didn't last long.

"Speaking of my... assets." She pulled me into a tight hug. "Let's elope over spring break. I want to be married to you before I do this, so I have someone to come home to."

"Holy crap, Angel. My head was already spinning from your wanting to go undercover. And now you want to elope?"

"We're already engaged," she answered.

"That's true. I told Dad I wanted to get engaged because I wasn't sure how much longer we could suppress our urge to have sex. I wanted God and the world to know my intentions if we did."

She looked a little surprised. "That's why they didn't argue about our engagement?"

"Yeah." I turned and started walking again, holding her hand. We weren't far from my house. "I need some time to think, Angel. My head is spinning."

She jerked my hand. "Dan, I love you. You will support me, won't you?"

I stopped in front of the garage of my house. "Of course I will. But I need some time to clear my head. Go spend some time with your mom." I kissed her softly, then leaned in for a hug. "Please tell me you have no more surprises for me this weekend."

"Who knows? Maybe I'll give you a peek at my ass. You said, it was your job to look at it."

She let go and started walking backwards. "I love you, Daniel Brock."

"I love you, too." She was determined to do this. She had a plan, and she will make it happen.

Finally, she turned and walked away. Then, she wiggled her ass a little for me without looking back. I had to smile, but the fear and frustration bounced around my skull as I watched her. The physical attraction and the desire to have sex were the last things on my mind right now.

Dad walked out of the garage. I had not heard him leave the house. "Are you okay, son? You look conflicted."

"I don't know, Dad. Our relationship just took a strange turn."

"That's nothing new. Your relationship with Angel has always been under outside stress. But you have overcome it. And I suspect you will this time as well. I'm here if you need to talk."

Outside stress. Is that what you call attempted murder? The murders of Sarah and Officer Cotton? He was right about the outside stress, and I didn't say what I was thinking. Our lives would have been normal if Donny Ray and Little John hadn't pushed us so much.

I looked at Dad and asked, "If I ask you a question as a church member to his pastor, you're supposed to keep it secret, right?"

He nodded. "There are exceptions to the rule if someone's life is in danger. You've got me worried now, son. What's going on?"

I was getting more and more anxious about Angel joining the State Police. "I told Angel I would keep it a secret. But I won't be able to convince you to do something for me if I don't tell you the secret."

Dad looked at me for a minute. He was thinking about what to say. Then he finally said, "That's not very clear. Let's see if we can do this without you telling me the secret. I can tell you're conflicted about something, so let's start with what you want to convince me to do?"

"Conflict is certainly the right word. Angel wants to elope over spring break. But I want you to marry us. I want our families there."

"You're right," Dad answered. "I will not conduct a wedding for you without a good cause. I agreed to your engagement, but you promised to wait until after college. You're not out of high school yet. Please don't tell me she has cancer or something like that."

I shook my head. "Nothing that bad. But it could be as deadly."

"She's going after her dad's killers, isn't she?"

I stared at him with my mouth wide open. "Close your mouth, son. Or you will start catching flies. Well? Am I right?"

"Yes, and no," I said. "She's been recruited to be an undercover officer. To specifically go after Donny Ray and Little John."

"Now I see why you're worried. Why is this supposed to be a secret?"

"The primary cause of undercover officers being exposed is family members bragging about what they are doing."

"And she wasn't supposed to tell you either. Right?"

I nodded.

He sighed heavily. "Y'all are afraid she won't make it out alive, and you want to have your honeymoon before she joins."

I stared at him again. "Am I that transparent? She said she wanted to know she had someone to come home to."

I hadn't told Dad the second part of the secret. He had guessed it. There was no need to hold back now. I told him about her experience at the cemetery. The feeling that a plan was being made for her. I told him about her having the revelation that seeking revenge because of hatred was wrong. And that seeking revenge through legal means, because of love, was better. I told him that my feeling that day were fear and pain.

"God was at work that day. I also had a feeling. I knew I needed to trust and support both of you. Now that you brought me into your conflict, let me see if I can help. When I was your age, I did not want to be a soldier in Vietnam. I didn't want to go kill people. But I accepted a support role as a medic. Angel is willing and ready to go to war. She is going in with a rational mind because she is thinking about how much she loved her dad, and how much she loves you. She knows that anger clouds a person's judgement and makes them do rash things. There is still danger even when you focus and think clearly. You will have the support role. The role of the medic. You will have to heal her and put her back together when she comes home," he said. "The hard part will be the waiting and not knowing when the danger will strike."

"If she comes home alive," I whispered.

"You must have the same faith that she has. You must let go of the protective role and give it to God. I know you want to protect her, or you wouldn't be so torn over letting her do this. It's not your decision; it's God's decision. He has chosen her to be the tool of their destruction. Trust her. But most of all, trust God."

He was right. I wanted to take control and protect Angel. I wanted to be the one to do the fighting. But I knew my anger would get the best of me. I had to turn it over to God, or I would stick my nose right in the middle of the investigation and get one of us killed for my efforts.

"Let me think about your request. I'm not saying I'll marry you, but I'll pray about it. I don't know how I'll convince your mom. Any ideas?"

"Sorry Dad. I'm still conflicted, as you said, over Angel becoming an undercover officer, and her wanting to elope. Plus, Donny Ray and Little John are back in Arkansas."

Chapter 22

Dan

We were married on the first Saturday of spring break. Dad never told me, but I think the television news reports were the deciding factor that convinced them to let us get married. The threat of elopement didn't hurt either. Donny Ray and Little John were arrested for the murder of Angel's dad. But a judge threw the case out for lack of evidence. I couldn't identify anyone, and Angel only identified the former Marine, who was still at large. The murder of a police officer was always big news. Dad also knew the truth about Angel joining the Sheriff's Department and joining the task force as an undercover officer. He admitted to being as frightened as I was. They had attempted to murder us twice. No one believed we could survive a third attempt. Mrs. Cotton and Mom reluctantly agreed to our getting married as long as we waited to have kids.

We held the wedding on the lawn between my house and the river.

We didn't invite many people. There were a couple of friends from the cross-country team, as well as Ben and Robby, and our mothers. Dad performed the ceremony. I wore my grey suit, and Angel wore a white fitted pantsuit. She was beautiful. She ruled out wearing a dress because she didn't want to waste time changing clothes for our trip. We didn't have a reception because there was little time. We had to go to the airport to catch our flight. Robby agreed to drop us off, and Ben agreed to pick us up. Maybe we were paranoid, but we weren't leaving a car at the airport for anyone to put another firebomb in.

We flew from Little Rock to New Orleans and stayed at the Four Seasons close to the French Quarter. It was spring break, and all the beach resorts along the coast were full. New Orleans was also packed with spring partiers. The good part is we blended right into the crowd.

We were probably like most honeymooners. Inexperienced sex addicts. What we lacked in knowledge and experience, we made up for with energy and excitement. We didn't leave our hotel room for hours.

Hunger finally made us come to our senses. We slipped out of the hotel room around noon and quickly realized that walking was going to be a challenge for both of us. We talked about room service, but decided to see a little of the city. Thankfully, New Orleans has trolleys, and we bought passes for the week. We rode down Canal Street and found the Creole House Restaurant. I ordered the Taste of New Orleans, a sampler dish, and Angel ordered the Cajun Alfredo with blackened chicken. The food was delicious, but a little on the spicy side.

There were things we wanted to discuss and plan. Not about our future together. We already had that planned. We were realistic about the fact that Angel might not survive this job. I hoped that Donny Ray and Little John would be brought to justice before Angel completed her training and went undercover. But so far, they had avoided any charges.

I reached across the table and grabbed her hand. "What do you want to do now? Do you want to explore the city? Or something else?"

"It's looking like rain. Why don't we go back to the room and do something else?" And she winked at me.

"Sounds good to me. I'll take care of the bill." I had a good idea of what the something else was.

*****

It was pouring rain when we woke up Monday morning. The view from our upper-floor window was gray, cloudy, and miserable when I walked out of the bathroom. Angel was looking out the window toward the Mississippi River. She was wearing a pair of my boxer shorts and a tiny spaghetti-strap T-shirt. I walked up behind her completely naked and hugged her from behind. She leaned backwards against me, and we savored the moment. I used one hand to caress her belly and the other to hug her tightly. I kissed her ear, and she turned her head to kiss me.

Then she turned to face me, and we kissed again.

I lifted her up. She wrapped her arms and legs around me, and I carried her to the bed.

*****

I woke up to the sound of the weather forecast coming from the television. Angel walked out of the bathroom, wearing only her smile. "Wake up, sleepyhead," she said as she crawled on top of me. "I'm starving. Let's find something to eat, and then we need to discuss my future with the State Police."

I lifted the sheets and said, "I thought we were already doing undercover work."

The thought hit me hard. "I'm sorry," I said. "You're not expected to have sex with someone else as an undercover officer, are you?"

She looked horrified at my question. My stomach sank, and I felt the anger rising in me. I sat up and rolled her off me and went to the bathroom to pee. My mind was spinning.

"Dan," she said as I walked away. "Dan!" she said a little louder. "I'm sorry. I hadn't thought about that. It's not going to happen."

My response was to relieve myself. Piss on this whole situation. If it weren't for Donny Ray and Little John, we wouldn't be in this situation. And that's exactly what she was trying to do. End this situation. Could I live with her sleeping with Donny Ray or Little John if it put an end to all this and put away those killers?

I told myself I could if it freed us to live the rest of our lives peacefully. But I was lying to myself. I wasn't okay with it.

She was standing in the bathroom doorway, watching, as I finished peeing and washed my hands. "We need to talk about this. About everything I might have to do. I need you to support me, Dan. I won't do this without your blessing."

"Are you having second thoughts?"

"If it means I lose you, then yes."

"You're not losing me," I said as I cupped her face in my hand. "But you're right. We need to talk about a lot of things. One moment of indecision on your part could get you killed. You must do whatever it takes to bring them down. You must be a step ahead of them at all times."

I leaned down and kissed her. Then, I wiped a tear from her eye and picked her up in my arms.

"Again? Are you never satisfied? I'm so sore I can barely walk," she protested.

"It's time for a shower," I said. "I think there's room for both of us to shower together."

"You can't change the subject. We need to discuss this."

I kissed her again as we stood in the shower.

"Do you love me?" I asked.

"Yes! More than anything."

"Will you love anyone else during the undercover operation?"

"No. Of course not. Why are you asking me that?"

I turned the water on and tested the temperature. "It's difficult for me to say, but there will be a difference between being intimate with me and you having to use your body to bring down a killer and rapist. If it means that we live the rest of our lives in peace, raise our kids and not have to watch our backs all the time, then I will deal with it. I won't like it, but I will deal with it."

The water was hot, so I pulled the stopper to divert the water to the showerhead. I turned to Angel, and she was watching me and crying. I pulled her into a hug. We stood there hugging for several minutes under the shower until I tilted her head back and kissed her. I had said everything I wanted to say. I had given her permission, but I wasn't sure she had accepted it.

She whispered, "I'm not sure I can deal with it." This conversation wasn't over, and it was going to be a tough one for both of us. Outside, the rain was still pouring. The Weather Channel was reporting on a tropical depression moving ashore, but said it would blow through by the next day. I think the depression part settled over me and Angel, and I wasn't sure how long it would take for that to blow over.

Chapter 23

Angel

Why didn't I think of it? All this time, I had been hyping myself up. I'm going undercover to take revenge on Dad's killers. I'm going to finish this once and for all. All I saw was the danger, the glory, and the results I wanted to see. The real challenge had not occurred to me, like the dirty stuff I would have to do to gain their trust. I hadn't thought about the sex, the drugs, or the human trafficking I would see.

Dan had lifted a bed sheet and made a joke about undercover work, and we both stopped cold. We both realized that I might have to sleep with someone, or worse, allow myself to be raped, to get inside their operation. I had told myself and Sergeant Johnson I could handle the undercover work. Now that I faced the reality, I still felt I could do it, but I didn't want to anymore. I didn't want to be with anyone but Dan or go through the pain I was feeling right now. It felt dirty, and I felt ashamed even though I had done nothing yet. The thought of my having agreed to it repulsed me. What kind of person was I?

If Dan had said he didn't want me to go undercover right then, I would have changed my mind. I would have backed out of the promise I'd made to Sergeant Johnson.

I expressed my thoughts to Dan while we were drying off after the shower. His response summed it up neatly.

"If you do this, you are going to feel dirty and ashamed you didn't do more and do it sooner. If you don't do this, you are going to feel ashamed and remorseful that you had a chance, and you did nothing. I can't make that choice for you. I won't do it."

"How can you let me do this?" I asked. I thought once I expressed my second thoughts, that he would agree and talk me out of it. "If you think I'm going to have regrets, then why should I do it?"

"You're doing it for your dad, for Sarah and other girls like her. You're doing it for Sheriff Tatum, and to let our children grow up with you and me there to raise them and love them the same way we were. So we won't be looking over our shoulders for the next attempt on our lives."

He was right. Our future children deserved to grow up on a farm with love and support from their parents. It wasn't about taking revenge for Dad anymore; it was about the freedom to raise our kids. If I survive to have kids. What had once been a simple decision was now muddier than the Mississippi River we could see from our room.

I had accepted that responsibility because I wanted to be the hunter and not the hunted. I truly believed this was God's plan, and I was his tool. Sometimes tools get used, abused, and broken. So be it.

We were still standing in the bathroom. I looked at our reflections in the mirror. We were just two naked teenagers on a honeymoon we shouldn't be having yet. We were having a deep philosophical discussion about life and the possibility there might not be a future.

"It feels like the weight of the world is on my shoulders, but why is it my responsibility?" I asked Dan.

"Dad once told me and Ben, 'Be careful what you ask God for; you might get it.'"

He threw his towel down and drew me to him. "Let's get dressed and go eat. I feel like we are fighting, and I don't like that," he said.

"We're not finished with this conversation."

"No. We need a break to think about it, but not to talk about it. We both think better when we're moving and doing something."

"It's pouring. But I think it's supposed to clear up soon," I said.

"It doesn't matter. I think our moods are stormier than the weather." He grabbed my hand and led me out of the bathroom. "Come on, let's get dressed."

I looked at my hair in the mirror. There was no need to blow-dry it, but I needed to brush it.

New Orleans was the same, rain, or shine. The locals still had jobs to go to, and the tourists still had places to see. We crossed the trolley tracks to the Riverwalk Outlets, a shopping mall, where we finally found the restaurants and had lunch at Mr. Shrimp's Kitchen.

We had spoken little since we had left the room. But we held hands as we walked and window-shopped. It still felt like we had argued, and I was upset about it. But we hadn't argued. I was upset that I hadn't realized that undercover police work in this situation might literally mean between the sheets of a bed. Now, I didn't want to follow through with my commitment. I didn't want to hurt Dan. I will put myself in danger, but I didn't want to hurt him.

One thing Dan had said stuck with me. "One moment of indecision on your part could get you killed." I had to be all in, be in the moment, and be one step ahead. I couldn't afford to have emotional moments when I missed Dan or Mom.

We were walking through the French Market. "I'm sorry I upset you earlier," I said to Dan.

He stopped and pulled me into a hug. "Listen to the music, to the words of the song," he said.

I heard Michael Jackson's *The Man in the Mirror* playing on the radio. The words were basically saying, if you want to change the world, start with yourself. "I'm trying," I said.

"Don't try. Do this. Make a difference in the world. Not just our lives, but many other lives. I'm proud of you for wanting to do that. I love you for being a take-charge person. But it will not stop me from worrying about you."

We listened to the rest of the song while people walked around and past us in the market. I saw Dan's reasoning. I could change the world for someone else, but that change had to start inside me. He wasn't as concerned about what I had to do on the job as he was about me staying focused and being all in. I had to change myself to be someone else, and to be convincing when I became that person.

I let go of our hug, stood on my toes, and kissed him. "Thank you. It's amazing how powerful a song is sometimes."

It was almost dark, and the rain had become a light drizzle. We made our way to Bourbon Street and found a restaurant that specialized in gumbo and etouffee.

Afterwards, we walked up and down the street wondering what the attraction was that people found here. I guess it was all about the decadence.

That's where we met Lydia. Her real name wasn't Lydia. It was her street name, her prostitute name. We met her when she proposed a threesome. For a price, of course. She was wearing a short red skirt that exposed her butt cheeks and a thin white silk blouse open to the waist, revealing she wasn't wearing a bra. I could see the curve of her brown-skinned breasts while the silk blouse tried but failed to hide her pointed nipples.

Dan stopped and asked, "How much?"

Before she could answer, I yanked his arm. "Dan!"

He pulled back. "Trust me." He looked at the hooker again. "How much?"

"A hundred an hour. Five for all night."

"We don't want the sex; we just want to talk," he said and pulled a hundred-dollar bill out of the pocket of his jeans. "I'll give you another hundred when we are done." The crowd pushed us closer to her.

"What's the catch? Are you cops? Naw, y'all are too young to be cops."

"Is there a quiet place where we can get some drinks and talk?"

Finally, she smiled, grabbed the bill from Dan, and said, "Follow me."

We walked down the street to an alley, and she handed the hundred to a big black man. "Willy, we're going to get a back room at Walker's. The kids want to talk dirty."

The big man raised an eyebrow at her but said nothing. She turned down the alley, and we followed. Dan dropped my hand, and we both loosened up. We were leery of being attacked now, and I was questioning Dan's intentions.

The noise from the street lessened as we got further from Bourbon Street. Lydia stopped. "Relax. Ain't anyone going to jump you as long as you're with me. But before we go any further, I need to know why you just want to talk?" She took a cigarette out of purse and lit up.

Dan said, "In short, how do you do it? How do you separate your job from your everyday life?"

She looked at him suspiciously, but then I understood. He knew I needed to know how to deal with psychological trauma. "You want to know how? Don't you mean why?" She put her fists on hips in a challenging way.

"No. My wife," he hesitated for a second. "We're not cops. But my wife has an opportunity to go undercover in another state to bring down some traffickers. How do you separate yourself from doing what you do, to being your real self when you are not at work?"

She looked at Dan for a long time, then she turned to me. "Do you think Lydia is my real name?"

"No. You wouldn't want the guys knowing who you really are."

"Exactly. Not just guys, though. Women swing both ways too. They can be worse than men sometimes." She took another puff of her cigarette. "Traffickers? You mean they're kidnapping girls and selling them?"

She asked me directly and ignored Dan.

"Yes. They killed one of our friends." I didn't tell her everything. She didn't need to know anymore.

"Shit," she said and took another drag on the cigarette before dropping it on the pavement and stepping on it.

"Come with me." She opened a barely visible back door to another restaurant and bar. We entered a back room that was filled with shelves, stacked boxes, and the large doors for walk-in coolers and freezers on the other side.

"Stay here. I need to talk to the manager." She moved through an open door and disappeared, but was back before I could say anything to Dan. She came back, followed by a man larger than the one at the end of the alley. He paid no attention to us. His large flat face and flat nose made him look like he was used for boxing practice. He unlocked a door and opened it.

"Sweetie, would you bring me a sweet tea and a platter of Cajun nachos? You kids want something to drink? We can share the nachos."

"Sweet tea," Dan and I replied. We entered an immaculate office with a desk facing the door, in front of two tall file cabinets and a computer desk against the wall filled with three computer screens showing camera scenes and a combo printer and fax machine. Pictures adorned the wall, showing the manager wearing New Orleans Saints and New York Giants uniforms.

Lydia moved to the table and pulled out a chair. "Have a seat," she said and sat down. Her blouse slipped off her shoulder as she set her purse on the floor, exposing a perfect chocolate brown breast.

Dan pulled out a chair for me, and I sat down. Lydia watched Dan's actions and pulled the blouse up enough to cover her exposed nipple. She leaned back in her chair and stared at Dan until he sat down. Then she looked at me.

"There are very few men in this world who will love you for you, no matter what you do or who you do it with. They will forgive you and love you as if nothing ever happened. That man out there is one of them. He's my man. We've been married for ten years. He bought this bar and restaurant and overpaid for it. I do what I do to help pay the bills around here and at home. I can make four grand a month before I pay Willy for a spot on the street and protection. We have a business agreement. I don't belong to him. He doesn't beat me or force me to do drugs. It's not like the TV shows. That's the why."

Her husband came back carrying two trays. One full of nachos and another with three glasses and a pitcher of sweet tea. Lydia took a nacho off the platter and put it in her mouth.

"Sorry. I'm starving. Tell me a little about the job you are going to be doing."

I gave a brief rundown of what I thought I would be doing. Then I asked, "I love him dearly, but how do I not feel guilty about it?"

"It takes practice. I didn't always feel comfortable walking around without a bra and with my titties and ass exposed. You develop a distinct personality. I can switch from my actual personality to Lydia like turning a light switch on. Out there, I'm an actress in an X-rated movie. When I come home, I leave Lydia on the street. You understand what I'm saying?"

"Yeah," I said. I looked at Dan because he had been extremely quiet. He had been nibbling at the nachos and sipping the sweet tea. He looked at me, and I read the sadness in his eyes. But like Lydia said, men who loved you regardless of what you did were rare. It bothered me that Dan wasn't demanding that I not do this.

"Why are you willing to let me do this?" I asked Dan.

"Because the odds are low that you will get inside their organization. And if you do, it may not happen the way you think it will. This is something you need to do, or you'll never forgive yourself. You're not doing this to cheat on me. You're taking a chance to be the one to put them in jail."

I just stared at him for a minute. It was Lydia who made me understand. "He doesn't want you to go. He knows you need to go, and he's supporting you. Men like yours and mine are hard to find. Hang on to him. Now your time's up. I need that hundred you promised and another twenty for the teas and the nachos. Good luck, young lady. Bring the bastards down."

"Thank you. I'll do my best," I answered.

We exited through the alley. Lydia walked back to Bourbon Street with us. Just before we reached the street, she said, "N'awlins is a wonderful place to let loose and pretend to be someone else. How many titties have you seen on the street? How many women have you seen wearing lots of beads?" She leaned in, smiled at me and then continued, "Let loose. Go back to the hotel with your man. Create a street character and give her a name. Come back to Bourbon Street tomorrow night wearing something sexy. Then play the game of 'How many beads can I collect?' Don't wear a bra and show your titties. Talk dirty to your man in public and private. Get into character on the street. Turn it off when you leave. You're too stiff; you need to practice."

As we reached the street, she turned to another couple walking toward her. "Look at these gorgeous people. Y'all interested in a little threesome?" They ignored her and walked away. "Your loss," she said.

Chapter 24

Dan

Behind the closed doors of our hotel room, it was easy for Angel to pretend to be a horny, sex-starved pervert with me. On Bourbon Street, it was harder for her to let go of the moral values she was raised with. I tried to help by taking on my own street character and pretending to be Danny B. I would hug Angel in public. I groped her butt and her breasts in public. It took the remaining four nights in New Orleans for us to feel even a little comfortable doing the things we were doing in public.

On the last night before we left New Orleans, we took one more trip to Bourbon Street. We didn't go looking for Lydia, but we found her searching the crowd, looking in another direction. We slipped up beside her, and Angel leaned in and asked, "Hey there, Mocha Momma, how about a little threesome action?"

Lydia turned to find us staring at her. "Well, hello there. I didn't expect to see y'all again. You want to talk some more? Surely, you don't really want a threesome?"

We had discussed the fact that we were inexperienced at sex. We knew one way and three or four positions. Angel felt she needed to know more. Particularly, how to get a guy off without having to have sex. We had experimented with oral sex before marriage, but we didn't know what we were doing.

"Yes and no," Angel said. "We want you to teach us some of the kinkier stuff." My stomach was nervous just hearing the question. We didn't want her to take part. Angel wanted to learn more for her preparation, just in case she needed to hold up her end of the character she was going to play.

"What do you have in mind? It's been a slow night. These college kids are running out of money since spring break is almost over."

That was the night Angel and I graduated from Lydia's school of sex education. To Lydia, sex was a job. She said there was no love or passion in what she did. That was reserved for her husband. Most of the acting was in the talking, and the exaggerated desire. "Fake it until they can't take it anymore," she said. "Then you act disappointed they couldn't do more."

The next morning, while Angel was in the shower, I called the camera shop in Memphis where I bought my security camera system. We made a deal for him to sell Donny Ray a camera system for the Wood Duck Lodge. Neither of us said it out loud. We both understood that I paid him for the camera system, the installation, and the back door password into the system. He could sell it or set it up as a demo for free. I didn't care if he made extra money. What I wanted was the cameras installed and to have the password. I had dreamed of installing them myself. But doing that increased the chances of getting caught or killed.

Chapter 25

Angel

Dan and I stole one more weekend away before graduation. He rented a cabin close to the farm on the Little Red River. It was secluded, and that was what we wanted. We didn't talk about it, but we both knew it might be the last time we ever had to make love. We planned to attend each other's graduations. His was on Friday night; mine was Saturday afternoon. I was to report to the police academy in Camden on Sunday and begin classes on Monday. Time flew faster than we wanted, and we had to say goodbye.

I had packed for the Academy before the weekend, so I could spend as much time as possible with Dan. Then I stopped by the post office and was on my way to Camden after I mailed letters to Dan and Mom.

I was committed, and Dan supported me. Before I left, I took my wedding ring set off and put the rings on the gold chain Dan had given me. The set included the promise ring, engagement ring, and the wedding band. I put the chain around his neck.

"Take care of those. I'll be back for them."

"You better," he said. "I'll keep them next to my heart until you do."

With one last long hug and kiss, I said goodbye.

I used the name Angie Lewis. Angie was a variation of my real name, Angelina. And Lewis was Dan's biological surname before he and Ben were adopted by the Brocks. They weren't fake names; they were important to me.

The first day of the academy arrived, and my undercover life began. We checked in, had our physicals, and received our training clothing and books that morning. In the afternoon, we did physical fitness evaluations.

It was obvious after physical fitness training that some cadets might not make it. The evaluation determined how much training each cadet would need to meet the minimum physical fitness requirements.

On the first day, I passed every standard. I set a record for female cadets in the one-mile run, and beat the minimums for sit-ups, push-ups, and pull-ups.

Only ten male cadets and I met all the minimum standards. The others weren't happy with us.

The next morning started at eight, with routine physical fitness. Stretches, sit-ups, push-ups, jumping jacks, and then a mile and a half run. I woke up at five a.m. and had already run three miles around the track before PT.

We lined up to begin our run, but the PT instructor called me aside. "Cadet Lewis, a word." It was going to take time to get used to being called Lewis.

"Yes, sir?"

"How many laps did you run this morning?"

"Twelve, sir," I answered.

"You know you still have to run another mile and a half?"

"My daily average is five miles, sir."

"Do you plan to run every morning before we start?"

"If I'm allowed to, sir."

He smiled. "You're allowed. But do me a favor and run with the ones that need encouragement. Show me you're a leader." Me be a leader? I was the youngest person here.

It was my turn to smile. "Yes, sir."

The rest of the class had already started. Today's run wasn't timed. It was a training run. The ones struggling were only half a lap ahead. I caught up with them easily.

There were three overweight guys running side by side.

"Well, look at this. Little miss show-off running at the back of the class." One guy huffed.

"I'm not here to show off," I replied. "I'm here to become a deputy. My dad was a marine, and I was an only child. I grew up a tomboy."

If I had expected that explanation to get me any respect, I was wrong. There were several negative comments from them before I shut them up.

"There's three women in this class. Are you going to let all of us beat you?"

With that, I ran to the next person ahead of them, one of the other two women. She looked at me in surprise. "Have you lapped me already?"

"No, I just caught up with you. I'm encouraging the people struggling. Let's pick up the pace a little. There are three guys behind you who don't enjoy getting beaten by women. Let's make sure they stay there, okay?"

She smiled then. "Okay."

We picked up three guys and completed one lap, a quarter of a mile, before we reached the third woman.

"Come on. Keep the pace. This will be the minimum pace you need to pass. We will increase a little each day."

"How do you know this is the minimum pace?"

"Let's just say I've run a lot and won a lot of races. I know my pacing."

We lost the first woman, Marti, halfway through the last lap. If she stuck with it, she would pass at the end. Sticking with it would be the hardest part. After crossing the finish line, I doubled back and walked with her to the finish line.

"I'm not a quitter, I'm just not a runner," she said.

Once we finished the run, we hit the showers, ate breakfast, and headed to the classroom. Another test to evaluate our knowledge. They wanted to know how much we knew. I didn't know as much as I thought I did. Everyone failed the test. The class was mixed with soon-to-be deputies, city patrol officers. We were cadets until we graduated. The academy trained Arkansas police officers equally. We wore our police force uniforms to class, and the instructors inspected us each morning.

After inspection, our instructor called the roll, then asked, "Did I miss anyone?"

I raised my hand. He looked at me for a full minute before he asked, "What's your name?"

"Angie Lewis, sir."

He checked what I assumed was a list of the cadets and found my name. He looked up at me and nodded. What did that look and nod mean? What did that list say?

"Your training here will include classroom and field training. The classroom portion will consist of lectures from experienced officers, video training, and role-playing scenarios. The field training has already begun. You're not training to be Marines, but you need to be in shape. Besides physical conditioning, you will learn hand-to-hand self-defense techniques and the use of firearms."

He hesitated a moment and looked at the cadets around the room. "Before we begin our classroom training, I want to remind you that loaded weapons are only allowed on the shooting range. If you had read your introduction material, you would know that. If you missed that piece of information, then you will get a pass today. Radios and cell phones are to be turned off during class time. Use your phones during breaks and after the day's training."

I had not missed the information printed in large bold letters on nearly every page of the welcome packet. My personal Glock 19 was unloaded and in my shoulder holster under my jacket. As a cadet, I had everything a deputy carried on the job. When I became an undercover officer, I would leave the issued field weapon, uniform, badge, and ID behind.

With the announcements over, we began our training with a video introducing us to the training program. It was boring but informative.

The afternoon was reserved for shooting instruction. Again, we were tested to set our baseline scores.

They taught us how to hold our pistols with the two-handed Weber stance and grip. The instructor checked we were holding our unloaded weapons properly, pointed downrange at our targets. Dad had taught me how to do that years ago, and it was also one technique we used in shooting sports.

When it was time to practice, the targets were at fifteen yards. I had shot over a thousand rounds through my pistol, and I rarely missed a bullseye at ten or fifteen yards. I missed a few at twenty-five, but never at the closer distances. The first five rounds hit the bullseye. The instructor tapped me on the shoulder. I laid my pistol down, pointed downrange and turned around. He was looking at my target through binoculars.

He dropped the binoculars that hung on a strap around his neck and tapped his ear protection. I removed the ear protection from my right ear, and he said, "Show me how good you really are. Start at the five ring and shoot the numbers out going down to the bullseye."

I replaced the ear protection and grinned. "Challenge accepted, sir."

There are ten rings on the target. The outermost ring is worth one point. Each ring closer to the bullseye is worth one more point until you reach the bullseye, which is worth ten points.

Any shot outside the rings is worth zero points. A perfect score is one hundred points. You must squeeze the trigger so that your aim stays true.

Pulling the trigger hard causes your aim to be jerked off center. Usually to the right and down for right-handers and left and down for left-hand shooters. Most shooters use a system of taking a deep breath and slowly exhaling while squeezing the trigger.

We had to shoot in groups and turn our targets in to another instructor, who scored the targets. One of the fat guys I talked to on the track that morning was behind me. "How'd you shoot, Miss hotshot?"

I didn't answer. I showed him my target. "Impressive," he said. "How about you?" I asked. Our targets were almost identical. I laughed. "Impressive," I replied.

The scoring instructor recorded a score of eighty-five, and I protested. "We want our cadets to have room for improvement," he said. "You showed us a perfect score without getting a perfect score."

The guy behind me said nothing because he had heard the explanation given to me. As I walked away from the scoring table, he asked, "Hey, can I ask you a question?"

"Sure," I said, thinking he might not like the answer.

"Can you help me get a better time in the mile run?"

He was being sincere, which surprised me. I just looked at him.

"I'm sorry about this morning. You helped and encouraged those other people. I can't afford to fail at this."

"Okay, apology accepted. We start on the track at five in the morning. While I run three miles, you'll walk as fast as you can and for as many laps as you can while I'm running."

"What will walking do?"

"It will help you condition your legs and your lungs. You will still have to do the PT run in the mornings, so you don't want to overdo it."

"Okay."

"Five o'clock, not five fifteen or five thirty, okay?"

"Okay."

I held out my hand. "I'm Angie Lewis. What's your name?"

"I'm Sam. Sam McKinney."

"Sam, you may have some company in the morning. I'm going to invite some others to do the same thing."

Chapter 26

Angel

Five cadets were waiting for me when I hit the track to stretch.

"Alright, Coach, what do we do?"

"Walk," I said. "Walk fast. I had a wreck last fall and cracked some ribs. The breathing hurt like hell when I tried to run. So, I walked five miles a day until I could run again. Before that, I ran five miles a day to prepare for a three-mile cross-country race. Three miles is easy when you can do five. One mile will be easy if you can do one and a half or two. Got it?"

"Were you good at track?" Marti asked.

I turned to begin my run. "State champion in cross country, and state champion in the eight hundred meters. Let's go."

They were tired when it came time for the mile and a half PT run. But they stuck together and encouraged each other. They walked the last lap and still finished ahead of the two slowpokes.

I walked the last lap with them. They were feeling as though they had let me down until the PT instructor fell in beside them on the last lap. "Don't you stop now just because you put in extra work at five this morning. Yeah, I know where you were this morning. You keep it up, and you'll get up to go for a run every morning for the rest of your life. You'll feel better, and you'll have more energy for those double shifts."

He kept talking until they had a hundred yards left. "Now let me see what you have left. Run to the finish line!"

There were several cadets waiting at the finish line, and they joined me as I yelled encouragement. Poor Sam gave it everything he had. Then he hit the infield and puked his guts up. I told them all they did well and made them promise me they would be there at five in the morning.

It was raining the next morning at four thirty. I smiled, wondering how many would show up to walk and run with me. I was on the track at ten minutes before five. No one was there. But then they started showing up. By five, everyone was there.

"Do we still do this in the rain?" Sam asked.

"How many wrecks occur in this kind of weather? How many tornadoes?" I asked. "It's water. You shower with it. You'll be okay."

I turned to run and saw three more cadets coming to join us. Two of them were Sam's buddies from the first day.

I told everyone to start without me. Marti and Sam started jogging. The rest started walking.

"Sam told us to show up this morning. But we didn't think you would do this in the rain."

"Like I told them, this is what you will work in during tornadoes. Wrecks occur in this weather. It won't keep you from working, so don't let it stop you from exercising. Walk fast this morning, but save a little for PT later."

I turned and started jogging. I didn't wait to see what they did. But when I passed them, they were putting in an effort. And everyone was still going when I stopped twelve laps later.

Because the weather had changed to thunderstorms, PT was cancelled because of possible lightning strikes. Instead, we had introductory self-defense in the gym.

This instructor was new. We hadn't met him yet. He started the class by talking about situations where officers were injured, and even killed because they didn't know how to protect themselves.

He grabbed a volunteer and demonstrated a chokehold where he grabbed the volunteer from behind with his right arm around his neck. Then he asked the volunteer to escape. The first two volunteers failed. Then he asked me.

He barely had me in the chokehold before I made my move. He held me tighter than he needed, and that made it easier for me to be aggressive. Dad had taught me the Marine Corps method of escaping chokeholds.

I pulled down on his arm with both hands, twisted my body left and got my left leg behind his right leg. Then, I pushed his body backwards over my leg, tripping him onto his back. In five seconds, I had my knee in his chest and my hands around his throat.

He yelled, "Stop!"

I stood up and offered him my hand to help him up. He took it, and as he stood up, he said, "Stay here."

"I've been thrown by cadets in this class before, but never as quickly and easily as she did it. The method she used is a basic combat move taught in the military. Two things worked in her favor. One. She has practiced the move until it's muscle memory. She doesn't have to think about it. Two. She didn't wait for me to get set. She started moving as soon as my arm went around her neck. A swift reaction time can save your life."

He looked at the class, and they stared back. A few of them looked at me and smiled.

"Now, let's walk through this process step by step and show everyone how you did it. You were so quick I didn't even see it."

The class laughed, and I found myself liking this instructor.

I was picking up the classroom lessons easily. I realized how much Dad had taught me, and how much I had listened. Before I knew it. We were at the halfway point. The lead instructor was doing midterm reviews with the cadets. When it was my turn, I found Sergeant Johnson in the office with the lead instructor, Mr. Paulson.

"Hello Angie. Sergeant Johnson and I are reviewing your progress," he said.

Sergeant Johnson followed with, "Your success has created a minor problem for us."

"What do you mean?" I asked and took a seat.

"You're at the top of your class. Every cadet knows you and looks at you as a leader. Even the ones who are years older than you." Mr. Paulson said.

"An undercover officer is supposed to blend in. Be inconspicuous. You, on the other hand, have stood out." Sergeant Johnson continued. "We must do something to protect you after you graduate. You see, top cadets are recognized at graduation. Photos are taken and often published in their local papers. We can't have that happen with you, because you can't afford to be affiliated with any law enforcement agency."

"What do I do then?" I asked.

"Well," Mr. Paulson began, "We can't have you perform at a mediocre level now. Your classmates know how good you are, and they would start questioning you. They respect you, and would offer you encouragement and assistance."

Sergeant Johnson took over. "We are going to do a special presentation on undercover work. I'll talk about the importance of undercover work, and how to protect your fellow officers should you recognize one. We are going to take a midterm class picture with you in it. You won't be in the graduation picture, nor will you be at graduation. Your classmates will get a copy of the midterm picture to replace their graduation picture when your undercover work is done."

"Can I stay and watch them graduate?" I asked.

"I'm sorry. Your assignment will have already begun."

Chapter 27

Angel

My act at the strip club in North Little Rock was to be a bad girl. I tried to weave a theme into my dance routines. No one cared besides me, but it helped me focus on the real reason I was there. That's where I met the new and improved version of Donny Ray.

"Angie, come down here. Someone I want you to meet," Fat Man, the bar owner, said to me when I was finishing a dance. During the two months of dancing there, I never heard his real name. He was simply called Fat Man.

I was the only dancer on the stage, and I danced to Kung Foo Fighting. Most of the dance was part of a kata, or karate exercise. But the observers never realized I was doing a series of real karate moves on stage. They did not care that I had become a brown belt in Tae Kwon Do, or that I was working toward my first-degree black belt. They wanted to see me dance naked. The closer I got to the edge of the stage, the more tips I got.

I had become comfortable being naked on stage, but I was leery of being naked on the barroom floor. Showing my titties on Bourbon Street actually helped. I was wary of being on the barroom floor at all. Men were often reaching out and groping the dancers. We had a rule never to have sex with the customers.

I had decided the only person I would have sex with was Donny Ray. And that choice was one that Dan and I both had a difficult time with when we discussed it on our honeymoon. If the opportunity arose, I had to make him fall for me long enough to learn about his operation.

"Angie, this is Mr. Donny Ray. He just bought your contract," said Fat Man.

"Contract? I don't have a fucking contract with you."

"Whatever you say, Angie, you're fired then." And Fat Man walked away.

This wasn't the Donny Ray I remembered. I forgot I was standing there barefooted and wearing a thong that hid nothing, holding a handful of one-and five-dollar bills from the stage. Fat Man confused me. That wasn't the cue he was supposed to give me when Donny Ray showed up. There was no contract. He had no right to sell me to someone else. I was about to follow and cuss Fat Man out when I heard Mr. Donny Ray speak. He spoke quietly and confidently. That's when I remembered my actual mission here.

"Angie, please have a seat so we can talk about this," Donnie Ray said with the purest Southern accent I had ever heard.

I glared at him for the first time. He looked me directly in the eyes, not at my breasts or my naked body. He looked me in the eye, and this caught me off guard, too. Then I noticed the suit and tie, the fresh clean haircut, and the smooth shave. Gone were the long, stringy blond hair, and the unkempt beard. I wondered what kind of game he was playing now that he had the decency to look me in the eye when he was talking to me. He wasn't looking at my body the way Fat Man looked at me.

I thought I remembered him being tall, but I couldn't tell since he was sitting. I'd seen him before, but it was at a distance. He was young, in his mid to late twenties. He was very handsome. The suit fit him well, which meant tailored, I thought.

I pulled out a chair and wiped it off with a few napkins and sat down with my legs crossed and my arms folded across my breasts. I looked for Fat Man, but he was gone.

Donnie Ray said, "I own a little bar and hunting lodge up on the White River. I like to have a few pretty servers around to encourage the customers to keep coming back." He spoke in that melodic Southern voice that I'm sure would charm the panties off most young women. "There's usually two or three young ladies working for me, and most of them live in my house or the lodge. There's plenty of room, and I don't charge rent. I protect them from good old boys who want to do more than flirt with them."

I knew this was a lie, but I pretended to buy it. It wasn't Donny Ray's sales pitch. It was the good looks; the close-cropped haircut, the smile, the baritone voice, and the eye contact that nearly convinced me. He had a charisma that made him even more attractive. If I hadn't known what he could do, I would have believed him. And that made him even more dangerous. This was a man who could say 'I love you' while stabbing you in the heart.

"So, what do you think?" Donnie Ray asked. "You don't want to spend the best years of your life working at a strip joint in the bad part of North Little Rock. You want more out of life than that, don't you?"

Of course, I thought, everyone wants more out of life. I want to put you and your cronies in jail. Now let me get into character and get started. But I never finished my thoughts. Donnie Ray was talking again. He told me I have beautiful eyes.

"Stop," I said. "I'm sitting here completely naked, and you're telling me I have beautiful eyes? What kind of bullshit are you feeding me?"

"No bullshit," he laughed. "You really have beautiful eyes. And a beautiful body, too."

There was that damn Southern charm. This time I blushed. I hadn't seen him look at my body, but he had obviously watched me dance. I knew I had an attractive body. Every man I talked to told me that. But it was only my body they wanted. They didn't want to know what I thought or what I wanted out of life. They only wanted sex, but they weren't getting it from me. The only man who wanted me for what I am is Dan.

"Would I be dancing at your bar, Mr. Ray?" I asked. Trying to avoid letting him know what I was thinking.

"Please call D-Ray, or Donny. Mr. Ray was my dad.

"Dancing, maybe," he replied. "But not stripping. Some of my customers wouldn't approve of that; others couldn't handle it. They would have you raped before I could shoot them."

"You would shoot a customer for raping me? Fat man would just demand payment, like he was pimping me out," I said.

"I protect my staff to the best I can," Donnie Ray said.

That surprised me. He used the word staff, not girls or women, and didn't directly answer my question either. He was the smoothest liar I had ever met. But what did I expect? I had expected him to be a rough around the edges country boy. A hunting and fishing guide. He seemed to have transitioned into a businessman who was trying to appear as an old-fashioned Southern gentleman. I was seeing through the act, though. He was good, but I was better. I had to be, because my life depended on it.

"Alright, I'm in, since I don't have a job here anymore," I said, like I had a choice. I was about to earn my real paycheck.

Donnie Ray smiled at me and, for the first time, I saw his eyes drop to my breasts. I had to admit, his looking at my body excited me. *He killed your father, Angel. Never forget that.*

"Go get dressed," he said. "I'm hungry for some BBQ ribs. There is a place on the other side of town. Have you ever eaten at Gaucho's?"

"No, but I've heard it's good."

I stood, turned away, and walked through the dressing room door.

Fat Man was waiting for me when I got to the dressing room.

"What the hell is going on, Fat Man?" I glared at him. "Is that really Donny Ray out there? That's not the cue you were supposed to give me."

"It's him. He's changed, Angie." Fat Man whispered. "He wanted to buy a girl. I'm pretty sure he deals in sex slaves. And, and, and..." he stammered as he looked me in the eye.

I knew he was frightened, because he was looking me in the eye. He wasn't staring at my tits like he usually did. I grabbed a little black t-shirt from the makeup table and slid into it. He was a pervert and a creep.

I finished his sentence for him.

"And you played your role like you promised. But this version scares you, doesn't it?"

"Right," he replied. "This Donny Ray is a cold-blooded killer. I called your roommate. She has Donny's name, his description, and the plate number on his truck." My roommate, Rebecca, was my undercover partner at the strip club. She was two years older and more of a training officer to me. As a Pulaski County deputy, she and I were part of the task force to infiltrate Donny Ray's organization. The plan was for one or both of us would get in. One of us worked every night the club was open.

I was shocked. Fat Man was showing some concern and some initiative. That was unusual.

Then I asked sarcastically, "How much did he pay you for my contract?"

"It's not good, Angie. He gave me five thousand in cash."

I stopped with one leg in my Cruel Girl jeans and found the chair. Once seated, I stared at Fat Man.

"I'm sorry, Angie. I had to warn you so you could be careful."

He turned away, and I thought I saw him wipe a tear from his eye.

"I'm sorry," he said again as he walked away.

My mind was a blur of thoughts. I needed all my skills and cunning for this assignment. It was happening. I was really going undercover.

Fat Man was back by the time I got my jeans on. He was carrying a single piece of paper.

"Rebecca works fast," he said as he handed me the paper.

I looked at the paper and had to agree with Fat Man. It was a one-paragraph report to Sergeant Johnson. It said I was leaving with the suspect, and I was going deep undercover as planned. I signed it and gave it back to Fat Man.

"I'll fax this back to her," he said.

He turned away and stopped. He looked back at me and said, "I'm just an old pervert. I look but don't touch. If he is a trafficker, take him down, Angie." And he walked away.

Fat Man had been arrested for allowing some of his dancers to prostitute themselves to the customers. He never admitted to pimping his dancers, and the dancers never said he did. To avoid charges, he spilled his guts about the twin brothers Donny and Danny Ray buying the contract of one of his dancers and agreed to allow the state police to run the operation to sell me or my roommate, Rebecca, to Donny Ray.

I threw my things into a small duffle bag, stepped into the hallway and stopped at the next dressing room, which two dancers shared, and stuck my head in.

"I'm done for good, girls. My dressing room is empty if one of you wants it, and you can share the rest of my dance spots."

Chapter 28

Angel

Dinner was pleasant, but it wasn't great. I didn't like eating after eight o'clock. I preferred fasting for ten to twelve hours between dinner and breakfast. My strict routine was out the door and entirely up to the new and even more mysterious and dangerous D-Ray. He wanted to go straight back to his home. But I insisted on getting some clothes from my apartment.

We had planned for this possibility. The apartment was sterile, decorated with generic furniture and wall decor. It had only one picture each of me and Rebecca. Otherwise, it could have been a long-stay hotel room. Which was exactly how we treated it.

I texted Rebecca to let her know we were coming. She activated the camera system and left the apartment. We didn't want Donny Ray to see the other roommate in case something went wrong with the first undercover attempt. The second person still had a chance at the operation, although it would be very slim.

I invited Donny into the apartment by asking if he would help me with the suitcase. We didn't want him to become suspicious of anything. Insisting that he not come in could have caused a problem.

It took only a few minutes to pack my clothes while Donny looked over the apartment. "You don't have much," he said.

"No, I'm barely off the street. I was homeless for several weeks before I started stripping. That's where I met Rebecca. She offered me her spare room." Our backstories had been meticulously planned and rehearsed. Being homeless was supposed to explain not having a car or a lot of possessions and being desperate to succeed.

He watched me put the last of my clothes into the old suitcase that came from Goodwill. "I never want to be homeless again." Turning, I walked to him, wrapped my arm around him and pressed my body against his. "I'll do anything to get ahead and never be homeless again."

"Anything?" he asked.

"Anything," I responded. And as I intended, he leaned down and kissed me. Part of the plan was to become his girlfriend. If he didn't want a girlfriend, then we were to become his favorite girl, which meant doing anything, including sex and drugs.

I had said I could do it, but now that the time had come, I had to force myself. You could say I went on the attack. His kiss led to me pretending to be turned on, and before I knew it, he was turned on and I ended up on my back in bed one last time before I left it for good.

I had worked on this persona of Angie Lewis with Dan and with Rebecca. Slipping into that personality had been a challenge at first, but the more I worked as a stripper, the easier it became. I did not think about Dan, my mom, dad, or the farm. I walked out of the apartment, as Angie and I left most of Angel behind. Angie Lewis was a horny, badass stripper who would do anything to get ahead in life. Step one was accomplished.

Step two was to become important to him. Become someone he wanted to keep around. The trip to the lodge was a little over an hour. I carried on with idle chatter. Telling lies about my life growing up and ending up on the street. Asking him generic questions like where he was born? Where did he grow up? Questions about his family. He answered everything smoothly until I asked about brothers or sisters.

Then he hesitated and said, "I have a twin brother." I wasn't supposed to know about Danny Ray, or that he was dead. It surprised me he said, "I have," instead of "I had." I didn't know if that was a verbal slip or a mental state that I needed to be aware of.

"Will I get to meet him? I won't accidentally end up fucking him by accident, will I?"

"He won't be around," D-Ray said.

"Too bad." I teased. Maybe he was still in denial about his brother being dead. I needed to be cautious on that subject. Better yet, I would ignore it.

We turned off the highway onto a gravel road. We had barely made the turn when he stopped. The headlights shone on a snake crawling across the road. It was still warm in September.

"Water moccasin," he said. "I hate snakes. He must be moving because they cut the rice field today." That explained the movement. It wasn't cold enough for them to hibernate yet, but they rarely moved much on cool nights.

He opened the console between us and pulled out a pistol.

"I could use a little target practice," he said as he opened the truck door. I got out of the truck as well.

His first three shots missed and only caused the snake to curl up in its defensive striking position.

"Let me try," I said.

He laughed at me. But he handed me the pistol and said, "Let's see how close you can get. Hurry, he's crawling away."

Should I show off or not? Why not? Something told me Donny wasn't attracted to the helpless type. He might fuck them, but that was it. I took a two-handed aim and shot the head of the snake before it could crawl off the road. Then, for the hell of it, I shot the snake twice more, cutting the tail off with the third shot.

I pulled the slide back and ejected the live round from the barrel. I picked the cartridge up from the road and handed the pistol back to Donny Ray. "That's how you shoot a snake," I said.

He didn't say a word. I know he watched me walk back to the truck. I could see his reflection in the windshield. There was a reason I unloaded the pistol. I wanted a little warning if he decided to shoot me in the back. But I was back inside the truck before he reloaded the pistol and walked up to the snake. Even though the snake's body was still twitching, he could easily see that I had made three perfect shots.

He looked at me differently when he got into the truck. "Where did you learn to shoot?"

"My daddy taught me when I was a young girl. Before he passed away," I said.

He nodded, but he was obviously thinking about my shooting ability. I may have just made a mistake. I hoped it would be my only mistake.

He became more talkative and talked about the farmland we were driving through. Some of it was owned by other family members, but it all was once owned by his grandfather. "The family has an agreement. If someone wants to sell, they must offer it to other family members first. I'd like to buy it all back someday.

"My dad was the oldest, and he got the house. That's where we are going now."

It was an old two-story house. Even in the dark, I could tell it had once been a showplace. It was built on a hill overlooking the White River. I couldn't see the river. But the single night light showed a large equipment shed with tractors, combines, and trailers parked under it.

"Do you farm also?" I asked.

"No, we lease the farmland to a cousin who farms and uses the shed to store old equipment," he said as we drove by the shed and parked behind the house.

D-Ray, as he called himself now, didn't move when he turned the ignition off. He was thinking about something. I didn't want him growing suspicious of me.

"Nice place," I said. "Let's continue what we started at my place." I reached over the console and rubbed his crotch until I felt his arousal.

*****

I was awake at five a.m., but everything was foggy. It had to be a hangover, the result of sniffing cocaine with D-Ray last night. I was accustomed to running at five in the morning, and I hated to stop.

I went to the bathroom and took one look in the mirror. The guilt hit me immediately. Was I cheating on Dan? We had talked about what I would need to do. I didn't want to be with Donny Ray. This, I reminded myself this was a job requirement for the persona of Angie Lewis, the undercover officer. I was separating Angel Brock from this investigation. Angel Brock could be hurt, even broken. Angie Lewis was a nymphomaniac who would use sex and her body to get ahead.

I pushed Angel aside. *Alright, Angie, let's go for a run. Then come back and fuck D-Ray's brains out and see where this day takes us.*

I ran down the driveway and turned onto the dirt road. I don't know how far I ran. When I started this job, I never thought I would spend most of my time in silent prayer. During this run, I cried and I prayed. Then I cried and prayed some more. I never dreamed how afraid I would be, or how much comfort and confidence running and prayer would give me.

I was shaking when I returned to the house. My body needed coffee and something to eat. To my surprise, I found a couple sitting at the kitchen table drinking coffee.

"Good morning. I'm Angie," I said, offering my hand.

The woman took my hand and shook it lightly. "I'm Blake. This is Mike. He doesn't talk much until he's had three or four cups of coffee. You must be the one who kept us up half the night last night."

"I'm sorry. What do you mean?"

"D-Ray's bed was banging against the wall last night for over an hour. How the hell do you have the energy to get up this early and go running?"

"I do it every day," I said. "Is there more coffee? I'm sorry we kept you up. Where are the cups?"

"Probably all dirty," Blake answered.

I looked at the dishes piled up in the sink. There wasn't a dishwasher. The house was built before their time. I turned the hot water on and looked for dish detergent. Finally, I found a nearly empty bottle in the cabinet under the sink. I washed a single cup and poured the remaining coffee into it. The coffee was hot, but weak. I made another pot, my way. If no one liked it, they could water it down.

I started adding dishes to the soapy water.

"Are you really going to do the dishes?" Blake asked.

"I'll do whatever it takes to earn my keep."

"Obviously," Mike finally spoke.

He was staring at me when I turned around to look at him. "He speaks," I said. I turned back to the dishes. "This pot of coffee will be a little stronger. You will like it, Mike."

He stood up and grabbed his and Blake's cups and walked to the pot. He poured two cups and took a sip before moving away from the pot. "Ah, now that's coffee. D-Ray needs to keep you around just to make coffee."

I smiled and allowed myself a brief memory. Dan had taught me the secret of making excellent coffee. My smile disappeared quickly when I heard a voice say, "Who are we keeping around to make coffee?" Little John asked. That was the last voice I wanted to hear and the last face I wanted to see.

I didn't think Little John was the quiet type. He wasn't. His mouth spoke whatever he thought. "I bet little miss sweet ass can do more than make coffee and do dishes."

I felt one hand grab my butt, and the other on my shoulder. The plate dropped back into the water, and I grabbed the hand on my shoulder. I turned my body to him and put my leg behind his and pushed backwards on his body, tripping him to the floor.

His pistol fell out of his pants and onto the floor beside him. I grabbed it before he did. Then I stood and put a round into the floor beside his head. I nicked his ear, and it bled. I hadn't intended to hit him, but he moved. The sound was deafening, but we could still hear cursing and falling sounds from upstairs. "What the hell is going on?" D-Ray screamed from upstairs.

Little John regained his composure. "Now, put that pistol down. You could have shot me with that thing."

Footsteps pounded down the stairs.

"If I wanted to shoot you, I would have hit more than your ear," I said.

"I'll take that thing away from you and spank your ass," he yelled.

"Little John, don't move," D-Ray commanded. "She didn't miss you. Your ear is bleeding."

Little John slowly raised his hand to his ear and looked at the blood on it.

"Who the fuck are you?"

I continued to hold the pistol on him and gave him my best fake smile. "Hi. I'm Angie. D-Ray's new girlfriend."

"Since when?" Little John yelled.

"Since last night," Donny Ray answered as he walked to me. He gently reached for the pistol and took it from me. "Keep your hands off her, Little John. She'll kill you quicker than you can open your mouth."

Blake giggled. Mike muttered, "I ain't seen anybody faster than his mouth." Everyone but Little John laughed.

D-Ray looked at Little John. "Get up. You're bleeding on the floor. You know how I feel about blood on the floor. Clean it up."

He looked at Mike and said, "Aren't you talking a little early in the morning?"

"You need to try her coffee," Mike said before being quiet again.

D-Ray turned back to me, put his hand on my shoulder, and kissed me gently. He looked at his hand. I'm sure he could feel the sweat from my morning run. Then he looked at me. "Go take a shower. We need to go to work."

Chapter 29

Dan

The sale of the cameras to Donny Ray turned out to be easy. He even wanted more than I had agreed to buy. So the installer made him a deal he would be stupid to refuse. The camera shop owner was thrilled with the money he made. But he was greedy. He wanted more money for the password. I had no choice but to pay him more.

I still needed cameras in the house, but I couldn't afford to spend any more money. Money leaves a trail. Luckily, I had bought extra cameras from the shop owner, thinking I would install cameras in the lodge myself. My class schedule kept me from having the time to do that. I finally got cameras into the house so I had access to the cameras at both places.

It became my pattern. Running five miles and doing farm chores early in the morning. Then, I would spend fifteen to twenty minutes scrolling through videos before heading to my classes.

Angel and I would talk late at night while she was at the Academy. I never understood the pain people felt when they said they missed someone. I did now, though, and I wanted to hold Angel in my arms and feel the rise and fall of her body against me as she breathed.

The EMT program ended in July. I passed the exams and began working part time for the ambulance service in Searcy while taking nursing classes at Harding. Angel's Android phone was identical to mine. They both had an extra slot for a second SIM card, which meant we could have two phone numbers. The night she left the academy, we talked for two hours as she drove to North Little Rock. When she arrived, we said a difficult goodbye. We took our second SIM cards out and threw them away. We were afraid that if her phone was checked, the information on the second card could be traced to me and expose her for who she really was.

It was time to trust her, but most importantly, it was time to trust God and let Him protect Angel.

It was ten weeks later that I saw her. I almost didn't recognize her. She had really cut her hair short. It was short on the neck and a little long on top, with a comb-over. She was now a bleach blonde. She puckered her lips a lot, making her face look thinner and sexier.

It was her body and her movements I recognized. I watched her longer than I should have and was going to be late for class. I realized that if I barely recognized her, and she was playing the Angie Lewis persona, she might pull this undercover operation off. But seeing her also made me miss her more. Now the real worrying began. I could tell myself a thousand times that she was under God's protection, but it didn't keep me from worrying.

Dad and I talked and prayed for an hour that evening. I did most of the talking, which meant he did most of the praying. It took me forty-five minutes just to tell him everything I knew. I had reached a point where my young mind needed his wisdom and experience. When I finished, he told me how proud he was of me, how proud he was of Angel.

"I know there is more going on than meets the eye. I have watched how busy you always are. When you're not working or at college, you're on your laptop, or working on the farm. I've never known an eighteen-year-old to work as hard as you work.

"Son, Angel has picked a very dangerous battle. I'll pray for her safety every day. She needs your love and support regardless of what she must do. You must overlook her actions and forgive her, because her ultimate goal is righteous."

"Yes, sir."

"Then memorize this verse from *John 15:13. Greater love has no one than this, that he lay down his life for his friends.*

"This is the verse that got me through the Vietnam conflict."

That verse confused me. I didn't want her to die, and I knew she didn't want to die either.

"You've never told us about your time in the army, just that you were a medic," I said.

"I am sorry, son, but that is all I will tell you. Those were days I do not wish to remember. Now, think about this question. At the end of the day, who protects those who choose to become the guardian angels, and who seeks absolution for the avenging angels?"

He hesitated before continuing. "Angel needs your help and your unconditional love, son. You do whatever it takes to help her, because she is laying her life on the line to protect others. She is out there in the midst of the battle. Your job is to be here to support her. Can you do that?"

"Yes, sir."

"And Daniel," he only called me Daniel when he wanted to make a point. "Talk to me anytime you need to because two heads are better than one. I'm on your side, son."

Chapter 30

Angel

I had thought of Donny Ray and Little John as a kind of country outlaws. They were that and much more. They were businessmen. D-Ray was handling the legitimate side of the business, and Little John was handling the other side. From what I could tell, the legitimate side was doing very well, and explained D-Ray's cleaned up appearance.

D-Ray ran the bar and restaurant, the hunting lodge, and the guide business. Little John ran the drugs and the girls under D-Ray's strict supervision. He occasionally painted a house, which was his own legal business. The girls looked older when they wore make-up, but they were fifteen to seventeen years old. There were three of them at the lodge, and they were frightened drug addicts who did whatever they were told so they could get their next release. Little John was a meth addict, which explained why the drug they were addicted to was also meth.

I had often wondered why they didn't come after Dad, or me and Mom more frequently. The first week I spent working at the bar and restaurant explained the reason. D-Ray had a business to run, and it was a good business. The restaurant served catfish and barbecue out of a kitchen run by Blake, who was an excellent cook. Mike was the main bartender, and he was in charge of the barbecue pit.

D-Ray had seven or eight hunting and fishing guides working for him and would sometimes work as a guide himself. The lodge only had twenty rooms, but it stayed half full most of the time with hunters and anglers. A local woman named Suzanne ran the lodge. She was another cousin or had been married to a cousin. She didn't like me, apparently, because I had all of D-Ray's attention.

I didn't see much of Little John the first week after I kicked his butt for touching me. Blake didn't like Little John, either. She told me, "After you went to take a shower, D-Ray told Little John about you shooting the snake last night. He told Little John to leave you alone. That you hit whatever you aimed at. And he added he wanted to see where your relationship leads."

She asked me how we had met. I told her about the strip joint, my fake story and said I had nothing to lose. So, I decided to see where this ride would take me. "I mean, who wouldn't be interested in a good-looking businessman like D-Ray, right?"

Her hesitation to answer told me more than her final answer. "He is good-looking."

I got her talking again when I said something about Little John being handsy. "Girl! He will screw anyone or anything. But be careful around him. He fears Donny Ray, not you."

I don't know what I thought undercover work was going to be, but it wasn't working twelve to fourteen hours a day in a bar and restaurant. But I worked hard, did everything I was asked to do, and I tried not to complain. I did complain to D-Ray, "We don't spend any time together. The only time we see each other is just before bed." My motive was to learn more about his operation. I didn't want to spend time with him. As a businessman, he was boring and too focused on his job. I wanted to learn more about the people involved.

I needed more information and more access to see what was happening behind the scenes. Picking up bits and pieces of information here and there was fine, but it wasn't enough.

The Wood Duck Lodge was laid out with the restaurant and bar at one end and the lodge offices at the other end. In between were the rooms, with five rooms on each side of the hallway on the first and second floors.

My luck changed on Friday. Suzanne, who ran the lodge, called in sick. D-Ray asked me to run the lodge in her place. His office was next to the lodge office, so he was close by if I had questions.

It was boring. I watched the news on the internet. That was more news than I'd had in a week. I watched YouTube videos for a few minutes, but that wasn't for me, because I needed to be moving and doing something. I stuck my head into D-Ray's office to ask what I could do to stay busy, but he stared daggers at me before relaxing. He put his cell phone against his body and said, "Give me a few minutes, and close the door behind you."

I did, but I wondered what could be so important that I couldn't hear. I looked at my phone to see the time. Eight fifteen. We started working at seven a.m. every morning. He seemed to disappear for phone calls at eight in the morning and five in the afternoon. What were they about? It was like a conference call for a business. It intrigued me, and I decided I would watch closer to see if he was having private calls at eight and five.

The closet with cleaning supplies was down the hall from the lobby. I swept and mopped the lobby — in front and behind the counter — and I was standing on a chair, washing the windows, when I realized D-Ray was watching me.

"I can't remember seeing those windows cleaned in the last ten years. They must have been, but I don't remember it."

"They're filthy. And I was bored. I'm used to doing something, which is what I was going to ask you. Who cleans the lodge rooms? Are there more cleaning supplies than these?" I stepped down from the chair and walked to him. Outside the house, he was all business. No fooling around or flirting, but without Suzanne here, he acted differently. He leaned down and kissed me.

"Suzanne does it all. She cleans, does the laundry, and runs the front end. But she's lazy, too. She's got a new boyfriend, so she'll probably be gone for a week. Too high, or too drunk to work."

A white van pulling into the parking lot interrupted us. It looked familiar, like the one I'd seen trying to kidnap Sissy at the football game. That memory was a mental jolt that reminded me of why I was here. I didn't see Little John or Donny Ray that night, but that didn't mean that wasn't the van.

The van belonged to Little John. I didn't want to be around him. I told D-Ray, "I'm going to the restroom. Keep him away from me, please."

Chapter 31

Angel

When I returned, they were out in the parking lot, leaning on the hood of the van and talking. I went back to cleaning windows and watched them talk for twenty minutes. I heard their muffled voices, but couldn't make out their words. D-Ray handled Little John sternly, but with love. He treated him like a little child in a grown man's body.

Little John got into his van and drove away. D-Ray returned with a brown bag.

"What have you got?" I asked playfully.

He lifted the bag. "Boat parts." He went to his office. When D-Ray returned, he showed me where the laundry room was and how to use the washer and dryer. It was not that different from cleaning at home.

He lied about the bag. That bag had cash in it. I'd seen Little John drop a wad of money into it before handing it to D-Ray. He wanted me in his bed. Wanted me to work in the legitimate business, but he didn't want me to know about the illegal business.

I had already figured out some of the cash from the drugs was run through the restaurant and lodge income. Now that I was working at the lodge, I could hear more of what Donny Ray said when he was on the phone in his office. So far, it had been everyday business.

I was trying to be the perfect girlfriend. He was a hard worker and enjoyed the legitimate business he was running. When I saw him stress out, it was about Little John and the drug business.

It was around five that afternoon when a black BMW convertible pulled up to the lodge. Two guys not much older than me got out and came inside. The first opened the door while texting on his phone, and said, "Suzanne, our regular room, please."

The second guy was looking at me as I smiled sweetly at him. He tapped his buddy on the shoulder and said, "That's not Suzanne." He was staring at me now.

"Hello gentlemen, my name's Angie. Which room is your regular room?"

The first guy looked up from his phone. "Well, hello, Angie." He said in a sexy voice as he smiled and answered, "That would be any room you are staying in. Now, can we make that happen?"

D-Ray stepped out of the office. "Sorry, boys, her room is my room."

"D-Ray! My man. You know I'm just kidding, right?" The guy had false self-confidence. He sounded like a politician.

"Angie, this is Matthew Thomas, Senator Thomas's son. And this young man is Teddy Boone, Judge Boone's son. Whatever they want is on me."

I gave them all a big smile as the wheels churned in my head. No wonder he sounded like a fake politician; he learned it from his daddy. "All right. What room will it be, boys?" These were two of the bastards my dad arrested that started the threats against him. This was getting harder than I thought it would be. I had to push Angel aside and return to being Angie.

D-Ray stayed around the desk until they headed to their room. "They haven't been here for a while. They're important political connections to me. Teddy's dad will probably show up later. They'll party all night. Don't even try to clean their room tomorrow if they are here. In fact, stay close to me this weekend. I don't trust them."

"Why not?" I was curious now.

"They think the law doesn't pertain to them." He turned and went back to his office, but stopped before entering. "I'm going to need Little John around this weekend. Try to get along and not kick his ass. Okay?"

There was a story here that I wanted to know. I would not push D-Ray, though. I had a feeling I would hear it soon enough. The old cliché of *the enemy of my enemy is my friend* didn't apply here. D-Ray was using them, and they were using him.

The judge came in a little later and wanted a room beside the boys. The old man was a pervert. He said the correct and polite things, but his eyes were all over me. I'd had men stare at me at the strip club, but this man undressed me with his eyes in a way that sent shivers down my spine. Thankfully, D-Ray was there.

He grabbed D-Ray by the arm and walked him into the office. They didn't close the door. "D-Ray, I want a piece of that ass. What's it going to cost me?"

"She's not for sale, Judge. She's my girlfriend."

"Come on, D-Ray, girls come and go. You know you still owe me for the favors I've done for you."

"Not this time. This one's different."

"Well, if you change your mind, I'll be down the hall."

My suspicions came together. D-Ray needed Little John, which meant drugs and girls. They didn't pay for anything, because D-Ray was paying back favors the judge had done for him. Which probably meant the dropping of charges and the throwing out of cases. I remembered Sarah's shoe from the Hummer. Case dismissed. The murder charges against them for killing Dad. Dismissed. I would guess this was the man behind the dropped charges. Since D-Ray was covering the cost, that meant there was no paper trail to show they were ever here.

I didn't have any proof. But I had a link. The free rooms, food, alcohol, drugs, and prostitution all equaled a payment, or payback.

Little John just nodded at me when he came in. He went straight to D-Ray's office and closed the door.

The weekend turned out to be busy. The lodge was full. Hunters, anglers, and guides were in and out all weekend. The restaurant and bar were packed. D-Ray had a good, legitimate business going here. Why was he screwing it up with the illegal drugs? There was even a Sunday after-church business at the restaurant.

Everyone ignored the Judge and the two young men, and they behaved themselves because of D-Ray.

I closed the lodge lobby down at ten on Saturday night and headed straight to the bar. "Need help?" I asked Mike.

"Damn straight. Wash up the dirty beer mugs. We're about to run out. When you're done with that, help me with the beer orders. I'll do the mixed drinks."

It was after one in the morning when we closed the bar down. D-Ray had come in and taken over for me, and asked me to help Blake clean the kitchen. Two off-duty deputies had helped usher customers out at closing time.

I took a shower while D-Ray talked to Mike and Blake. He was downstairs on the phone with Little John when I got out of the shower. I could tell it was Little John by the tone of his voice.

The bar was closed on Sunday, but some alcohol was still served in the restaurant. D-Ray was back and forth between the restaurant and his office. By five in the afternoon, the lodge was empty, and I was busy cleaning rooms.

The worst rooms were the Judges and the boys' rooms. There were empty beer bottles and an empty whiskey bottle in the Judges' room. Used condoms on the floor beside the trash can, and even a line of coke left on the little table in the boys' room. Their rooms were next to last. I'd clean the girls' room last. I figured the condoms were used for them. Poor girls, they didn't deserve this kind of treatment.

I left their room, ready to kill Little John and D-Ray. Cherrie was the only one awake when I entered and when I left. She wouldn't answer my questions; she gave me her name when I asked. I quickly cleaned the bathroom and left clean sheets. I saw very little clothing and even fewer toiletries. There was a bar of soap and a bottle of shampoo. One brush and a comb to be shared was my guess. I was shaking and on the verge of tears.

Time was short. I had to get those girls to safety. I became angrier when I realized I was supposed to be in that room as well. That's what D-Ray bought me for. I had to be careful and smart, or I could still end up there.

Chapter 32

Angel

Everything but the lodge was closed on Monday, and it was not busy. D-Ray asked me to go to the kitchen and fix something to eat and take it to the girls' room. He said nothing about why they were there, or that they couldn't leave, or anything. He either assumed I knew what was going on, or thought I was naïve enough not to know.

I was smart enough not to ask D-Ray questions. Slowly, I got the girls to talk. I learned their names and actual ages, but they wouldn't tell where they were from.

D-Ray was in his office on Monday afternoon. I was playing solitaire for the thousandth time. Little John pulled into the parking lot and backed up to the door of the lodge. He always pulled straight in. Something was up.

"D-Ray? Little John is backing up to the door," I called out.

I stood up and walked around the counter. Little John opened the back doors of his van. He pulled a pair of motionless legs to him. It appeared to be a girl as he moved her to the door. Was he trying to hump her right in the parking lot?

"What the hell?" I screamed as I rushed through the door and grabbed his shirt and flung him away. I ripped his shirt right off him, exposing his body as nothing but skin and bones. It reminded me of the starved prisoner of war pictures I'd seen in school.

He didn't yell or curse at me. He just asked, "Is she dead?"

I quickly turned and reached for the brunette's hand. I checked for a pulse, like we were taught at the academy. No pulse. Crawling further into the van, I checked for a pulse on her neck.

"I didn't mean to kill her. I thought she was gorgeous," Little John said softly.

Again, I found no pulse. My face grew hot. "You stupid son of a bitch. You killed a girl!" I screamed.

I lunged out of the van at Little John. D-Ray caught me and pinned my arms behind my back. "Dammit, Little John. Clean up your mess."

I struggled to get free from D-Ray. I wasn't thinking about fighting tactics, because I was so angry I wanted to beat Little John to a bloody pulp.

"What do I do?"

"Plant her in the garden with the rest. Dig the hole with the backhoe, but wait until dark to finish the rest. What happened?"

"I'm not sure. I used chloroform to put her to sleep."

"Stupid. You used too much," D-Ray yelled.

D-Ray kicked the lobby door open and pushed me inside and screamed, "Go to my office and stay there unless you want to join that girl."

Thoughts ran through my head in no cohesive pattern. I stopped fighting. It was the first time D-Ray had threatened me. Little John had just committed murder. But D-Ray had just threatened to kill me.

Little John killed the girl. I touched a dead person. Can you kill a person with chloroform? D-Ray was yelling and screaming at Little John. My head was roaring like the sound of a waterfall. Why was Little John so skinny?

My stampeding thoughts stopped when Little John yelled, "Don't you know who that bitch is?" And he pointed at the lodge. At me.

"Of course, I know who she is!" D-Ray yelled back. Then, a little softer, he said. "She's my girlfriend. Go clean this up."

I shook uncontrollably. Did they know who I was? I ran to D-Ray's office and heard the lobby door open just as I turned the corner. He shouted a string of curses as he walked to the office. I had just sat in the chair across from his desk when he entered and slammed the door behind him.

I stood when he came to me. He pushed me back into the chair. "Don't come between me and Little John. He's the only family I've got left since Danny was killed." He finally admitted that his brother was dead.

My hands were gripping the arms of the chair. He leaned down over me and grabbed my wrists and crushed them against the chair arms. "You're hurting me," I said. But he continued to squeeze.

"Why are you mad at me? Little John killed the girl. Not me."

He let go, turned and screamed, "Damn it!"

I still wasn't thinking clearly. Still shaking in fear. I had stood my own against Little John earlier. But D-Ray was a different story. To fight effectively, I needed space and to be clearheaded. With D-Ray, I had to get close and be vulnerable like an actual girlfriend would. And it didn't help that the Angie persona had developed feelings for D-Ray. As Angie, I had to be believable. I didn't want to be Angie anymore. I didn't want to be undercover. This game was ending, because I knew too much now.

When I stood, I hugged him from behind. "I'm sorry. I'll be kinder to Little John. What's wrong with him? Why is he so skinny?"

He let out an enormous sigh and relaxed. "When we were fourteen, he started acting weird. Doing some crazy shit. He had no emotional switch, and didn't care if he hurt someone. He would cut himself for fun and laugh because he didn't feel it. That's when the doctors found a tumor on his brain."

D-Ray gently opened my arms and turned to hug me. "The tumor was basically inoperable. They gave him five years to live. He's lived fifteen, but I don't think he has much longer."

I held him while he talked. "He wanted to experience life before he died. We hunted and fished, and found him girls. We tried alcohol and drugs and discovered that meth helped him control his lack of emotions. He became his normal self when he was high. It made sense when we discovered that methamphetamine was once used to treat ADHD. It gave him another ten years, but it's killing him too."

If I didn't know who D-Ray and Little John really were, it would be easy to fall for the lies, feel sorry for him, and to love him. But I had overheard them say they knew who I was, and I knew Little John had murdered a girl and D-Ray had instructed him to bury her in the garden. No, he said, 'plant her' in the garden. D-Ray was talking again.

"When we were kids, we called ourselves the three amigos, like in the movie. When we got older and started experimenting with alcohol and drugs, we became the three Banditos. Now we're the two Banditos, and soon it will be the lone Bandito."

I was afraid to say anything. Luckily, I didn't have to. There was a knock on the office door. "D-Ray? You in there?"

D-Ray pushed me away. "Yeah." Then quietly he said, "It's my cousin, the Sheriff. Give us a few minutes alone."

I unlocked the office door and stepped back to let the sheriff in. He stared at me until I smiled and said, "Hello Sheriff, come on in. I must get back to my desk." He stepped in, and I slipped past him and went to the restroom instead. I got my shaking under control by taking several deep breaths. I washed my face with cold water. Apparently, D-Ray wasn't finished getting his money back out of me, but that could happen any day. I went back to the front counter. I forced myself to stay busy. There had been no calls, and we had no reservations for tonight.

A few minutes later, D-Ray emerged from his office. "Go get Cherrie and take her across the hall to room nineteen. The Sheriff needs to ask her some questions."

I muttered, "Okay." And I did what I was told. I went to the girls' room and asked Cherrie to come with me. For the first time, I noticed both rooms had a deadbolt that required a key on both sides. I opened the door for her and said, "I'm sorry." She watched me close the door with big brown eyes. She was frightened, and I was frightened for both of us. The girls were prisoners, and it was my responsibility to free them. Yet here I was, handing her over to the Sheriff. He would not question her. He was going to rape her. For me, having sex with D-Ray was a choice. She didn't have one, and that turned my stomach upside down.

Chapter 33

Dan

I spent more time at Ben's apartment since starting nursing classes at Harding. I would even crash on his couch some nights when I had a late shift on the ambulance, or an early morning exam. Moving was not an option, since I still had farm chores to do.

I met a lot of Ben's college friends and even attended church with him a few times. That was how I met Amy and Audra. They were students who lived across the street from Ben.

Amy stopped by one afternoon when I was there studying between classes and work.

"Is Ben home?" she asked when I opened the door.

She looked upset, wringing her hands and moving from one foot to the other.

"Ben's at work. Are you okay? Do you want to talk?" I asked.

"Audra, my roommate has been missing since last night."

"Oh no. Come in. Do you want a bottle of water or something?"

She came in and sat on the couch. "No, thank you. I just wanted someone to talk to and pray with me."

We talked for a while. The police found Audra's car in the Walmart parking lot. But the security cameras had revealed nothing, and the security that patrolled the lot saw nothing. Calls and text messages went unanswered, and eventually the message changed to her being unavailable, whatever that meant. She was concerned about her friend and roommate, but she was concerned for herself as well.

I thought about a few of the leftover cameras I had. The ones I had trouble getting to work. They needed to be reprogrammed, and I hadn't taken the time to do it. I told her I had an extra security camera that she could use. I would put it over her door and help program her phone so she could see who was at her door, no matter where she was.

It was obvious she liked Ben, so I promised to have the camera ready in a few days. Ben would call her when it was ready to be installed. She thanked me, and we said a quick prayer before she left.

*****

There were three micro-cameras left over from the trailer and fair displays. I hadn't used them because I had issues getting them to work. I also took my laptop and a micro USB adapter needed to reprogram the cameras. They were tiny, no larger than a micro USB plug, and easily hidden. The quality of the pictures they produced was amazing.

Some cameras had tiny microphones, but the ones I had today did not. I was at Ben's dining table, rebooting each camera individually until I got it working. I had two working; the third was not cooperating with the reboot, so I downloaded new software to it and it was trying to work.

My laptop was showing two screens from the working cameras. One was on the refrigerator and kept being activated because I was moving. The second was outside of Ben's apartment, above his door. It was only active when someone walked by or came to his door.

Ben came in, and I watched the camera. I needed to adjust its location to get a better picture of the face.

"Hey Dan. What are you up to?" He asked, looking at the screen of my laptop.

"I promised Amy I would install a security camera above her door."

"Do you have one above my door?"

"Yep. There's another one on your fridge. See if you can find it."

"There's nothing on the fridge but the clip holding my shopping list."

"Keep looking," I said.

He looked at the laptop picture, then at the fridge. He moved his hand around until his hand blocked the picture. Then he picked up the notepad and the clip holding it. He looked at the clip and finally put it back on the fridge.

"Found it. That is scary. That camera can be hidden anywhere. Are those what you used in the trailer?"

"Yeah. I can get notifications and see what it sees with just a few second's delay."

"Can you wear one?" Ben asked.

"It can't refocus. It works best in a permanent location."

He opened his refrigerator door and grabbed a bottle of water. "You want some water?"

I shook my head no, and he closed the door.

He sat at the table across from me and drank his water. "Amy thinks she has a lead on where Audra may be," he said.

"Where would that be?" I asked.

"She wants me to go with her. It felt like she was asking me on a date."

"She likes you. You should ask her out."

"Between classes and work, I don't have time."

"Where are you going?" I asked.

"Some place called the Wood Duck Lodge."

I froze and looked at Ben. "Do not go there. It belongs to Donny Ray. The guy responsible for killing Angel's dad and nearly killing us. If he sees you, he will think you're me and kill you, Ben."

"I have to go. Amy said she would go without me if I didn't go with her. Why don't you go with us? There's safety in numbers."

"No, Ben. Besides, I'm scheduled to work for the next two nights. Please don't go. It's dangerous." It was dangerous, but I also didn't want him seeing Angel and exposing her undercover operation.

He didn't answer. Angel and I had survived the attempted murders, but Ben hadn't experienced those close calls. He didn't feel the fear that I felt every day for Angel's safety. It was useless to say anything about her to him, because he would be more determined to force me to go with him.

I put a piece of double-sided tape on the back of the last camera and stood up. "I have to go to class."

This camera needed to work so I could put it over Ben's door. I went to the bathroom. I wasn't sure where to put it and decided against putting it over the bathroom door. It ended up over Ben's bedroom door, and I pointed it straight down.

Ben was silent while I packed my stuff up.

"I'll try to talk Amy out of going again. But she refused to listen to me, and I made her promise not to go without me."

"When are you going?" I asked.

"Tonight."

I was standing with my hand on the door, ready to leave. "They attempted to kill me and Angel twice. They killed her dad, and you think you're going to walk right in and ask about Audra, then walk away without a scratch? Don't do this, Ben."

"I have to protect Amy."

I understood, because I wanted to protect Angel, but I had to trust her training.

"Take your Glock. They had pistols at the lake. Remember?"

He nodded. I opened the door to leave and said, "Be careful, Ben."

I got into my truck and slammed my hands against the dashboard. "So much for going to class," I said to myself.

I pulled my phone out and hit the speed dial. "Sheriff, I need a favor."

I left Sheriff Tatum's home armed with a combat shotgun, my pistol, and an extra pistol the Sheriff loaned me, a Kevlar vest and a badge that said I was an auxiliary deputy sheriff. The sheriff gave me strict instructions not to interfere unless Ben or Amy's lives were in danger.

"Look at me, Dan. I want these guys as badly as you and Angel. Danny Ray put me in this wheelchair. Give Angel time to gather evidence and bring down their entire operation. You understand me?"

"Yes, sir."

"Call me if you need advice."

"Yes, sir."

I left in an unmarked car and drove back to Searcy. I didn't need to follow Ben and Amy, but I followed them at a long distance and prayed they would turn around. They didn't.

I parked on the restaurant side behind some trucks and opened my laptop. It took several minutes to find the right cameras. There were two cameras in the restaurant, but neither showed Ben and Amy. For selfish reasons, I added the camera near D-Ray's office and the Lodge desk where Angel was working. I wanted to see Angel, and I was glad I did. I watched and listened as Little John told D-Ray about Ben, but he thought it was me. Angel slipped into the picture and was listening to the conversation. Little John wanted to kill Ben and drug the girl for his pleasure. I was watching so intently that I forgot I should have been checking my weapons.

Angel said, "Don't kill them. I've seen enough dead bodies this week. Drug them both and take them back to his place. Then we strip them and put them into bed together and leave. They won't remember anything. Once we are out of the parking lot, I'll call the police and say I think someone is being raped, and request a welfare check."

D-Ray and Little John laughed. "Let's do it," I heard D-Ray say.

I breathed a sigh of relief. It would be embarrassing for Ben, but he and Amy would be alive. And what dead body had Angel seen?

They must have used Rohypnol because I didn't have to wait long. The dinner crowd hadn't even cleared out before they made their move. Angel came out of the restaurant and used the alarm button on the key fob to find Ben's car. She drove it around the building to the lodge entrance. I moved the car so I could see when they left. I was lucky and recorded them being carried out of the lodge and put into Ben's car.

D-Ray and Angel drove Ben's car. Little John followed in a truck, and I followed him.

It took twenty minutes to get to Searcy. Once there, I took another street and got ahead of them. I was barely in the parking lot with my headlights off when they arrived.

I recorded everything outside the apartment. They weren't in Ben's apartment five minutes before they left in the pickup. I kept recording on my phone. I was wondering whether Angel had called the police. It took the police twenty minutes to respond. That was way too long if a rape was actually in progress. I continued recording as two officers knocked on the door. When no one answered, one walked to the manager's apartment.

They called an ambulance shortly after entering the apartment. An hour later, everyone was out of Ben's apartment, and the apartment manager locked the door. Ben and Amy were both still knocked out. Amy would be fine. But Ben would probably wake up handcuffed to a hospital bed. I called Sheriff Tatum for advice. He reminded me that my priority was protecting Angel. My second priority was to clear Ben's name. I combined all the videos from my phone and Ben's apartment and organized them in order on a thumb drive.

I remembered Angel's comment about seeing enough dead bodies this week. That was the only thing I could think about driving back to Sheriff

Tatum's. I prayed one wasn't Audra's. Wavering between anger and relief, and shaking from frustration, I had to keep reminding myself that everyone was alive and safe.

I gave the thumb drive and all the borrowed equipment to Sheriff Tatum, and he said he would take over from there. He would keep my name out of any police or court records, but he couldn't promise anything. He would call my uncle Vernon if he needed legal help.

It was nearing three in the morning when I got home. I reset my alarm to get at least four hours of sleep. If I could sleep.

Chapter 34

Dan

I have stayed away from Ben and avoided his calls and texts. When we finally talked, I said, "You're lucky to be alive."

"This wouldn't have happened if you had come with us. Amy won't answer her phone or return my texts."

Ben was angry and confused. He remembered talking to me about going, but he couldn't remember going to the lodge. He couldn't remember anything else until he woke up in the hospital. One of the side effects of Rohypnol is that you remember nothing. You have no memory of anything that happened while you were out. It's illegal in the U.S., but so are cocaine, meth, fentanyl, and the other drugs Little John and D-Ray probably have.

"You're right. We'd be dead."

We ended our call without resolving his issues or needs. I wanted to help him, but that required my telling what was really going on. Dad and Sheriff Tatum already knew. That was too many.

I spend too much time watching the cameras. There are over thirty cameras at the lodge and six more in the house. But I rarely see Angel on any of them. When I see her, she is in and out of the camera's view quickly. I've learned to watch shortly after five in the morning when she gets up to run. I can watch her at night on the camera from Donny Ray's bedroom. But I don't. I can't watch my wife having sex with a man who tried to kill us, and probably killed her dad. The camera I reviewed the most was the lodge camera close to D-Ray's office. It was the camera Angel appeared on the most.

I still have problems recognizing her as Angel with her short blond hair. But it's her. I know her face and her body. I pray several times a day for her safety. The situation could change at any minute.

Ben's visit to the Wood Duck Lodge happened on a Thursday night. Angel had been there almost three weeks. If she had seen a dead body and was taking part in drugging people, she was in deep. Deeper than either of us had dreamed. The question now was how long it would be before this was over?

I watched the camera in real time on Saturday night. Donny Ray was bringing two cups of coffee back to his office. He came out of his office with one cup, stopped and dropped something into it before taking it to the desk.

Twenty minutes later, he picked up a sleeping or drugged Angel and carried her down the hallway. The hair stood up on my neck. That's not good.

I open screens in all the rooms. I quietly apologized to the people in the rooms that I'd seen in various stages of undress until I found the room he was taking her to.

Watching him lay her body on the bed brings back flashbacks of Ben and Amy. I want to scream as I watch him undress her and rape her motionless body. And then he allows another man to rape her. Until now, Angel had been having consensual sex with Donny Ray. But this was rape. And he let someone else rape her. Whenever I watched Angel and Donny Ray go to bed, I turned the video off. I couldn't force myself to watch. But I couldn't turn this off. It turned me cold inside, and I shook with anger. The undercover operation had to end soon. This was the part we had worried about. The part she couldn't control. The part I couldn't control. I watched her lie drugged on the bed for an hour after they left. I was too traumatized to cry or scream.

In my room at home, I had been closing my bedroom door more often. When Mom asked me why, I said, "I'm not sleeping well. The late shifts on the ambulance, the classes and worrying about Angel are bothering me. Any little noise wakes me up." She hugged me, apologized, and said she would be quieter. I was monitoring the cameras, and I was falling apart.

I dressed quickly and was leaving my room when Dad stopped me. Mom must have said something to him.

"Let's go to your room to talk, son. You've got your mom worried." We stepped into my room, and he closed the door behind him. "What's going on?"

"I'm going to get Angel."

"No, you're not. We've been over this. Let her do her job."

He must have read my reactions, because he reached out, palm forward, to stop me. "Shhh! Tell me what happened."

I opened my mouth to tell him, but the words didn't come out. I squeezed my eyes tightly and fought back the tears. The tears could not be stopped. Dad stepped forward and pulled me into a hug. I finally whispered, "They drugged her and raped her."

Dad didn't speak. He hugged me tighter and let me cry.

"It will be over soon. There will come a time when I tell you to go. But not today."

Chapter 35

Angel

I woke up dazed and confused. I lay still until I got my bearings. My head was pounding like a bass drum in a marching band. I stayed still and slowly opened my eyes. It was daylight. I could hear a shower running. It took me several minutes to realize I was in a bed in one of the lodge's rooms.

I tried sitting up. Oh, that would not work. I groaned out loud. D-Ray walked out of the bathroom naked. "You're awake. How are you feeling?"

"Like a herd of elephants has run me over," I answered.

"You passed out at the desk last night. I brought you up here and stayed with you." He started dressing.

"Thank you." I couldn't remember anything. The pounding in my head was in rhythm with my heartbeat.

"I've got to go open up the front desk. Rest and come down when you are feeling better. I'll ask Blake to bring you some coffee and a Danish when she has a break."

"Thanks," I replied. I finally sat up after he left. I pulled my legs up, hugged my knees, and waited for the pounding to go away.

That was the beginning of a strange week. D-Ray and Little John were no longer hiding anything from me. They spoke openly about the drug business, the dealers, and the suppliers. I was frightened because I was learning so much so quickly.

D-Ray still closed his door for the eight a.m. and five p.m. phone calls. Most of them were less than five minutes long. But some calls lasted half an hour. I was curious about who this call was from. I would sneak to the restroom, type notes on my phone and upload them to a Dropbox account Sergeant Johnson had set up.

It was mid-afternoon on Friday, and customers were showing up at the lodge. Little John entered and went straight to D-Ray's office. I finished with my customers and started toward the office but stopped.

I heard D-Ray tell Little John, "You don't get to tell me what to do. Remember?"

The rest of the conversation chilled me to the bone. The undercover operation was over. It was time for me to leave.

Chapter 36

Dan

I've become obsessed with watching the videos from the lodge. Obsessions are unhealthy, I know. The trailer was loaded with two calves for me to deliver to the Dalliers in Colorado. I was ready to leave the farm when my phone notified me of a video. I watch and listen as Little John and Donny Ray argue about Angel. Little John knows about Donny and the man raping Angel. He called him a judge.

"You don't get to tell me what to do. Remember?" Donny said.

"Donny! We have to get rid of that bitch. Do you know who she is? She is the game warden's daughter. That bitch is not here for a good time. She's here for revenge."

"I've known who she is from the beginning," Donny Ray answered. He pointed his finger at Little John. "I'm taking my time getting my revenge for Danny." He hesitated and said, "Last weekend was the beginning of the end. The judge will owe us favors for a long time now because I have him on video with her. Besides, I paid five grand for that tight little ass. I wanted something for my money. I'll get rid of her soon."

"Let me kill her, Donny. I deserve that much. That little whore has embarrassed me enough. I want to be fucking her when I put my gun in her mouth and pull the trigger."

"She'll kick your ass like she has before. You're no match for her."

"I'll drug her, like you did. But I want her to know what's happening."

Donny Ray scratched his head. "Think you can do it?"

"With your help, she'll never know what's coming."

"Alright. I'll dig a hole in the garden tomorrow morning. We'll plant her when you're finished."

Little John pumped his fist when he turned and walked away. Danny Ray didn't move. The mic on the camera barely picked up his voice. "I won't drug her very much, though. With any luck, you'll kill each other." Then he turned and walked out of the camera's view.

I closed the app. I had listened to Dad and had waited for Angel to complete her job and come home so I could help her put the pieces back together. But this changed everything. Donny Ray hoped that Angel and Little John would kill each other. If I didn't act, and act now, there might not be any pieces of Angel to put back together.

I had planned this trip for three weeks. Ben had wanted to go with me after Angel and I told him about the Dalliers Ranch. I would pick him up in Searcy, and we'd swap out driving. I called Ben and told him I needed to work an emergency shift on the ambulance and asked him to make the trip alone. After some complaining, he agreed. I hated lying to Ben.

Next, I called Robby, Angel's half-brother. He had sold his dad's house, moved to Little Rock, and was going to college. He would do anything for Angel, and I was counting on him for a big favor. I promised him I would explain when he picked me up in Searcy. I would have to tell Robby a different lie.

Finally, I went to my room and gathered some clothes and a few other essentials. My last stop was the mudroom and the gun safe. I didn't have a plan yet. I was winging it and grabbing what I thought I needed, like a pair of thin cloth gloves. Ben and I used them when hunting because they kept our hands somewhat warm, and we could still shoot with them. I was thinking about using them so I wouldn't leave fingerprints.

When I met Ben and Robby in Searcy, I was still agitated, and they both saw it.

"What's wrong, Dan?" Ben asked. Robby was curious, but he stayed silent. I had mentioned helping Angel to him, and he said nothing. If I said anything to Ben, he would insist on going with me. I couldn't allow him to do that.

"I'm just aggravated about covering this shift. I wanted to make this trip with you, but I have to return this favor."

"It's okay. I can do this," Ben answered.

"Thank you. Call me if you have any questions."

We said goodbye, and Ben drove off.

I hated lying to Ben. But if he had known the truth, he would have insisted on going with me. When I turned to Robby, he crossed his arms, and asked. "What's really going on? You can't lie to me like that. What's this got to do with my sister?"

"Let's talk in the car," I said, and turned to his car.

"Where am I taking you? If you had needed a ride to work, you could have had someone else pick you up, or used your brother's car. He'll think of that eventually."

It was time to add one more person to my inner circle. I pulled a tiny battery out of the pocket of my jeans and held it up. "Angel didn't join the Marines. She's working undercover for the state police. I need to replace the battery in one of the hidden cameras."

He stared at me for a full minute. Then he slowly put the car in reverse, and asked, "Where are we going? And why can't she replace the battery herself?"

"We're going to Des Arc. She doesn't know the cameras are there. She is going to take down Donny Ray and Little John."

"Oh, shit." His face went pale, and his hands shook. "They'll kill her."

"Not if I can stop it."

He stared at me as if he didn't know me. "Watch the road, please. No more questions. Forget everything I told you, because it's about to get... complicated." I had to hesitate to think of a good word.

Yeah, complicated was the word. I didn't have a plan, and that was unusual for me. The camera in Donny Ray's bedroom did need a new battery. I'd already been there before when I installed the camera originally. I hoped the combine where I'd hidden the first time, when I installed cameras in the house, was still there. The cab protected me from the army of mosquitoes that lived along the river.

"Alright, I know nothing. But if Angel dies, I will kill you."

"If Angel dies, I will beg you to kill me."

The combine was still there. It was going to be my hiding place until the sun rose, lighting the old farm equipment, which appeared as shadows within the shadows of my fear of being found. What was I doing here? Did I have a prayer of stopping Donny Ray or Little John? Once inside the cab of the combine, I monitored the cameras from my phone, and didn't expose myself. Looking at everything that could go wrong was out of the question. Because anything and everything could go wrong when there was no plan.

Morning finally arrived after a sleepless night. I watched every camera in the house except the one in Donny's bedroom. The battery finally died. I waited thirty minutes after everyone left before leaving my hiding place. The run from the equipment shed to the back of the house was the hardest I ever ran. My heart was in my throat and beating so fast I couldn't calm it down. I slipped on the cloth gloves and avoided the cameras. Easing up the old creaking stairs was impossible. I quickly replaced the battery in the camera and prepared to leave the house.

The sound of a tractor starting stopped me in my tracks. "Shit." Without thinking, I went to the window in Little John's room. Donny Ray's truck was at the equipment shed. The backhoe was moving toward the garden. I had my pistol, but I didn't want to use it. I searched Little John's room. It didn't take long. He had an arsenal of weapons hidden in the obvious places. I found a Ruger nine millimeter in his nightstand, loaded and ready to use. Of course, it was loaded with one in the chamber.

I stepped into the hallway and realized I'd been on camera. Before I moved, I used my phone to delete the footage of me in the room. It also reminded me to activate the camera in Donny Ray's bedroom.

Angel could take care of Little John. I was making it my job to take care of Donny Ray. The screen door slammed behind me as I marched toward the backhoe. Donny Ray had finished digging the grave and looked up to see me walking toward him.

He climbed off the backhoe and took a few steps toward me. "Well, well, well. What have we got here? A modern knight in sweatpants and a sweatshirt comes to save his damsel in distress."

"Give it up, Donny Ray. Turn yourself in because it's over."

"It's just getting started."

"I won't let you kill Angel."

He looked shocked for a second. Then he laughed at me and said, "There's at least twenty bodies buried in this garden. I ain't doing life in prison. You're here for Angie, or should I call her Angel? She is a sweet fuck, you know."

Then he pulled his pistol. I stepped to the left, and his shot hit my arm. It spoiled my aim, and my shot hit his knee. I missed the second shot. He missed his second shot. They sounded like one shot. My third shot was through the chest. It knocked him backwards and killed him. His body turned, and I hit his shoulder with my next shot, before he fell into the pile of dirt next to the grave.

Using my foot, I pushed his body onto his back and shot him between his eyes. I was sure he was already dead, but I wasn't taking any chances. I shivered as a dragged his body to the grave he had already dug. Donny Ray was dead, and I killed him.

Stay focused, Dan. Clean this up and leave.

His pistol lay on the ground, and his phone fell out of his pocket as I was dragging him. That reminded me of one thing I needed to do. He used a combination of his fingerprint and a login code to access his phone. He was very paranoid about his phone, apparently.

Stay focused, Dan. I had to kill him before he killed Angel.

I grabbed his dead hand and put his finger to the back of his phone, then I used the same finger to enter the password I'd seen him use on camera. Taking my gloves off was out of the question; I wasn't leaving fingerprints. He didn't know there were cameras in his house. So, I used his finger to connect his phone to the house system. I stuck the phone into his back pants pocket and rolled him into the grave. Then, I threw in both pistols. I smiled, realizing the pistol I used probably had Little John's fingerprints on it.

I hadn't used a backhoe on the farm, but my tractor had a front bucket, and so did the backhoe. Five minutes and he was buried in the grave he had dug for Angel and Little John. I turned the backhoe off with the bucket resting on top of the grave. He had haunted Angel and me for over a year while he was alive; leaving that bucket on top of the grave was an effort to keep his memories from haunting us for the rest of our lives.

I sprinted to the equipment shed and grabbed my backpack out of the combine. I wiped the door-handle off with the gloves I was still wearing.

Stay focused, Dan. It's almost done.

I hit the woods along the river, running at a controlled pace. When I was a mile away, I called Robby. That's when I felt the injury on my arm, and saw the blood. That's when I began shaking and threw up. The blood was mine. I was alive and not in the grave.

Chapter 37

Angel

I had a lot of information about the drug operation. But most importantly, it was time for me to get out. I'd decided overnight that I needed to kill D-Ray. If I stole his truck and ran away, he would call his cousin, the sheriff, to track me down and arrest me. Then he would have Judge Boone throw the book at me. It would take time for Sergeant Johnson to get control of the situation. By then, D-Ray would find another way to kill me. Why not send Sergeant Johnson a message and wait for her? It could be hours before she checked the online Dropbox.

A busy Friday night at the restaurant and bar made it easier for me to stay busy and avoid D-Ray. I didn't want him to see the fear in my eyes. I had proven I could handle Little John. But D-Ray was bigger and stronger. Matching him in a fight would be difficult. It's true I had sparred with Dad and Dan, but they both took it easy on me.

D-Ray was surprisingly gentle when we reached the house. We did the usual line of coke and had sex, then he cuddled with me while I pretended to sleep. I couldn't sleep because I kept thinking of how to kill him without being killed. I didn't come up with the answer until the morning, until he had to go back to the house for something he forgot.

He dropped me off at the lodge and drove back to the house. Little John's van was at the lodge, but I didn't see him. He was probably in the restaurant kitchen. I didn't enter the lodge. I began walking the mile back to the house. There were plenty of pistols stashed all over the house. I would use one of them to confront D-Ray.

I was almost back at the house when I heard the backhoe stop. A thicket of briars and sumac blocked my view. Dammit, I was too late. I ran forward to the edge of the thicket when I heard voices.

"Dan?" I whispered when I recognized him. "What are you doing here?"

I froze in place. This couldn't be happening. I took a step forward to run to Dan. I wanted to go home. Then D-Ray drew his pistol and fired at Dan. I dropped to my knees, watched and counted the shots. One, Two. Three and four. D-Ray fell after Dan's first shot. Dan flinched, and his pistol lowered after D-Ray's shot. Dan walked to D-Ray and shot him one more time.

Oh Dan. What have you done? I wanted to run to him, but I couldn't move. I wanted to call out, but I couldn't speak. Then, I shook uncontrollably and watched him bury D-Ray and run away.

It was after he ran away that I realized I could have left with him. I still needed to leave, but it was too late to catch him. He was a fast runner. He would be a mile or more away, and I wouldn't catch up to him.

I don't remember walking to the house. But I found myself curled up in bed, where I had slept with D-Ray last night, holding a pistol with both hands.

He had been so gentle. It was almost like making love instead of the raw physical sex we usually had.

How long had I been in bed? What was wrong with me? It was shock. That was it. I had to be in shock. We had talked about this at the academy during tactical training. Tactical training involved preparing for active shooter situations. Stay focused on the danger. Eliminate the danger.

There wasn't any immediate danger, unless it was Little John. I sat on the edge of the bed, trying to focus on a plan. I was stronger than this. Pack my stuff up. Even that wasn't important. Take D-Ray's truck and leave. Simple plans are better. Until they aren't.

I heard the back door slam shut. "D-Ray!" Little John screamed. "D-Ray, where the fuck are you?"

I was too late. I grabbed my phone from the nightstand and stuck it in the waistband of my leggings and backed away from the door.

Heavy footsteps were coming up the stairs. "Who the fuck did you bury in the garden? I know you wouldn't do that bitch without me."

He was in the doorway, pistol in hand, staring at me. He was high and pissed off.

"You? Where's D-Ray?"

"Dead. Planted in the garden," I said. I wasn't sure I could take him down in this state. People high on meth found unusual levels of strength and stamina. I held my pistol two-handed, but still pointed down. I had to get an edge.

"Naw. You couldn't take D-Ray down. There's no way."

"I didn't do it. You did. Don't you remember?"

"Liar. I wouldn't kill D-Ray."

"He was in love with me. He changed his mind about killing me. You became angry, shot him, and ran off."

"No!" He lunged at me and shot while raising his arm. I shot twice, hitting him in the leg and the chest. When his body slammed into me, my head hit the edge of a dresser, and I blacked out.

I opened my eyes. My head pounded to the beat of my heart. My left shoulder screamed in agony. Little John lay sprawled across by body. I was sitting against the dresser. The pistol I used lay across the room, and I couldn't move.

I couldn't move. I closed my eyes. My eyelids moved. I opened my mouth and said, "Help." Something was seriously wrong with me. My left arm was trapped under Little John. I tried to move the fingers of my right hand. Am I paralyzed?

"Oh God, help me, please."

I tried to turn my head. Pain shot through my entire body. I tried to tilt my head up and down. The pain in my neck and head exploded in my ears, and my vision went black.

When I awakened again, I was lying on my left side. I think Little John had moved. Was he still alive? The pounding in my head had subsided some. I tried moving the fingers of my right hand. They moved. Oh, thank God, they moved. My phone — where was my phone? It was still in my waistband. It seemed like it took forever to get my phone out.

I couldn't call 911. Sheriff Pendleton would come. If I called Sergeant Johnson, she would call 911, and Sheriff Pendleton would come.

Chapter 38

Dan

Ben called shortly after Robby picked me up. He was returning from the Dalliers in Colorado when a bearing froze up on the trailer. I talked Robby into taking me to Oklahoma and then taking Ben home.

I was at the Flying J truck stop in Roland, Oklahoma, when Angel called.

"Hello?" I answered.

"Dan, come get me. Little John tried to kill me. I'm scared Donny Ray is going to come and finish me."

"Are you okay? Are you hurt?" I asked her.

"I'm hurt. Little John and I fought. I can't move, and I can't think, Dan. Come get me before Donny gets here."

"Don't worry about Donny. Help is on the way. I love you."

"Hurry, Dan."

"Okay, I've got to go."

I was four hours away from the Ray farm. Robby and Ben were maybe an hour ahead of me. I called the one person I trusted, even though I really should have called Sherriff Tatum or Sergeant Johnson. But I wasn't supposed to know about Angel being undercover.

"Dad, I need your help."

I explained the phone call from Angel and what I had seen on the video before calling him.

"Okay, son, I've got this. It's time to get Mrs. Cotton and your mother involved. I'm going to need someone to drive if she needs medical care. Now, how do I find her?"

I knew she was at the Ray House. She was in Donny's room, so I told Dad where to check.

"I'm almost in Arkansas, Dad. I'll be home as soon as I can. Be careful."

"I will, Daniel. It's not my first battle."

It's interesting how families rally together in times of need. No one asks questions; they just focus on what needs to be done.

By the time they reached the hospital in Searcy, Dad had passed out. But not before he called me. Dad said it looked like Angel had been drugged and had received several hard blows. One blow was to the base of the neck. The injury had caused swelling around her spinal column at the base of her skull. She had shot Little John twice and knocked him out with a blow from the pistol. He had pushed her against the dresser, and fallen on top of her, trapping her. She was too weak or paralyzed to move him. Dad dragged him off, but Little John woke up swinging fists and kicked Dad in the chest several times before Dad knocked Little John out with the butt of his pistol.

Dad often had difficulty breathing from Agent Orange exposure. Multiple diseases are associated with exposure to the dioxin in Agent Orange. Most of them attacked the immune system and prevented the body from fighting infections.

Dad refused treatment at the hospital. He did not want to be hooked up to a respirator and have multiple drugs dripping into him, preventing him from being aware of his surroundings. He had told us many times that if he was going to die, he wanted to be at home and not in a hospital.

Chapter 39

Dan

The clouds hung low, and the drizzle was soft as morning came to our house on the Little Red River. Dad often said that the Lord was shedding tears of joy because He was calling an angel home whenever it rained on funeral days. I hoped he was right because today we were burying my dad.

It had been five days since we brought Angel home to my grandparents' house on the farm. Angel's mom and I had taken turns sitting with her for the first forty-eight hours after bringing her home. We brought Dad home the same day. When I wasn't sitting with Angel, I was with my dad.

When Dad dragged Little John off Angel, Little John woke up enough to kick Dad in the chest. His kicks had broken a rib and punctured Dad's lung. Dad was admitted to the hospital at the same time as Angel. He had had health problems since he had returned home from the Vietnam War. But he made it home and met and married Mom and adopted Ben and me. Even when he had bad days, he never made excuses. He just kept going. And I was doing the same now. I was forcing myself to keep going, just like he did. In the last few days, we had talked and prayed for hours. He talked to each of us. Me, Ben, and Mom. We thought he was getting better, but he was saying goodbye.

I don't know why I was thinking about this today, of all days. I was barely functioning. Five days awake with little sleep were making me emotional. I slept for another six hours last night. Twelve hours of sleep in the last ninety-six. Most of that time was spent sitting at Angel's bedside, treating her wounds and bruises, and watching for issues from the head and spinal injury.

She finally woke up yesterday morning, but she didn't want to talk to me. Instead, she talked to her mom for several hours. She pushed me away, probably feeling the need to explain to her mom what she had really been doing. Her mom and mine thought she had joined the Marine Corps. Dad had to tell them the truth when they went to get Angel from the Rays' house.

I was thinking about our conversations and listening to the rain on the porch roof when I felt a pair of arms encircle my waist. I had not heard her, but I knew it was Angel. She had often hugged me this way when I stood on the farm and appraised what I, or we, had done or planned to do.

Her right hand often found its way under my shirt and played with the hair on my stomach while her left arm held me tight. My stomach was ticklish, and she loved to tickle me. But this time, she must have felt me tense, because she held me tight. My hands found hers, and we intertwined our fingers and squeezed. We stood there for several minutes. I felt the warmth of her body against me and her head on my back between my shoulders. I waited. This was her first move to be near me, to talk to me since she went undercover.

When she started to sob, I loosened her grip on me and turned around. I took her into my arms and held her tight. Her sobs came in torrents then, like the rain on the tin roof, and I cried with her. She sank to the cool floor of the porch, and I eased my body down with her, never letting her go. We sat on the floor and cried until we could cry no more. When I finally looked at her face, she had fallen asleep in my arms. I picked her up and carried her back to bed.

What was I going to do? We had secrets. Her secrets would soon be told to the world. I worried she wouldn't tell me her secrets before everyone knew. I wouldn't push her though, because I had secrets too.

Angel's mom watched me lay her down and cover her up.

"What did she say?" She asked.

I shook my head. "Nothing. We held each other and cried."

Mrs. Cotton nodded. "She's afraid you won't be able to forgive her, Dan. She didn't explain why, but this was something she had to do on her own. The man not only killed her father; he tried to hurt us too. She had to get revenge. She said she needed to protect me and you."

"I don't blame her, but why didn't she find him and turn him over to the police? I don't understand..." I trailed off as I waved my hands in the air in frustration.

"Dan, she has a lot to tell you." She hesitated for a minute and finally said, "She has a lot to tell the State Police. She went to the police academy and joined an undercover operation.

"Dan, she wanted you to know that much. The rest she wants to tell you herself." Her mom told me.

I was supposed to believe she had joined the Marine Corps, and I was supposed to be surprised that she was a deputy sheriff assigned to a State Police Task Force. But I knew everything, and my head was spinning from the lies I had to tell, and I was having trouble remembering what I knew and what I didn't know. I needed to avoid any further conversation.

"I need to go to Mom's and get dressed for the funeral. Will I see you there?"

"You know I will be there," she replied.

As I started my truck to drive the few hundred yards home, the clouds burst open, and the drizzle became a torrent. Was the rain here to wash away my tears or to drown me? I didn't know. My head ached, and I just wanted to close my eyes and go to sleep forever.

Chapter 40

Dan

The Hiram Baptist Church, where Dad had preached for the past sixteen years, was a small community church that seated about a hundred people. But I never remembered it holding that many people. Most Sundays there were twenty-five to thirty attendees, and most of them were retired. It had over a hundred members on the rolls, but I had never seen them all there at once. Today might be the exception.

There were only five or six kids who attended every Sunday, and Ben and I were two of them. Shortly after high school, Ben started attending services at Harding University. I kind of switched back and forth. We both worked in Searcy, and there were nights when I crashed at his apartment.

We should have found a larger facility for Dad's funeral. It was going to be standing-room only. But his wish was to have the funeral in that church and to be buried in the cemetery beside it. This was the church that he had painted every five years and that Ben and I had painted the steeple just two years before. It was where Ben had stood up and preached for the first time at twelve. Where he and I were saved and baptized. We knew every inch of this church. It was strangely calming.

Ben would conduct part of the service, and an old army buddy of Dad's would deliver the sermon. The funeral was to start at eleven, and knowing Ben, it would start right on time. It was my assigned task to greet and take care of the Reverend Sonny Towns before and after the funeral. It was going to be a challenge for the Reverend because he used a wheelchair.

I was surprised, but not shocked, to find Reverend Towns was a black man. He and Dad talked weekly, sometimes daily, and I never suspected. Dad was always emphatic that the color of one's skin wasn't important. It was the color of their hearts that mattered.

My first impression of Reverend Towns was that he had an enormous heart. His smile could brighten any room. And his booming, "Hello, Daniel," when I opened the van door for him, stirred me to my toes.

"Reverend Towns, it's a pleasure to finally meet you."

"And you as well, but not under the current circumstances," he said.

Just being near him kind of revived my spirit and lessened the sadness I felt. "No sir. Let's see if we can get you inside without you looking like you were just baptized."

"Ha, ha. You have your father's sense of humor. If you will open the side doors of the van, Andrew will work the controls to let the ramp down."

Andrew was his driver. He was a middle-aged black man who didn't look happy to be here. I held an oversized golf umbrella in my left hand and carried two oversized firefighter jackets in my right.

"I've brought two firefighter jackets for your use while you're here. They will help keep you from getting completely drenched," I joked. "They are brand new, so they don't stink yet."

We managed to get into the church without getting too wet.

"Everyone will be soaked today," laughed the reverend. And he was right.

Ben was prompt, as I expected him to be. At five minutes till eleven, I found my mother and sat beside her. My mother was the strongest woman I knew. She and Dad had been partners in life for nearly thirty years. They raised me and Ben to be the men we were becoming. They raised us with love, discipline, and to be in control of our lives, and we loved them. I reached for Mom's hand as I sat down, remembering that she and Dad had talked for hours during the last few days of his life. She gave me the smile that mothers reserve for their children. The smile that says *I love you, I'm proud of you,* and *you better behave yourself* all at the same time.

The usher stopped at our pew to show Mrs. Cotton in. There was a young lady in a deputy uniform behind her. I had to stare at her for a moment to realize it was Angel. My Angel. I don't know why I did it. I looked at the back of the church and was startled to see several police officers I didn't recognize standing in the back. They looked like deputies from another county. On the side immediately behind me, there were two state troopers and another deputy sheriff.

I twisted around to find Angel sitting beside me, holding a deputy's ball cap in her hands.

"Angel, what's going on?" I whispered.

"It's just a little turf war," she said hoarsely. "Nothing to worry about."

I know I had to have turned twenty shades of red. "This is not the time or the place for a little turf war," I hissed at her. I was doing my best to hold my temper. Rarely was I an angry person, but this was my father's funeral. I had enough emotions to handle already.

I began to stand up when Angel leaned toward me, grabbed my arm, and whispered, "They think they're here to arrest me for the attempted murder of Little John. But the state police are handling it. They won't interrupt the service. Please sit down."

There was no time to say anything. Mom said calmly, "Stay seated, Dan." I settled back, and Ben started the service.

I must confess, I don't remember much of Ben's part of the service, because I was reeling from Angel's arrival, the police presence, not to mention my father's funeral. And the damn rain fell even harder.

I lowered my eyes and studied the hands I was holding. These were the two women I loved more than anything in the world. Preoccupied with this thought, I didn't come to my senses until the Reverend started preaching. His booming voice filled the church and reached to the heavens for God to hear.

"God has called another angel home. And this man, my brother, in more ways than one, was a living, breathing angel."

There were several scattered amens in response. I looked up and towards the pulpit, but the Reverend wasn't there. He was in his wheelchair by my dad's casket. From where he sat, he could not see my dad's body.

"I first met Lloyd Brock in Vietnam in 1972, when he was a medic. Brother Lloyd didn't carry a rifle. He carried two Colt 1911s. We were only issued one. He wouldn't tell me how he got a second one."

That brought a few laughs. "His response when I asked him the third or fourth time was, *The Lord works in mysterious ways, Sonny.* I can still recall how all the soldiers said, 'We want Lloyd on our patrol anytime we're going out.' I had the good fortune to have him along with me the first and only time I went on patrol."

The Reverend lowered his voice a little. You could tell he was a master storyteller. Most good preachers were.

"I don't know where we were in Vietnam or even what day it was. We were ambushed, and of course, the newbies got to take the lead. That day,

I was the newbie. What I do remember from that day was an angel racing to me with his sidearm, firing in all directions. When he reached me, he holstered his pistol and pulled mine out of my holster. He then threw me over his shoulder and carried me back to safety while emptying my pistol. I know he made a couple of direct hits that must have been fifty yards out. Shots past thirty-five yards are lucky shots."

The Reverend paused for a moment. I was eager for him to continue because I had never heard this story before.

"I asked Lloyd two questions when we were safe. The first question was, why did he need my pistol? His response was, 'I'd already emptied both of mine.' The second question I asked him was how he'd become such an accurate shot with a pistol. He said, 'I don't shoot people. God guides those bullets where they need to go. If it is by his hand that enemy soldiers die, then it is his will, not mine.'"

A chorus of *amens* echoed through the church. "That was the first time Lloyd saved my life. The bullet that hit me broke both bones in my left thigh. The medics on the chopper joked that the avenging angel had saved another one. I asked them, 'Who's the avenging angel?' They told me Lloyd was the medic who saved me. He would go in, pistols blazing in both hands, and carry the wounded out. I never found out how many men he saved. But that day, he was my avenging angel." He hesitated. More for the dramatic effect than for any other reason, I believed.

"When the surgeons finished, my left leg was two inches shorter than my right. Depending on which leg I was standing on, I was either six feet tall or six feet two inches. The army immediately decided they didn't need someone who couldn't decide how tall he was, so they sent me home.

"Lloyd came to the hospital tent to check on me when the patrol came back. He sat beside my cot, and we talked like we were old friends. He helped me come to grips with the fact that I would never be a professional athlete."

The Reverend laughed and said, "I would not be one anyway. I was one of those rare black kids who wasn't good at sports. I think we must have talked for three or four hours that day," he said, and smiled at the memory. "Before he left he asked me, *Sonny, will you pray with me?* I told him, if you believe in God, I can too."

"That was the second time Lloyd saved my life, and he also saved my soul. I prayed with him that day and asked God to forgive my sins and to help me find my way in life."

"Thanks to God and Brother Lloyd, my wife and I raised thirteen children. Six of them were adopted," he said, holding up his right hand and getting a laugh. "Seven were biological, including my oldest son, Andrew, over there."

The Reverend became very somber. "In over thirty years, Lloyd and I haven't missed a week when one of us hasn't called the other. He finally told me just last week how he got the second pistol. A green second lieutenant left him the Bible that I'm carrying today," and he lifted a tattered Bible above his head. "And he left his pistol, with instructions to save as many men as he could in God's name." The Reverend hesitated. "And I am just one of many."

The Reverend sighed deeply and bowed his head. Quietly, he said, "Andrew, Ben, help me stand up. I wish to look at my brother and my friend one more time."

With Andrew and Ben on each side of him, the Reverend Sonny Towns stood and said goodbye to my father. He placed his hand on my father's hands. "I will see you soon, my friend, and then we will know the answers to all the debates we've had over the years. Until then, I will miss you dearly."

He spoke softly to Ben and Andrew, and they helped him turn to face the audience. "Black preachers are known for their long and fervent prayers. But I can't stand here that long, and I don't have the strength for it. Please join me in the Lord's Prayer."

Ben took over after they helped the Reverend back into his wheelchair. He announced that because of the weather, the interment would be postponed until the next day. He requested that graveside services be attended by family and church members only. I had my suspicions about that announcement and turned to find no police officers at the back of the church. Not even Sheriff Tatum, who was in his own wheelchair.

The ushers were starting with the front row to direct people by the casket and down the main aisle. Mom had held up well and was accepting condolences from the attendees. I turned to Angel to find her crying and looking exhausted. Suddenly, I remembered we hadn't attended her father's funeral because we had run away from the threats on our lives. This must have been very difficult and important to her at the same time. I let go of Mom's hand and turned completely toward Angel to pull her into a comforting hug.

She shuddered in my arms. "Oh Dan, I'm so sorry."

"Shhh, it's okay," I said. "You're home now."

"I'm so sorry," she whispered.

"It's okay, Cotton Top. I'm here and I will not leave you."

I'm sure everyone thought we were grieving for my dad. Maybe we were. But I knew we were grieving for her dad and my dad. We were grieving for ourselves, and for the innocence we lost over the last year and a half.

Reverend Towns' story about my dad pulled me out of my self-pity. Dad never told us war stories, and I now knew why. There were more terrible memories than good ones. No matter what had happened, I still loved Angel and was going to fight to protect her.

A tap on my shoulder forced me to loosen my hold on Angel. It was my mother. She had a worried look on her face.

"What's wrong?" I asked.

"The sheriff needs to see you and Angel in the adult Sunday school classroom. What's going on, Dan?"

"I don't know, Mom. We will go find out," I assured her.

I looked at Angel, and she shook her head, sniffled, and wiped her nose with a tissue. Mrs. Cotton had not moved. She had been holding Angel's other hand for the whole service.

Mrs. Cotton said, "Go. I'll stay with your mom."

"Thank you."

I stood and helped Angel up. She was very weak. Just a shadow of the young woman I loved.

Most of the church had cleared out. There were only a few people left. Several were gathered around Ben and Reverend Towns, who were swapping stories about Dad. Andrew was standing away from the group when we walked toward him to head to the back of the church. I had my arm around Angel, almost holding her up when I reached him.

Stopping, I extended my hand. "Andrew, thank you for bringing your father today. I learned something about my father I never knew."

He smiled for the first time, took my hand, and held it. "And I owe you an apology. I tried my best to talk him out of coming today. But he would have none of it. Now I understand why. I'm forty-two years old, and I've never heard him mention Vietnam. He never talked about it. I learned something about my father today as well."

"Andrew, this is my wife, Angel. We've been summoned by the sheriff."

"Go. I can get Ben to help load Dad back into the van."

"Again, thank you for bringing him today. If Ben or I can ever do anything for you or him, just call us. Please."

"Thank you," he said, smiling again.

Chapter 41

Dan

Before we reached the Adult Sunday school room, Angel stopped me. She took a deep breath, straightened her uniform. She grabbed my hand, and we stepped into the classroom. Classrooms in churches varied a lot. This one had a mixture of old and new folding chairs in several rows set up facing a podium at one end of the room. At the front of the room were several people.

I knew Sheriff Tatum; he was still sheriff and would serve the last few months of his term before retiring. I remembered Sergeant Johnson of the State Police. The other three officers, I didn't know. There was another white male state trooper, a black female Pulaski County deputy, and a white male sheriff from another county.

Angel stopped abruptly, stood at attention, and saluted Sergeant Johnson.

"At ease, Deputy Brock," she said.

"What the hell is this?" the visiting sheriff said. "Her name is Angie Lewis."

"No, Sheriff, this is Deputy Angelina Brock. A member of my Task Force Investigation team. She has spent the last six months working undercover cases for us," the sergeant answered.

"It's good to see you again, Sheriff Pendleton," Angel said.

Sergeant Johnson raised her hand to Angel. "Enough, Angel." She turned to the sheriff. "Sheriff, we are going to depose Angel this afternoon. From earlier reports, we expect that there will be a lot of charges brought against many people. We will compare her statements to those of a DEA informant who was close to your cousins as well."

Sheriff Pendleton was staring at Sergeant Johnson. I could tell his mind was working overtime. He wanted to say something, but apparently, he thought they knew he was guilty of something, and Angel and Sergeant Johnson were giving him a stern warning.

"Who is the DEA informant?" Sheriff Pendleton finally asked.

"The federal prosecutor has not disclosed that information, Sheriff."

"Federal Prosecutor? Why are the Feds involved?" Sheriff Pendleton barked.

"Sheriff Pendleton, I think I've said enough. Your name has come up several times during this operation. I recommend you return home and get a good lawyer," replied the Sergeant.

Sheriff Tatum finally spoke. "Charlie, I trust you can find your way out."

The Pulaski County deputy nodded at Sergeant Johnson and followed Sheriff Pendleton out of the room.

When he walked out the door, Angel swayed in front of me, and I caught her. "You need to sit down, dear."

"Okay," she whispered.

I grabbed the nearest chair and slid it around for her to sit on. When Angel was seated, I looked at Sheriff Tatum and Sergeant Johnson.

"Can one of you please tell me what's going on?"

Sheriff Tatum looked at Sergeant Johnson. "Dan, I'm going to have to let the sergeant answer your questions. I was here for Lloyd's funeral and in here as a courtesy to Sergeant Johnson. I'll see you tomorrow."

"Thank you, Sheriff," I replied.

I turned slowly back to look at Sergeant Johnson. "What is going on? Angel is not well. My father just passed away, and I've had very little sleep in the last seven days," I growled.

Sergeant Johnson raised her eyebrows at me and quietly said, "I understand your frustration, Dan, but we need to know what Angel knows immediately. Sheriff Pendleton came here to arrest Angie Lewis for the attempted murder of Little John and the disappearance of Donny Ray. He also came here to arrest someone who called himself the Avenging Angel for the attempted murder of Little John. When he discovered that was your father and that he was in poor health and had passed away, he insisted it was you. He wanted to arrest you, Dan, for the attempted murder of Little John, but your alibi is airtight. You were filling up your truck at the Flying J truck stop in Roland, Oklahoma, at the time that Angel was being rescued. We have copies of your receipt and video footage. You are in the clear."

She let me digest that information for a few seconds before she continued. "We must get Angel's information now. This is just the first step they will take to stop this investigation."

I was suddenly sweating. I couldn't believe the state police already had copies of the receipt and video footage of me from a truck stop just a few miles into Oklahoma. How did they even know I was there?

I just hoped they would stop their search of my trip there. I diverted the conversation.

"But if Donny Ray has disappeared and Little John is in custody, it's over, isn't it?" I asked.

"They were just the tip of the spear, Dan," Angel said, her voice barely above a whisper. "Sheriff Pendleton is their cousin. There is a vast organization that includes Sheriff Pendleton, other law enforcement officers, lawyers, prosecutors, and judges. There are lots of drug dealers and human traffickers out there. And I can identify a lot of them."

Sergeant Johnson spoke again. "There you go, Dan. They didn't know that Angel was undercover, or that there was a DEA informant. They will scramble now, just like we want them to."

I sighed and hung my head. "Okay, but let's get Angel back home. I can get her comfortable and watch her closely."

"That is what we had planned. This could take hours, Dan. Maybe even a few days. I apologize, but the state police and the Attorney General's office have invaded your farm."

She nodded to me. "We arrived just after you left. Sheriff Pendleton's plan was unexpected. We brought Angel her uniform and encouraged her to come to the funeral. We have taken over the Cotton house. Your farm will be under twenty-four-hour protection for a while. I'm sorry for the intrusion, but her location and real identity are known now. She may have a target on her back, and we must protect her."

I sighed and bent over until my head was beside Angel's. I kissed her and whispered, "Let's get you home."

Then I moved around the chair, picked Angel up, and carried her from the classroom. I heard one officer ask as I left the room, "Is he going to be a problem?"

As I moved down the hallway, Sergeant Johnson replied, "I don't think so. He wants these people as badly as Angel does."

I needed rest. Angel needed rest. Why wouldn't they leave us alone so we could rest? I would only be a problem if they pushed Angel too hard. Then, I would kick them off my property. Little John had beaten Angel over a week ago, and Sergeant Johnson shows up now? Where was she? Why hadn't she worried before now?

Once I got Angel into the Green Machine, I started the truck and pulled out of the church parking lot. She apologized. Telling me things didn't go as they were planned. I stopped her,

"Angel, please stop. Stop talking and listen to me for a few minutes, please."

She stared at me, shaking her head. Before she could start talking again, I said, "I need you to tell the state police about the hidden camera system in the hunting lodge and the Ray house. Donny has an app on his phone that he uses to monitor the camera system. The primary system for recording videos is hidden in the utility room. Do you understand me, Angel?"

She looked at me with big bug eyes. "You did it? You installed the cameras? How?"

I shook my head. "Not important. The state police need to believe the Rays installed the camera system. Okay? So, what did I tell you? Where is the main system at?"

She looked at the truck floorboard. "In the utility room. Donny has an app on his phone." She looked at me again. "How did you get the passcode for his phone?"

"I got it from watching the video cameras. That's not important. What is important is that it shows important people there doing things they shouldn't be doing with young girls. It's evidence. And the only way it's admissible is if it belongs to the Rays. You only know because you caught Donny watching a video. Okay?"

"What video was he watching?" She asked, with a slight smile appearing on her face.

"There's one of the Sheriff back at the church with a young black girl. Tell them about that one."

The smile evaporated. "Oh my God, Cherrie is only fifteen. I took her to that room." She had tears in her eyes, but she was doing her best to be strong.

"Tell them about the camera system first. The truth about the cameras will die with you and me, Angel. We can't tell anyone I had access to the cameras. Agreed?"

"Agreed. I love you. Thank you. That will make my testimony believable."

"The second thing you need to tell them is to dig up Little John's garden."

She gasped. "How do you know about Little John's Garden?"

"Some cameras had microphones," I said.

"Oh," she said. "Anything they need to look for?"

It was my turn to tear up as I turned into the farm road to find a State Trooper blocking the drive.

"Lots of bodies," I said. I didn't want to admit to anyone how much I knew about that garden. Especially to Angel.

I rolled down the truck window to speak to a trooper dressed in rain gear as he stepped out of his car. "I'm Dan Brock, and this is my wife, Angelina, I said."

"Yes sir. I'm sorry about your father. Is the funeral over?"

"Yes sir. There will be a lot of traffic in and out of here in the next few days," I told him. "I have security cameras at all the entrances to the farm. There's at least four ways you can get onto the farm without coming down this drive. You'd be better off watching the camera system than sitting here."

He gulped. "I'll tell Sergeant Johnson when she gets here."

Looking in my rearview mirror, I said, "You can tell her now. She's right behind me."

When I rolled the window back up, Angel asked, "How many bodies?"

"I don't know, around twenty, if the garden size fits the Google satellite image. They planted a garden there to conceal the fresh dirt on the graves. Some may have been there for years."

Before I turned off our farm road onto the driveway of my grandparents' old home, I looked at Angel.

"I love you, Angel. Remember, tell them about the camera system; you know little about it because Donny controlled it. He used an app on his phone. And then Little John's garden. Got it?"

"Yep. I love you, too." She replied as her thumb caressed a spot on my arm. Three layers of clothing, and bandages and covered that spot. There was no way she knew about that injury. She might have seen the bandage during the last week, but she couldn't possibly know how I got it.

I parked my truck in the shed where the Mustang should be parked. I helped Angel out of the truck and winced from the pain in my arm.

"Are you ready for this?"

"I am now. You just gave me the pieces I was missing," she replied.

I picked her up and carried her to the back porch of the house.

Chapter 42

Dan

I took Angel to her bedroom and helped her change out of her uniform and into sweats. She had lost weight. Too much weight. Most of it in the last week. The doctors had insisted on her sleeping and resting as much as possible. She needed time for the swelling to go down and relieve the pressure on the spine there.

The troopers and a couple of lawyers from the Attorney General's office were in the living room. I could either exert a little control over this situation or relinquish all control to Sergeant Johnson. I wasn't willing to relinquish all control. Sergeant Johnson had not been heard from since our parents had found Angel and taken her to the hospital. She should have been there, checking on Angel. To say I was upset and angry with her and the state police would be wildly misleading. I wanted to throw them all out, but I wanted to end this undercover operation and get Angel back home full-time. The only way to do that was to cooperate.

The lawyers from the Attorney General's office had rearranged the living room and put Angel in a corner with good lighting. A video camera and two separate voice recorders were set up and ready to go. The stage was set and waiting for the actor, or more accurately, the confession.

"Sergeant Johnson, I need to show you something if you're going to monitor and protect the farm."

"Dan, we know what we are doing."

"Are you watching the launch ramp from the river, the logging road that comes onto the farm? The road west of the pastures could be driven by one of your cruisers with no issue. A four-wheel drive could access the farm from either direction by coming down the power line. Do you have those points covered?"

"No. But we don't think it's necessary," the Sergeant replied.

"Then it's a good thing I'm not relying on you." I pulled out my phone and pulled up the app that showed all the cameras around the farm. I brought up a video showing a news van making its way slowly down the logging road west of the pastures. "You have this under control, then?"

"Shit. Why didn't you tell me this first?" Sergeant Johnson asked.

"I tried, but you told me you had it under control. Do you want access to my camera system now? And why is there a news van trying to get onto my farm?"

Sergeant Johnson looked at her cell phone, but she had no signal. She looked at me. "How do you have a signal?"

"Wi-Fi," I said.

Ignoring Sergeant Johnson, I looked at the trooper, who asked if I was going to be a problem back at the church and said, "Ignoring what I know about my farm is a mistake that could get someone killed. I won't be a problem unless you are the problem."

Turning back to Sergeant Johnson, who was holding her phone over her head trying to find a signal, I said, "They won't go much farther. I pulled a log across the road last week. They can't get around it."

She stared at me coldly. "What kind of game are you trying to play here, Dan?"

I stared back. "The game of life, Sergeant Johnson. I protected Angel for days before you got here. She's been here for five days, and suddenly you think she is in danger? I've seen Donny Ray on practically every security camera I have on this farm in the last year. I've been preparing for this for a while. Now, you can either work with me or continue to pretend I'm a country bumpkin who doesn't know his own farm better than you ever will. Which will it be?"

"She'll work with you," Angel said softly, entering the room behind me. "If she wants to know what I have to say."

"Why didn't you tell us Donny Ray was on your farm?" Sergeant Johnson growled.

"Because the letter you made my wife send me made me think she was in the Marine Corps, not working undercover for the Arkansas State Police." I hesitated until the count of three before I added, "But I told Sheriff Tatum."

Sergeant Johnson winched.

"I'm sorry," she said, holding one hand open toward me and one hand open toward the other trooper. That's when I realized he had his hand on his pistol.

"You're right. You're right. I've given you no reason to trust me. But understand I always had your wife's back."

I was ready to explode then. She didn't know how close Angel had come to getting murdered. And I couldn't tell her. The cameras were my secret, and now Angel's.

I was taking slow, deep breaths to calm myself down. It was Angel's hand on my arm that reminded me; I had started this confrontation for a reason. They needed to be off their game just enough to keep them from digging too deep. I needed them to focus on the information Angel was going to give them. I didn't need them digging too deeply into how she knew about it. Sergeant Johnson had failed to watch Angel's back. She didn't realize how badly she had screwed up, and I needed to keep my mouth shut because I knew things I wasn't supposed to know.

"I'm sorry, I have slept very little in the last week. Forgive me if I've overstepped," I said and turned to go to the kitchen.

Sergeant Johnson said to my back as I walked to the kitchen, "I'm sorry too, Dan. Maybe I underestimated you. Maybe I underestimated the Rays."

That was all it took to set me off. I wheeled on her, and my face was just a few inches from hers when I yelled, "Maybe? Maybe? When you are done with this interview, I want you off my farm, and I never want to see you here again. Am I clear?"

She stood her ground and stared right back at me. "Very," she said with clenched teeth, and turned away.

Angel, weak as she was, was pushing me toward the kitchen. I finally relented and stepped back into the kitchen.

"Stay here," Angel said. And she put a hand on my chest. "I won't let them take long today. We're both exhausted and need rest."

"Yeah," was all I could get out. Finally, I looked into Angel's pleading eyes and nodded.

"I'll put some coffee on," I said and gently pointed her to the living room door.

I stood in the doorway and watched her walk to the chair they had set up for her. She walked slowly, with one hand or the other always touching a piece of sturdy furniture or a wall.

She sat down in the chair and looked at everyone individually.

"Let's get started. I'm tired, and it's been an emotional week."

Sergeant Johnson spoke then. "Angel, we have a lot of questions, and we need answers as quickly as we can get them."

Angel looked at one attorney and ignored what the sergeant said. "Please start the camera."

Sergeant Johnson turned and glared at me. I gave her a flicker of a smile and turned to make coffee.

I listened to the conversation from the kitchen.

One attorney said, "Please state your name and position for the record."

"I'm Angelina Brock, also known as Angie Lewis, and I'm a Cleburne County Deputy Sheriff and member of the Arkansas State Police Special Investigation Task Force."

"What was your assignment?"

"I was undercover. I was assigned to get close to and learn as much as I could about Donny Ray and Little John Johnson."

"What was the nature of your assignment?"

"It was an undercover investigation."

"And how did you get close to the subjects?"

"I was working at a gentleman's club from where D-Ray, I mean Donny Ray, purchased the contracts of some dancers."

"What do you mean he purchased contracts?"

Angel cleared her throat before she continued.

"Before we get into that, there are two pieces of critical information you need now, so you can get search warrants."

"Stop the camera for a minute," the lead attorney said.

The coffee smelled good, so I peeked through the kitchen door to watch Angel.

Sergeant Johnson quickly told the attorney, "Leave it recording. Go ahead, Angel."

"About a week ago, I saw Donny on his cell phone. I peeked over his shoulder, and he was watching a video of Sheriff Pendleton with a young black girl named Cherrie at the hunting lodge. I think they were about to have sex. He shut the app down when he thought I might be watching. They have hidden cameras at the lodge. I think I found the main system in the utility room, but I had to get out before I got caught."

Sergeant Johnson asked the attorney, "Can their own security system be used against them?"

"Not sure," the attorney answered, "but no one wants their video posted on the internet for the world to see. It might get confessions from some of them."

Sergeant Johnson was getting excited. She asked Angel, "You said you had another piece of information?"

When I looked at Angel, it worried me how haggard she looked. I turned and poured her a cup of coffee and took it to her.

"They have a garden at the Rays' house that they call Little John's Garden," Angel said and reached for the coffee. I stepped back as she took a sip. She smiled at me and continued. "It's actually a cemetery. It's where they bury people."

"Now you can shut it down. Holy shit!" Sergeant Johnson said. "Shut it down. Get me search warrants for the lodge, for the cameras, and to dig up the garden at the house. Hell, get search warrants for the house, too."

She was still talking to the attorneys when I walked back to the kitchen. I had to hide the smile that was crossing my face. *We have the bastards now.* I poured myself a cup of coffee and stared out the kitchen window at the rain. It should blow through soon.

I reminded myself to stay focused. Dad wasn't here for me to talk to anymore. I had to remain in my callous shell and bury my feelings. I was exhausted, and I needed to think about every move and every comment before they came out of my mouth. Now that Angel knew some of my secrets, I needed to make sure she didn't say too much, either. That's why I hadn't told her any more than I had. I didn't trust how the drugs she had taken since leaving the hospital might affect her mental state. I didn't trust how weariness affected my mental state. It's why I didn't want to leave her alone. We were together again, and we needed each other.

Chapter 43

Dan

I gave Sergeant Johnson and one attorney the Wi-Fi password. I made the excuse that it was old and limited and might crash if too many people were on it at the same time. Truthfully, I didn't want anyone taking the time to explore the Wi-Fi setup I had around the farm. They might get ideas about the similarity between my camera system and the one in the Ray's hunting lodge. Donny Ray had a system identical to mine.

The attorneys left their business cards on the coffee table in the living room. It didn't take them long to pack up and load up their cars and vans. There was a lot of excited chatter among the attorneys. One said getting the warrants would be easy; the other thought they would get turned down because of the judge's connection to the Rays. Sergeant Johnson chimed in with a comment about calling the FBI if there was any doubt. As Angel saw them out, the Sergeant assured her they would get the warrants from a federal judge if needed. She was going to call an FBI contact and ask him to be ready to go.

"What you told us in there can give us physical evidence to put some of these people away. If it's there, we'll find it. We will be back in a day or two to get your statement to corroborate the physical evidence. Get stronger and healthier."

"Yes, ma'am," was Angel's simple reply.

Angel leaned back against the front door after closing it.

"You're overdoing it," I said.

"How many days have I been recovering?"

"Five since leaving the hospital."

"Five days, and I haven't reconnected with my husband," she said.

I walked over to her and pulled her into a hug. I whispered, "We planned this, remember? We knew the risks. I love you, and you love me. That's all that matters."

"Why are you whispering?" she asked softly.

"I wasn't lying about seeing Donny Ray on our cameras. This house has a hidden camera and a microphone. The state police have to be the ones who find the cameras Donny Ray installed," I whispered.

I leaned back far enough to look at her face. She searched my eyes, looking for an answer.

"Do you feel up to going to Mom's? The church is serving an early dinner. We can talk there."

"I think so, as long as I can rest later. I'm exhausted."

"We can go to my room after we eat a little. You can rest, and we can talk there. Your medicine is going to wear off soon, and you may start feeling pain again. I need to get you back here before it wears off." I told her.

Our mothers met us as we walked into the kitchen. After hugs, Mom looked at us and asked, "What's going on? Why were the police all over the church today? And, and stopping every car that comes here?"

I sighed and said to Mom, "Let us get something to eat, and then we will tell you."

"Oh no. You go find a seat. We will bring you a plate. Would you like sweet tea to drink?"

"Mom, you should be the one sitting. We can help ourselves."

"Daniel Brock." She stiffened and raised her voice, and I knew I had accidentally offended her. She softened and said, "I have to be doing something. I already miss him so much." The tears started, and I pulled her into a hug.

"I'm sorry, Mom, I miss him too." And I meant it. For the past five days, when I wasn't sitting with Angel, I was sitting with Dad. He was the only person who knew all my secrets, and he was no longer with us.

She pushed me away, but her hand lingered on the collar of my suit. "You need to change out of that suit. Hang it up in the bathroom, and I'll take it to the cleaners this week."

We said our hellos and goodbyes to Uncle Wheldon, Aunt Liz, Mike, and Sissy, who now asked to be called Angela, her given name. They were leaving as we entered the living room. There were a couple of folding chairs by the fireplace, and I helped Angel into one.

"I'll be back. I'm going to change out of this suit."

Ben was talking to a couple of church members. From what little I heard, they were trying to convince him to take over for Dad. I knew from previous conversations that Ben would help until they found another pastor. But Ben had other plans. He was already researching missionary opportunities.

When I came back, most of the people were gone. Ben was sitting beside Angel while she picked at her plate. There was a plate of food on the empty chair beside her, and I assumed it was mine.

"Hey Ben, I'm sorry I wasn't much help today."

"You had other responsibilities pop up. I'm just glad Angel could attend."

There were still two of Mom's friends from church there, and they pushed Mom and Mrs. Cotton out of the kitchen to sit with us.

There was a little chit-chat while I ate, and Angel pushed her food around her plate. When Angel finally set her plate down, Ben asked, "Okay, what's going on? Why is there a state trooper parked at the end of our road?"

Chapter 44

Angel

I took a sip of sweet tea before saying, "When I graduated from high school, I went straight to the police academy. Sergeant Johnson came to the state track meet to recruit me to go undercover for the special investigations task force. I never gave her the chance because I asked what I could do to bring the Rays down. I recruited myself.

"It was her idea to send Dan and Mom the letter about me joining the Marine Corps. With Dad having been a Marine, it seemed plausible. The trooper is at the end of the road to protect me, or us. I guess someone discovered who I really was."

"But Dan knew what was going on the whole time?" Ben asked.

"Partly," I answered. "We have both done our share of acting and lying the last few months. I didn't care what the sergeant said I needed to do. I wasn't hiding anything from Dan. We wanted what she wanted — to bring down this group or organization that Donny Ray and Little John were a part of. I told him everything until I left the academy."

Mom and Mrs. Brock gave me dirty looks. "I'm sorry," I said. "Leaks about undercover operations often occur from family members bragging.

"After the academy, I went to work at a strip joint."

"Angel, please tell me you weren't a stripper," Mom demanded. Mrs. Brock put her hand over her mouth.

"I'm sorry, Mom. I was an exotic dancer. Donny Ray purchased some dancers from the owner. When the strip club owner figured out what Donny Ray was doing with the girls, he called the police. He worked with the police to bring me and a Pulaski County deputy into the club as dancers. She was at the funeral today with Sergeant Johnson. Where did she go?"

Ben answered, "She followed the other sheriff out of the parking lot."

Dan raised his eyebrows and looked at me as if he had missed something critical. He asked, "You only used the name Angie Lewis, right?"

"Yes, why?"

"How did that sheriff know to come to Dad's funeral looking for Angie Lewis? When you're here, you're Angelina Brock, or Angel Cotton?"

"I don't know. He looked surprised when the sergeant called me Angelina Brock."

I could tell Dan's brain was racing. He was tired, and he wasn't thinking clearly. Then it must have clicked.

"Ben? Will you go to the Cotton's house? The attorneys left their business cards on the coffee table. Grab them and bring them back here, please?" He asked.

"Why?"

"I believe one of those attorneys is married to a Ray cousin," Dan said.

"Be right back." He said as he rose and left the room.

Dan looked at me and said, "I'll be back, too. I need to grab my laptop."

He started talking as he walked back into the living room. "The Rays' grandfather sired twelve children, and they went forth and multiplied, to use biblical terminology, and now that Danny Ray is dead, there are two hundred and seventy-nine cousins. Thanks to one of those cousins, I have a family tree that shows all the family members, their spouses, and their occupations."

He sat down beside me again and pulled up the website showing the family tree. When the page came up, he started scrolling down. He stopped at Sheriff Pendleton's.

"Is he the one who was at the church today?" he asked me. We both knew he was. I couldn't understand why he was asking me and pretending he didn't know. I looked into his eyes, and I understood. We still had secrets to keep. We had to be careful about how much of the truth we told. Dan might know a lot more about this investigation than I knew. He had access to the camera system.

I nodded. "He was around."

He scrolled down some more and stopped at Greg Wishborne, Attorney. Whoever did this website had put in a lot of work. If the person had an internet presence, their name showed up in blue, showing a hyperlink that would take you to more information. Dan clicked the link, and it pulled up his bio on the Attorney General's website.

He had been with the AG's office for three years. Before that, he worked for the Honorable J. P. Boone, Judge for the East-central district of Arkansas.

He pointed to the name and asked me, "Does that name look familiar?"

I shook my head. "I don't remember. If I could see his picture?"

He opened another tab in the browser and did a quick search. He found the Judge's picture and gave the laptop to me.

I felt my stomach lurch. "Yeah, he's been there." I knew the bastard. I knew him too well.

He pulled his phone out and handed it to me.

"If one of those cards belongs to Wishborne, then there won't be any chance of getting the warrants issued," Dan said.

Ben came back carrying the business cards. He handed them to Dan.

"Call Sergeant Johnson. She needs to go straight for the federal warrants," he said to me. "One of the business cards belongs to Wishborne."

I put the phone to my ear and dialed the sergeant's number.

Sergeant Johnson answered the phone. "Daniel Brock, why are you bothering me?"

"Sergeant, it's Angel. We have a problem." I explained what we had discussed, only to have her reply, "I'm aware. It's part of the plan. The federal warrants were requested as soon as I called the FBI agent. He was waiting for my call. If, I mean when Judge Boone denies the warrants, then it adds to the evidence of a cover-up."

"Okay, I'm sorry I bothered you," I replied.

"Angel, discuss none of this with Dan or anyone else. Am I clear?"

"Yes, ma'am."

I hit the end-call button and handed the phone back.

"She's ahead of us," I said.

"No," Dan said. "She set this up. She used Dad's funeral as part of her investigation."

"I'm sorry, Dan."

He smiled, "It's okay. I think Dad would have approved."

Mrs. Brock glared at Dan, pointed at Mom and said, "Dan, I think you and Angel owe us the truth now. We have both lost our husbands because of these people. And I shouldn't have to remind you that you nearly lost Angel. We want them brought to justice too. Apparently, you know more about what Angel has been doing than you have told us. So please tell us the truth. We promise not to talk about this to anyone."

"Okay, Mom," Dan answered. "We must be careful where we talk. Donny Ray planted cameras and a microphone in the Cotton's house and in the barn. I know where they are, but I left them."

"Why did you leave them?" Mom asked Dan. She gave me a frightened look.

"Because they aren't in any private areas, and I couldn't let him know how much I knew he was doing. We need the state police to find them. That way they can use it to build a case against Donny Ray," he explained.

Mom shook her head. "I don't care. I want them gone."

"Two, maybe three more days," Dan said. "The state police will remove them. Let us explain, please."

"Talk fast, you two," Mom said.

I resumed my story. "Okay. Anyway, Donny Ray showed up at the strip club, and I was the one he bought. But instead of being one of his hunting club girls, I became his girlfriend."

"How did you convince him of that?" Ben asked.

"Fat Man, he owned the club, must have told him something about me. But I played the role of a strong-willed, crooked girl, who would do whatever it took to get what I wanted." I would not tell our mothers and Ben that I screwed his brains out to get close to him, or that he knew who I was from the beginning. Fat Man wasn't as innocent as I thought he was.

I took another sip of tea and looked at Dan. He must have read my thoughts in my eyes.

He looked at our mothers and said, "You deserve the entire story, and you will eventually hear it. But when Angel says she is tired, then the story stops until she feels up to continuing. How are you doing, Cotton Top?"

I had to smile. It had been months since Dan had called me Cotton Top, and I wanted to hear his voice call me that every day.

"I'm tired. And I'm aching," I told him.

"Then let's get you home. The next few days will be rough," Dan answered.

Chapter 45

Angel

Our mothers were less than happy about not hearing the rest of the story, but there was one more thing I needed to do before Dan took me home. The guilt I felt because of it was overwhelming.

"Ben?"

"Yes?"

"Do you have the phone number of the girl who came to the lodge with you that night?"

"Yes. But she won't answer my calls or return my messages."

"Did you tell her who I was?"

"No, I never knew you were there."

"What was her name, Ben?"

"Amy, why?"

"Dan, I need to use your phone again, please."

"Ben, give me her number."

I dialed the number and hoped she would answer.

"Hello? Who is this?"

"Amy. This is Angelina Brock. I'm Dan Brock's wife and Ben Brock's sister-in-law."

"If you called me about Ben, this conversation is over. I want nothing to do with him."

"No. No. This has nothing to do with Ben. As a matter of fact, I owe both of you a huge explanation and an apology. Will you listen, please?"

There was a long pause on the phone. I looked up to see Ben staring at me.

"Okay, but don't ask me questions, because I don't remember anything."

"I won't ask questions, but I need you to listen to what I have to say. The night you came to the Wood Duck Lodge, I was working undercover for the Arkansas State Police. Ben didn't know I was there. They thought he was Dan, my husband.

"You didn't leave soon enough. Ben and Dan look a lot alike. Donny Ray decided he wanted to kill him, drug you, and sell you to his human-trafficking contacts. I suggested a better revenge. I couldn't let those guys kill Ben, and I couldn't let them turn you into a drugged sex slave.

"It was my idea to drug you both. Take you back to Ben's apartment, undress you both, and call the police, pretending you were being raped."

I took a sip of sweet tea and looked up to find Ben in tears. Mom and Mrs. Brock were in total shock. Ben was horrified listening to me.

"I'm sorry for the embarrassment I caused you. If I hadn't done that, Ben would be dead now, and probably you, too."

"You are crazy. How am I supposed to believe this?"

"Please watch the news," I answered. "There will be a joint state and federal investigation into the Ray family, the Hunting Lodge, and their activities. I'm so sorry, Amy. Goodbye."

Ben, my mom, and Mrs. Brock were in tears. Dan was watching me with no expression on his face.

I looked at Dan and said, "You don't look surprised."

"I'm a little surprised. But I watched it all go down that night. Sheriff Tatum deputized me. I watched from a distance, armed with two pistols, a combat shotgun, and a bulletproof vest. I wasn't letting anyone in my family die that night if I could help it," Dan said. "But the Sheriff gave me strict orders not to interfere with an undercover operation, unless someone's life was in danger."

Ben stood and yelled, "How could you, Dan? How could you let her do that to me? To Amy? I asked you to go with me, and you refused. Why?"

"I'm sorry, Ben, I was there, just not inside. I'm truly sorry, but if I had shown up there with you, we wouldn't be here today. We would be dead, Ben. Dead. You, me, Amy, and Angel. All dead."

Mrs. Brock looked at Dan. Her face twisted with anger and frustration.

"Dan, you and Angel need to leave now. Please don't come back home tonight," Mrs. Brock cried.

Dan didn't say anymore. He looked at me, and I nodded to him. I tried to stand up, but I didn't have the strength.

Before Dan could pick me up, Ben yelled at Dan again.

"There's no way they could have killed four people and gotten away with it. You and Angel are crazy."

I looked at Ben and said quietly, "Tell that to the people buried behind the Ray's house. I love you, Ben, and I'm not lying. Take me home, Dan."

Dan said softly, "Ben, I left those cameras in your apartment to test the motion sensors. I didn't know they would capture anything besides your movement. But how do you think Sheriff Tatum had copies of the videos and knew where you were the next morning? I did that, Ben. I took the video of their carrying you out of the lodge and into your apartment. That's why there were no charges filed against you."

"Why did you put a camera facing my bed? Was that supposed to be funny?"

"No. I pointed the camera at the bedroom floor. The camera got moved when Donny Ray carried you in on his shoulder and threw you on the bed. I didn't intend for that to happen. But it proved you were innocent."

As Dan bent down and picked me up, he said to Ben, "I'd rather have you alive and you never talk to me again than for you to be dead." He choked a cry back and said, "Good night."

The rain finally stopped. The light from the rising moon slipped through the thinning clouds. I was exhausted after the confrontation. I hadn't expected Ben's reaction to my story, but then I hadn't expected Dan's confession either. He'd been there. And no one knew it. Donny Ray and Little John had a sixth sense about people being around that weren't supposed to be. But they didn't have a clue that Dan was there.

We were backing the truck under the shed when I realized something. "Dan, how did you know what we were doing with Ben and Amy?"

Dan sighed heavily before he replied. "You were standing in front of a camera with a microphone. I heard the plan, and I trusted you. It worked, Cotton Top. You saved their lives."

"Why didn't you tell Ben what you heard?"

"Because I'm not supposed to know the cameras are there. I shouldn't have told them I was there. Even now, the lying and acting must continue for me. Let's get you to bed."

I loved him more than he would ever know. He truly loved me and had my back when I didn't know I needed him. I knew one of his secrets though, and now I wondered what else I didn't know.

"Stay with me tonight, Dan. I want you to hold me, please."

"I'm not going anywhere."

Chapter 46

Dan

It was nearly nine o'clock when we got settled into bed. Mrs. Cotton had not returned home yet. I left her a note telling her I was sleeping with Angel and would take care of her tonight.

I tried to curl up with Angel and hold her like she wanted me to. She tossed and turned and elbowed me in the ribs once and hit me in the face. Accidentally, of course. She finally fell into a restful sleep around midnight. I eased out of bed and went to the bathroom.

When I came out, the kitchen light was on, showing Mrs. Cotton was home. I walked into the kitchen to find her reading my note. She looked up and immediately headed to me and gave me a big hug and a kiss on the cheek.

She stepped back and said, "Your mom and Ben are very upset with you and Angel. But they are coming around. Your mom more than Ben. I had to remind them that your old girlfriend and Jonathan were murdered by one of them. And Roger was given laced drugs, and that your dad died from complications from being kicked in the chest by Little John. I even reminded them of the kidnapping attempt at the State Fair and your truck getting set on fire. Your mom understood, because she had already made that point tonight, herself.

"Ben is angry about being embarrassed and because the girl won't talk to him. He hasn't forgiven himself for what happened, and he can't forgive you, Dan."

"Thank you for understanding, Mrs. Cotton."

"Oh, I don't think I understand anything, Dan. What I understand is Angel did this because she loved Jonathan, and you did this because you love Angel. Am I right?" she asked.

"Yes, ma'am."

"There's a lot of other stuff between you and Angel that I don't understand. Your dad was very secretive with your mom about what the two of you talked about. Your mom and Ben talked about things you did that made little sense. I told them they needed to be quiet and trust you both."

Then she reached up and pulled my head down and whispered in my ear, "You and Angel need to get your stories straight before she talks to the State Police. We can't have you going to prison for something stupid. Your mom, Angel and I need you here."

"I understand," I answered. She had to be referring to my sitting outside the lodge, knowing Ben and Amy were in trouble, and knowing what Angel was doing. She couldn't have known the other secrets I was keeping.

"Good. Now, get some sleep. You look exhausted."

I said, "Goodnight." As I turned to go back down the hall.

"Good night, Dan."

My phone buzzed at exactly six a.m. It was Sergeant Johnson. I answered the phone with a simple hello.

She didn't say hello, how are you doing, or even ask how Angel was doing. She just started talking.

"We will be back today at one. Make sure Angel is ready to answer questions at one-thirty, okay?"

"Sergeant, I don't mean to be disrespectful, but we are having Dad's graveside service at one today. Can you push this to two-thirty? I understand you need information. But we need to grieve and say goodbye to my dad. Privately. I don't want any interruptions like yesterday. Please?"

I must have caught her off guard. She called, ready to argue with me, but I had made a simple plea instead. After a pause, she answered.

"I can do that, Dan. I'm sorry I've been so pushy. We need this information, and I've been totally focused on that. But I will respect your need to grieve. Especially after that circus yesterday."

"You didn't plan that?"

She raised her voice slightly then. "If you're referring to Sheriff Pendleton? I leaked some information to him, but I didn't expect him to show up at your father's funeral. Please accept my apologies for that."

"Apology accepted," I replied.

"How's Angel doing?" she asked in a lower voice.

"Sleeping soundly for the last six hours. She asked me to stay with her and hold her last night. There is a lot of tension between us and my family right now. Angel told the story about drugging Ben and his girlfriend last night and explained why she did it. Mom and Ben didn't handle it well."

"She saved their lives. The prosecutor called me to verify Sheriff Tatum's story before he dismissed the case and sealed the report. That was a smart move by Angel."

"Amy hasn't talked to Ben since then. She doesn't trust him. Angel called her last night and told her the story, but she didn't believe it," I answered.

"I hope Angel didn't say too much."

"She didn't. She needed to apologize and explain her actions."

"Dan. I owe you one, so I'll call Amy and talk to her. If she hears it from me, maybe she will believe Angel and forgive your brother. Now, please tell Angel to stop talking about this case. We need to get her testimony recorded as soon as possible. Can I get your help with that?"

I didn't ask why she felt she owed me anything. I wanted this whole thing over, and I wanted Angel back home, and our life to be normal.

"Yes, ma'am."

"Thank you. I'll see you this afternoon."

Sergeant Johnson hung up before I said anything. That was fine, because the conversation went better than I had expected any conversation between us to go.

I got up and went to the bathroom. I came back and checked on Angel. She was tossing and turning again, so I woke her up and helped her to the bathroom.

"You have to start eating something to build your strength back," I told her. "Come with me, and we will make breakfast, okay?"

I was surprised to find Mrs. Cotton already up, and to find Ben and Mom sitting at the dining table drinking coffee.

"Mom, Ben." I acknowledged them. Angel hugged her mom.

Ben spoke first. "Dan, I'm still angry about all of this, but I think I'm understanding the sacrifice you and Angel have made. I realized this morning that's why you and Angel got married. You weren't sure she would survive."

He was finally getting it. I nodded my head at him.

Ben continued, "Dad knew, didn't he? You told him everything."

I nodded again. "Yeah. He and Sheriff Tatum were my advisors from beginning to end."

"I have one question. How did you know what Angel was going to do that night at the Hunting Lodge?"

There it was. The question I couldn't answer. I tapped my ear and cut my eyes to look up at the light above the dining table. "I didn't know. And Angel and I are under strict orders from Sergeant Johnson not to say anything else about the investigation right now."

"Since when?" Angel asked hoarsely.

"Six a.m. sharp. They will be back at two thirty to continue interviewing you. Sergeant Johnson is going to end up talking to Amy and Ben as well."

Ben asked again, "How did you know?"

"I didn't know, Ben. I had to trust Angel." But I looked at him and then looked up at the light.

Mom gasped when she figured out I was telling Ben we were sitting under a camera. She grabbed Ben's arm and said, "You and Dan can talk about that later."

She hesitated for a moment before continuing. "Your father believed in what you and Angel were doing. He told me before he passed that you and Angel had been waging a war on evil, and that if you made it out alive, you would suffer from injuries and trauma that could not be seen. I understand that now.

"Angel? It took a lot of strength to confess what you did to Ben and Amy. After your mom reminded us of all the people they had hurt and killed, I realized you may not have made the best decision, but it was a quick decision that saved their lives. Thank you."

Mom stood. "Dan? May I speak with you and Ben outside, please?"

Angel reached for my hand as I stood, and I stopped. She gave me a questioning look. I kissed her on top of the head and said, "I'll be back shortly."

Mentally, I was preparing for an argument that I wasn't up for. I followed them out the door, and we stopped on the front porch. If Mom only knew half of what I was hiding in my head, she would tell everyone to back up and prepare for the nuclear meltdown. Dad had been the only reason I stayed focused and kept going.

Mom asked, "Can we talk here?"

"Yes," I replied. "I'm sorry about all of this. There is a lot Angel and I would love to tell you. But we can't."

"Why not, Daniel?"

I looked at Ben, and then at Mom. "Not everything we did was morally right. We need to be careful, or we could end up in prison and they could go free. I won't say anymore. I love you both, and I need to protect myself, Angel, both of you, and Mrs. Cotton."

"By not telling us everything?" Ben asked.

"Yes," I replied flatly. "I'm having a difficult time not telling you. Please respect my wishes. I'd rather not tell you than lie to you."

Mom asked me, "Dan, did you do something bad?"

I didn't look at Mom. I looked at Ben and gave him a pleading look. He raised his eyebrows at me, and his mouth dropped open as if he imagined the truth. He and Robby must have talked on the way home from Oklahoma, although I never told Robby what I did.

"I'm sorry, Dan. I won't push you anymore. Let's go home, Mom."

I turned to go back into the house. Mom touched my arm. "You will tell us everything soon, though. Right?"

This time, I had to be honest. "You will know everything the state police know. But some things are best left buried."

At the word 'buried' Ben's eyes told me he finally understood what I was dealing with, so he came to my rescue. "Let's go home, Mom. We're not helping him by bugging him for information he can't give us."

Without looking back, I returned to the house. The secrets were weighing on me. Angel's secrets would soon be told. Hopefully, mine would never see the light of day.

Breakfast to lunch was a blur. Angel hammered me with questions, but I refused to answer most of them. It appeared she was shaking off the effects of the injury better than I'd hoped. Every person was different. How their bodies dealt with the injury was different. It may have been less from the physical beating she and Little John inflicted on each other, and more of the mental stress of living the lie that undercover operations created. She had been Angie Lewis for so long; it was difficult to return to being Angel.

Angel stopped asking me questions and said, "If you will not answer my questions, how about I answer yours?"

I told her, "I know enough. You're alive, and that's all that matters to me."

"Damn it, Dan. I'm trying to reach out and reconnect. I've missed you so much."

Chapter 47

Dan

I went home at noon to get dressed for Dad's graveside service. Mom gave me a strained look. But Ben confronted me while I was changing. "What did you do when I was in Colorado? You didn't have an emergency shift to work, did you?"

I stiffened, remembering those two days. Angel's phone call, in particular. "Nothing I want to remember."

"Did Dad know?" he asked.

"Yes."

"But you don't plan on telling me or Mom, do you?"

"No," I answered. "Trust me, Ben. There are some things I will take to the grave, and this is one of them."

He huffed and gave me a worried look.

"Okay, I will drop it for now. I need to go to the cemetery." He turned to leave and stopped. Without looking at me, he said, "I love you, Dan, but I feel like this is tearing our family apart."

"I hope not, because I need your support. See you at the cemetery." I buttoned my shirt collar and began tying my tie. Dad had taught both Ben and me how to tie ties. This morning, I used a double Windsor knot. It was a perfect knot that many people confused for a clip-on tie. Most men used a single Windsor knot.

Angel stayed home to rest. She wasn't ready to go to the cemetery. Her dad was buried there, and she wasn't ready to visit. She didn't feel like she had kept her promise to him yet.

The ground was still wet and soft from the rain, but the sun shone brightly. There were two tents. One covered the grave, and another covered the chairs. There were about twenty people already gathered. My aunt, uncle, and cousins. The sheriff, his wife, and a few other church members.

There was also a state trooper's car. Sergeant Johnson stepped out of the driver's seat when she saw me heading toward her. Then, the passenger door opened. When I realized who the passenger was, I stopped in my tracks.

"I told you I owed you one, Dan," Sergeant Johnson said. "I had a long conversation with this young lady and her parents this morning, and she wanted to come and support you and your brother."

The emotions running through my head were crazy. I couldn't believe she had gone out of her way to talk to Amy. Perhaps this woman was human, after all.

"Amy, I'm so sorry about everything that has happened. Are you doing okay?" I asked.

"I'm totally confused. Hurt. Still embarrassed. But Sergeant Johnson said I... Ben and I got involved in something much bigger than we realized. That Ben had no control over what happened."

I stepped closer and saw the red lines in her eyes. She wasn't wearing makeup. I was just steps away from her when she asked, "Will you tell me what happened?"

I looked at Sergeant Johnson, but she stood there stone-faced, neither giving nor denying me permission to tell her. Then I remembered Sergeant Johnson was not aware I was at the lodge that night. She knew I was responsible for the cameras at Ben's apartment. But nothing more. I was going to be forced to tell more lies.

"Not until Sergeant Johnson tells me I can. I'm sorry for what happened and the embarrassment it caused you and Ben. But he had nothing to do with it. He was there to protect you, and he is embarrassed that he failed to do so. Can you forgive him for that?"

"I will try."

"Would you come sit with me and my mom? We will talk to Ben after the service."

We slipped into the seats beside Mom. She barely noticed. Ben had already started what would be a brief service. He never looked my way. I assumed he thought Angel was beside me. And I figured he was still angry at me for not trusting him. He spoke softly and elegantly. Telling a couple of funny stories about Dad. Then he closed with a long prayer.

Amy and I sat quietly as people started to leave. Mom stood and started speaking to someone.

I turned to Amy. "Are you nervous?" She nodded yes. "It will be okay. Ben cares about you more than you know. This has torn him up inside. Your being here will relieve a lot of pain he's been going through."

I stood up. "Come on. It's going to be okay."

She stood and grabbed my hand. "I don't know if I can do this."

Fear, reluctance, not even the devil was going to stop this reunion. I held her hand tight and looked for Ben. He was talking to the funeral director. I stepped in his direction and called, "Ben."

I felt like I was tugging Amy's arm off. She was reluctant to do this now that the time had come. I didn't give her a choice, and I didn't give Ben a chance to talk. He turned when I called his name.

"There's someone here who would like to see you."

Amy had been hiding behind me as we walked up. When I got close, I took a quick step to my right, surprising Amy, and Ben.

They stared at each other for what felt like minutes. I finally held her hand out to Ben. "There's no reason for y'all to be angry at each other. You had no control over what happened. You should support each other and talk through your issues. I'll give you a minute."

Turning, I walked out of hearing range to where Mom was talking to Uncle Vernon. I touched Mom's arm. She looked at me with a mix of anger, frustration, and sadness. Then she looked toward Ben. "I thought Angel was with you. Who is that?"

"That's Amy."

Mom gasped. "What happened? Why is she here?"

"The state police did me a favor and stopped by to talk to her this morning. After understanding Ben had no control over the situation, she wanted to come see him and support him."

As Mom watched them, a small smile appeared on her face. I turned to see Amy and Ben hugging each other.

"I'll go check on them," I said.

Mom grabbed my arm. "No. Let me. You need to talk to Uncle Vernon."

I watched Mom walk away. Uncle Vernon cleared his voice and said, "Your mom thinks you are in trouble and need an attorney."

I smiled and shook my head. "No. Do you see that state trooper over there standing beside her car?"

"Yes."

"That's Angel's boss. Angel is a deputy sheriff and has been working undercover with the State Police. I wasn't supposed to know, but I did. Dad knew as well, but we kept her secret. It's nothing to worry about."

The best lies are wrapped up in a kernel of truth. This wasn't a lie. I was avoiding the truth and his question.

"Thank you for your concern, Uncle Vernon. I need to talk to Sheriff Tatum. Excuse me, please."

"I'm here if you need me." He said as I turned away.

"Thank you."

I walked to where Sheriff Tatum was sitting in his wheelchair. His wife had returned to the van. "Thanks for coming, Sheriff." I held my hand out for him to shake.

"Don't be so formal, Dan. Tell me how you are doing while you help me to my van."

I turned his wheelchair around and helped him across the soft ground. "I'm tired of lying," I said quietly.

"It's not lying if you don't know anything, and you're not supposed to know anything."

"I know. I know."

"Keep them focused on Angel's story. That's what you need to do, Dan. Don't tell Angel any more than you must. Until she is completely well and finished with the deposition, you say nothing. Understood?"

"Yes, sir."

He let the lift down on his van and rolled his wheelchair onto it. "I'll be fine, Sheriff. We'll get through this."

"I know you will. Please follow your dad's plan."

"Yes, sir."

I walked to where Sergeant Johnson was talking on her phone. She had been on the phone every time I looked at her. I looked for Ben and Amy, and they were still talking with Mom.

When Sergeant Johnson saw me approaching, she said to the person on the phone, "Hold on a second, please."

"Thank you for bringing Amy. I think we can get her home. I'll see you at the farm." She nodded, returned to her phone call, and got into her car.

I talked to a few more people who had attended Dad's graveside service and thanked them for coming. Finally, I walked to where Ben, Mom, and Amy were talking.

I heard Amy asking, "I don't understand how it happened? It makes no sense."

"Maybe I can answer a few of your questions," I said. They looked at me. "Angel told me more of her side last night. I'm not supposed to say anything, but you deserve some peace."

They waited for me as I swallowed hard, deciding how much to tell. "Little John recognized Ben and heard you asking about your friend. Ben and I look a lot alike, and Donny Ray and Little John have tried to kill us on several occasions. He thought Ben was me and wanted to kill him. Angel argued against killing him and convinced them that embarrassment and revenge were better than killing. They liked the idea. They used a date-rape drug on you both. I can't remember the name right now. Then they drove you back to Ben's apartment, stripped you, and threw you in bed together. Angel called the police, pretending to be a neighbor, and said she thought someone was being raped and requested a welfare check."

I hesitated for a moment before I continued. "She said Donny Ray and Little John laughed all the way back to the lodge. They included Angel in practically everything after that. She said they asked for creative ideas about dealing with people and situations. You were the only ones she kept them from killing. At least one other person was killed while she was there. I can't tell you anymore."

"Oh my God," Amy replied.

I asked, "Are y'all okay? I told Sergeant Johnson we could get Amy back home."

Ben answered, "I think so. Is it okay if I take you home, Amy?"

"Yes," she said with a sad smile.

Ben and Mom looked around then. "Where is everyone?"

"They have gone home," I said. "You had been talking for twenty minutes before I came over. I thanked most of them for coming before they left."

The funeral director was waiting politely for us to move. Most of the chairs and one tent had already been taken down. I turned one more time to look at the casket. That was Dad's body in there, but his spirit and some of his wisdom lived on with me. I longed for one of his hugs and his reassurance that God would take care of everything.

Sergeant Johnson met me on the porch of the Cotton's house when I returned to the farm. Now I was afraid I would have to break my promise to the Sheriff. I might not be able to keep quiet.

"Your girl is talking and feeling stronger. I wanted to ask you a few questions out here."

"Okay," I responded. Here it comes.

"How long have you known she was working for the State Police Task Force?"

I sighed. There was no use in lying about this. She would find out eventually, and it was better for her to believe I had told her the truth.

"I've always known."

"Shit. How did she contact you?"

"Her phone has slots for two SIM cards. She threw the second SIM card away after the academy. We decided it was too dangerous if someone took her phone and found the second SIM card. It would lead straight to me."

"And she had no contact with you after the academy?"

"No, ma'am." And I wasn't lying about this. I had watched the cameras, and that was how I knew she was with Donny Ray.

She stared directly at me, but I didn't waver. I gave her an honest answer.

"How did you know to put cameras in your brother's apartment?"

"Those were cameras I bought for the farm but didn't work. I fixed them for Amy and one of her friends to put above their doors after their friend Audra went missing. I put them around Ben's apartment to test them and make sure they worked, but never had the chance to put the cameras up for them."

"You put one in his bedroom, though. Why?"

"It was above his door. It was supposed to be pointed straight down to test the motion sensor I was having trouble with. Somehow, it got bumped and pointed straight at the bed. I didn't intend for that to happen."

We both took a deep breath. "This happened three weeks ago. Why are you just now asking me these questions?"

"Because the young lady this morning asked me some tough questions, and I didn't have answers. I asked myself some questions. I thought about the

Ray's camera system. Then I remembered your camera system on your farm, and that brought up more questions."

"What questions?" I asked. She was putting things together much faster than I expected.

"How long have you had cameras up around the farm?"

"After my ex-girlfriend's death. The Sheriff will confirm that."

"So, you are familiar with remote cameras?"

"Nearly every hunter has a game camera or several. Most record locally, and you must retrieve the memory card from the camera to see what it recorded. Some are hard-wired and some work on Wi-Fi, but the Wi-Fi cameras are much more expensive. Most of my security cameras on the farm are Wi-Fi, and I have signal boosters set up in different locations. I set those up when we started getting threats."

"And you have seen Donny Ray on your farm? What was he doing?"

"Putting up his own cameras."

"You have to be kidding me," she said.

"I wish I were."

"Let me guess. The Sheriff knew they were here?" I nodded, and she shook her head before she asked, "Do you have cameras in the Cotton's house?"

"There are three cameras, one at each door, to show anyone entering and leaving."

"Did Donny Ray have any cameras in the Cotton house?"

"There is one hidden in the chandelier above the dining table," I replied.

"How do you know this?"

"Sometimes, I lose the Bluetooth connection to my earbuds or my cameras. So, I search for all Bluetooth items within a connecting distance of my phone or laptop. This happened before, and I found Bluetooth connections I wasn't familiar with. I experimented with them until I connected with them."

"And you left them there?"

"I knew they would eventually become evidence. But I haven't touched them."

"I see. Were you able to connect to any of his other cameras?" She never took her eyes off me.

"Just the ones on the farm. I know nothing about the ones Angel was talking about, but I figure they are like the ones here." A lie and a truth.

"How many did you find, and where are they?" I was tiring of this interrogation and reminded myself to keep it simple.

"Three. There is one at the end of the drive. One is in the barn, and the other is in the chandelier," I replied. "If there are more, I haven't found them."

"How did Sheriff Tatum get the video from Ben's apartment?"

"Sheriff Tatum is a family friend. We go to church together. I've helped him work cattle on his farm. He knows I have cameras on the farm. When Ben got into trouble, he called and asked if there was a camera at Ben's apartment. I got the video for him."

"Did you film them at the lodge and the apartment?"

"I didn't know there was more footage," I lied.

"Thank you, Dan. Your use of cameras and Donny Ray's use of cameras raised some red flags. But the use of game trail cameras explains it. Donny Ray would be familiar with trail cameras because he was a hunting guide, and you said you used them for hunting as well."

She took a deep breath before continuing. I got the sense that my answers helped her make a decision of some kind.

"You and I haven't gotten along well since we started this yesterday. I was pushy, and I'm sorry. You need to know that I knew where Angel was as soon as your family checked her into the hospital. I was on my way to check on her when I got a call from the Feds. They told me she was in excellent hands and that if I showed up, it might endanger her and another undercover operative. It pissed me off to be overridden by the Feds. But I was under orders not to contact Angel until yesterday, or I would have been with her before you were. This is an important case to me, and I didn't want to make any mistakes."

I know she was frustrated, but so was I. Now she was telling me she wasn't allowed to be there. That turned my anger and frustration with her upside down. I turned my back on her and stared out across the farm, putting my hands to my face and breathing deeply. It seemed Angel and I weren't the only ones who had secrets.

When I turned around, I said, "I thought you had lost contact with her and didn't know what was going on. I've been so angry with you because

I thought you'd abandoned her." I took a deep breath before continuing. "Why did the Feds tell you not to interfere?"

"They had to get their operative out safely. Little John was arrested as soon as he reached the hospital. We lost contact with Donny Ray, and we thought he would show back up. But he never has."

I kept quiet. I couldn't think of questions. Until I said, "That's why you felt like you owed me a favor."

"Yes. I let you take care of Angel. I knew you would do what was best for her. It was the best cover she had. To let them think she was doing this on her own. And it worked; Sheriff Pendleton bought it."

I nodded. It made sense, and it didn't at the same time. "I understand now, but I don't like it," I said.

"Trust me, I didn't either."

"Were you able to get the search warrants? Have you heard anything about Donny Ray?" I needed to move the conversation on. Any more questions along the camera line would lead nowhere good.

"The federal warrants were issued this morning. The state warrants were denied. And, no. No one has heard from Donny Ray."

She pulled her phone out. "I should have heard something by now. What's your Wi-Fi password again? Damn, I forgot there is no signal here."

I pulled my phone out and read it to her. I changed the password every few weeks. Before the Cotton's moved in, I had only changed it once.

As soon as she connected to the Wi-Fi, her phone started dinging, and then it rang.

Her first comment after she said hello was, "You're shitting me."

She finally said, "Thank you. I have a phone signal now. Keep me posted."

She exhaled heavily. "I probably shouldn't be telling you this, but you'll know soon enough. They have uncovered five bodies in the garden so far. One of them was Donny Ray's. They identified him through his wallet."

I acted shaken that his body had been found. I looked at her as blankly as possible and pushed the memories of that morning out of my mind.

"What?"

"Yeah. We don't have any answers right now. Let's check on our girl." And she turned to the door.

We entered quietly, and Sergeant Johnson made a T with her hands to signal time-out when one lawyer looked up.

Angel looked tired. Even though she had had a good morning, the constant questioning was wearing her out. Sergeant Johnson's questions had worn me out.

Angel finished answering a question about the people who worked in the lodge and bar, and then the lawyer announced a break.

"How's it going in here?" Sergeant Johnson asked.

"We're making slow progress. We still have a lot of questions, though."

"Good. I just got an update on the federal search of the Ray's lodge and house."

One lawyer had no reaction. But the other lawyer almost lost his balance at the words "federal search."

"They have retrieved the cameras and recording systems from the house and the lodge. They have recovered five bodies from behind the Ray's house. One of them was Donny Ray."

Angel was staring at me, but I remained calm and avoided her gaze. When I finally looked her way, I saw a tear rolling down her cheek. Did she have feelings for him? I guess it was possible. She was pretending to be his girlfriend. But the videos will reveal his actual plan for her soon.

The shocked attorney had to be Wishborne. He grabbed his phone, and I raised my hand to tell him he had no signal.

Sergeant Johnson slapped my wrist hard enough that the sound made everyone look at us.

"There is no need to call the judge, Mr. Wishborne. The Feds already have him in custody."

He looked at Sergeant Johnson, confusion, and anger spreading across his face.

"Mr. Wishborne, you are under arrest for obstruction of a police investigation, and aiding and abetting criminal activity, and I'm sure we will add many more charges. But that will get us started for now."

She looked at the trooper in the room. "Take him to the county jail. They are expecting him. Then, you are free to go home and see your family. Tomorrow will be a long day."

"Yes, Ma'am." He handcuffed the lawyer and read him his rights.

As the trooper pushed the lawyer out the door ahead of him, Sergeant Johnson turned to me. "I didn't mean to hit you so hard, but I didn't want you ruining my moment. That bastard has been a thorn in my side during this entire investigation."

She looked at the other attorney, who was smiling. "Did you enjoy that?"

"Yes, Ma'am," he answered, still smiling.

I looked at Angel again. This time, there was a slight smile and a look of relief on her face.

There were only four of us left in the house. Sergeant Johnson said, "Let's take a break. Everyone hit the bathroom. The next hour is critical. Dan, is there any coffee made?"

"I'll check."

Chapter 48

Angel

I wanted to tell them everything I knew, but the attorney, Wishborne, kept focusing on insignificant details. He was dragging things out with his questions. The other attorney, Moss, would ask a question, and Wishborne would dismiss it and continue asking silly questions. It confirmed that Dan was right. Wishborne was still loyal to Judge Boone and his cousins.

I tried to remain calm and answer his questions as if they were important to the case. They weren't. We all knew it.

I had not seen Sergeant Johnson, but I was seeing Wishborne's plan. When Sergeant Johnson showed up and asked about details, he could reply that I knew nothing important and they were wasting time. But that wasn't the case. He wasn't asking anything important.

I had been answering stupid questions for an hour when Sergeant Johnson and Dan entered the house. It thrilled me when they arrested Wishborne. They should add wasting time and asking stupid questions to his charges. I was exhausted from his pointless questions, which he repeated in two or three different ways.

I wasn't the only one thrilled. The other attorney smiled, loosened up, and became a whole new person.

I watched Dan closely when Sergeant Johnson announced what they had found at the house. He didn't move or flinch. He didn't smile or frown; he just stood, showing no emotion when she made her announcement. That was something new about Dan. He had always been a cheerful person. But now, he was unemotional. Hiding secrets was making him a different person. Everything he did, he did it for me.

After taking a break, we rearranged the interview area. The sergeant and attorney Moss sat on the couch, and I was in a chair across from them. I was more comfortable. It was now an interview and not an interrogation of impossibly repetitive questions.

"Angel, before we get started. There are two investigations going on. More than that, actually. But two agencies are involved. The state police is spearheading the first one with you as our undercover operative. Keeping you a secret has been a monumental challenge. Wishborne was working two sides and was told he was the lead on this investigation. But Mr. Moss here has been the genuine lead and can now take over."

Moss said, "And we are about to skip the trivial delay tactics and get started with proper questions."

"Thank goodness," I said.

"The other investigation," Sergeant Johnson continued, "the office of homeland security spearheaded, is with the DEA and FBI working together. They are the reason I haven't been here sooner. I'm sorry. I was on my way to the hospital right after you were admitted when I was called off by the Feds. They insisted you were in good hands and that I should back off until they could secure their operative and we could jointly plan how to proceed. I assure you I did not forget about you. I don't like being told how to handle my cases, but this one is big and the corruption led to some big people. Are you okay with continuing today? Please tell me you are."

"I'm good." And watched as Sergeant Johnson smiled. It was a little inside joke that let her know I was ready. "I've been too busy recovering to think you had forgotten about me."

"Mr. Moss, please resume your questions."

"Angel, please tell us about the Rays' major connections. Who were the important people you saw there? Who were their contacts?"

I smiled. No more petty questions. We are getting somewhere now.

"You already know about Sheriff Pendleton. He and two deputies ran interference locally. They were on the lodge's payroll as security. Judge Boone was a regular. He was there for the drugs and the girls. U.S. Senator Thomas was there once. I didn't see him do anything illegal. He may have been there on a legitimate hunting trip. I don't know. His son was there often and took part in everything from drugs, the girls, and illegal hunting activities. He was the one Dad arrested with Danny Ray. That's the arrest that got Dad murdered. Maybe the cameras will tell a different story about the Senator."

I stopped to take a sip of coffee. It felt good to be talking now. Talking about their actual connections.

"There was a farmer nearby who had a private airfield. Jones, I believe. He picked up the drugs in Mexico. Mostly coke, heroin and fentanyl. A skinhead group in South Central Missouri and Northern Arkansas handled human trafficking. Their leader's name was Mason. That's the only name I know. If the girls at the lodge survived a few months, they were traded to the skinheads for meth and marijuana."

"That's new information. We'll come back to that if the Feds have nothing," Moss said.

"There was one person I never met. Donny talked to him two or three times a day, always at eight in the morning and at five in the afternoon. It was like a conference call. I never met him, and Donny didn't talk about the calls. The contact will be on his phone. I think he was receiving orders. Sometimes Donny took notes. Sometimes things happened quickly and unexpectedly after the calls. That's the person you need to find."

I took another sip of coffee and let them catch up on notes. "There was an unmarried couple who were the cook and bartender at the lodge. Sometimes during the week, they distributed the drugs to the local dealers. If I had to guess, the woman was undercover. Little John didn't like her, but her boyfriend protected her."

Moss asked, "Do you know their names?"

I gave him the names of Blake and Mike as I knew them, but I felt they were fake.

I looked up to see Dan slip back into the room. He had taken his jacket and tie off and unbuttoned his collar. He sat in my original interrogation chair and sipped coffee.

Moss looked at Sergeant Johnson. "Do you want to dig deeper into any of these subjects before we move on?"

She answered yes just before her phone rang. She looked at her notes in a little pocket notebook and then at her phone. "Let's take a quick break."

She took her notebook and stepped outside. Dan stood and asked if we needed a coffee refill. Moss did, and Dan also refreshed Sergeant Johnson's cup.

Dan knelt in front of me and rubbed my legs. "How are you doing?"

"I'm better now that we are discussing the big picture. Wishborne was asking stupid stuff and repeating questions two or three times. It was fun to see him get arrested."

Dan handed me a note that said "DR phone code" and had six numbers on it. "Yeah, that was interesting. A lot is happening and is going to happen."

Then mouthed, "Remember the numbers." Then, he took the note back just before Sergeant Johnson came back into the house.

"Let's get started again. Dan, would you mind getting me some more coffee?"

"Already done," he said as he stood up.

Moss restarted the camera and nodded to Sergeant Johnson when it was ready.

"Angel, the Feds need the passcode to Donny Ray's phone. Do you know it by chance?"

I said, "One, one, one, nine, one, six."

Sergeant Johnson wrote it down and stopped and slowly looked up at me.

"Isn't that your birthday?"

I nodded, and for the first time during the questions, I started crying. "It's the day they murdered Dad. The day they took revenge for his brother."

"I'm sorry. Take a minute to pull yourself together. I have two more major questions they want answered."

"Okay, go ahead," I sniffled. I wanted to answer questions. I wanted the unknown man. I hadn't done this to take down a few small crooks. I wanted the man who thought he was too powerful to be taken down.

"The Feds want the names of the two deputies under Pendleton, and any other law enforcement officers that you know about. They also want to know about any other attorneys who may have been involved."

I nodded and named the deputies. As for the others, I told her his phone had all the details and contacts they needed.

"His phone has apps that access all the bank accounts. He had access to the cameras. He did everything on his phone and used a password app. Break into it, and you get all his accounts and access codes."

"Do you know the login for the passcode app?"

"No. But if I had to guess, possibly his birthday or something to do with his brother. If that doesn't work, try variations of 3 Banditos."

"Okay. We are going to wrap it up here for the day. The Feds and the AG's office want us down there to help them." She spoke to Moss as he turned the camera off.

"Angel, the passcode to his phone will speed things up drastically. The Feds are getting another warrant allowing access to his phone, and they are already issuing arrest warrants based on the information they are getting and the information you have given. They know about the Brotherhood in Missouri and are already working on that part. And I agree with you. I want the person behind those phone calls."

"What do we do now?" I asked.

"Get well. Be available at a moment's notice to answer questions. We will be back soon to do an honest and formal interview to get every question answered we need for prosecution."

"Okay," I answered.

"Dan, we will call Angel through your phone until we can process her phone and get it back to her. I hope you don't mind."

He nodded at her and replied, "It will be with me."

"Thank you for your cooperation. I'm sorry about yesterday's fiasco. But once the investigation was announced, we acted quickly to arrest people before they disappeared. And again, I'm sorry about your father."

"Thank you," Dan answered.

I stood and went to where Dan was standing and put my arms around him. We watched as Moss and Sergeant Johnson carried things out to his car.

I don't know why, but once they closed the door, I cried. I felt joy, pain, and relief at the same time. But I was so tired my knees buckled, and Dan caught me. Then the dread and fear hit me. I did not know where that was coming from.

Dan carried me to the couch and set me down. I just bawled. It was over. It was finally going to be over. Donny Ray was dead, and Little John was in jail. But I felt like the world was falling apart.

"It's okay, I'm right here," Dan said. "Your body is having some withdrawal symptoms from the medicine you've been taking. They will pass, but you may feel hopeless and out of control. I'm here to help with that, to protect you."

He pulled me tightly to him and hugged me. I knew he was right. "Take deep, slow breaths. It will pass."

I don't know how long it lasted, but I must have fallen asleep, because Dan woke me.

Chapter 49

Dan

I held Angel until she stopped shaking and fell asleep. It could have been withdrawals, but more than likely it was exhaustion and anxiety. She had only been asleep for fifteen minutes when I saw Ben pulling into the drive.

"We have visitors," I said, and shook Angel's shoulder.

"What?"

"We have visitors. Ben and Amy are here."

"Who?"

"Go wash your face and freshen up. I think we need to clear this up while we can."

"Okay."

It was too soon to wake her, but I hadn't told her what Sergeant Johnson had done. She was upset about what she had done to Ben and Amy, which is why she had called Amy the night before. That had created a blowup that took Mom and Ben a while to accept and understand. I still wasn't sure they had accepted it.

Angel staggered down the hall to the bathroom, and I went to the door. Ben pulled into the drive and was talking to Amy. They hadn't gotten out of the car, and I'm sure they were questioning whether this was a good idea. Last night we argued. I didn't want to argue anymore. Everyone needed to understand what had happened and why.

I waved at Ben to come in. When they didn't move, I walked to the car. He rolled down his window. "I'm not sure it's a good idea to talk yet," he said.

"It's the perfect time," I said. "We have some news you need to hear."

"Dan, I don't want us to argue or fight."

"Then we won't. I want you to understand our side. We can tell you more now than we could yesterday. Come in and we will talk."

My phone rang, and I didn't wait to see what Ben and Amy would do. I turned to walk back to the house and answered my phone.

Angel opened the door for me as Sergeant Johnson started speaking. "Dan, is Angel close to you?"

"She's right here. Let me hand her the phone."

I heard the car doors close and turned to see Ben and Amy walking towards us. I motioned for them to come in and put a finger to my lips, indicating they needed to be quiet. Amy reached for Ben's hand. I wasn't sure if that was for friendly reassurance or if there had been something else going on there before this happened.

I closed the door behind them and turned as Angel said, "Okay, thank you for the update."

She turned to Ben and Amy. "I'm sorry about everything you went through. It was the only way I knew to save your lives."

Ben was shaking his head. "Were there really people buried in the garden?"

Angel looked past Ben to me. "They have recovered nine bodies so far, and cadaver dogs have located at least eight more graves."

Amy gasped and sat down on the couch. Ben turned and looked at me. Suddenly, he looked pale and sick. He sat next to Amy on the couch. Angel sat in the chair she used earlier when being questioned by the lawyer, Moss.

Ben said, "We were watching the news, and they reported they had found at least one body. But nine?"

Angel spoke again. "One body was a girl I know Little John murdered. But the name I gave them didn't match any missing persons' names. It may not have been her real name. The only body they have identified is Donny Ray's."

Ben said, "Isn't he the one you were investigating?"

"One of them. They think he and his cousin had an argument and Little John killed him."

"Oh my God," Amy said. She looked at Ben. "If they will kill each other, we would have meant nothing to them."

Angel frowned and turned to me, then back to Ben and Amy. "I thought you two weren't talking."

Amy said, "I received a call from the State Police this morning. They urgently needed to speak to me. We planned to go to church, but canceled those plans to meet with Sergeant Johnson."

She squeezed her eyes shut, trying to control her emotions. "We thought she was investigating the incident with Ben. But she brought the videos. She showed us what had happened at the apartment. It's embarrassing, but it wasn't what I thought had happened. She explained why you did it, and that it saved our lives. I didn't believe you when you called me last night. But everything that's happened this morning and the news this afternoon must prove you were right."

Angel stood and walked to the couch and sat beside Amy and took her hand in hers. "They killed a friend of Ben and Dan's at the lake last year. She was a gorgeous girl. They tried to kill me and Dan twice. The second time, they killed my dad. Somehow, they got away with everything."

"Until now," I said.

"Until now," Angel repeated. "They arrested one attorney investigating this case, right here in this house this afternoon."

"Wishborne?" Ben asked, looking at me.

"Yes," Angel answered as I nodded in agreement. "They have also arrested the sheriff who came to the funeral yesterday, two deputies, and a state district judge. They have issued warrants for a U.S. senator and his son."

Amy stared at Angel. "You did all of that?"

"I helped put the pieces together," Angel answered.

We were quiet for several minutes. Ben and Amy were dealing with the conflicting emotions I'm sure were running through their heads.

I said, "I'm not sure Angel can legally tell you much more. She's probably told you more than she should have. She was saving as many lives as possible while getting evidence to shut them down."

Amy looked at Angel. "Where did you find the strength to do this?"

Angel let go of her hand and smiled. "God gave me strength. I have been a stripper, used drugs, slept with Donny Ray to gain his trust. But the hardest thing I did was lying beside Donny Ray while he was sleeping; knowing I could end his life right then, but letting him live. I wanted him in jail or dead, but I also wanted the judge, the sheriff, and the senator who protected him. Donny Ray and Little John were just a small piece of the operation. Getting rid of them would not have stopped the human trafficking or the drugs. They were replaceable."

Amy leaned over and hugged Angel. I had to wipe a tear from my eye.

As Amy let go, Angel asked, "Can you forgive me for what I did to you and Ben?"

Amy nodded. But Ben, who had been silent, said gently, "What's to forgive? You saved our lives, and who knows how many others? We should thank you."

He looked at me. "I understand why you didn't get involved that night. You were trusting Angel. If you had interfered, the entire investigation would have ended, and none of this would have happened."

"That's right, and we could all be dead," I said, and waited for him to ask how I knew to trust her. But he didn't ask. Maybe it didn't occur to him to ask. He was still reeling from the embarrassment and the sudden reconnection with Amy. That was for the best. I wouldn't have lied to him because I trusted him. But I didn't know Amy. I couldn't trust her. Yet. Only Angel would get to know I had access to the cameras at the lodge and the Ray house.

Time to change the subject before someone asked the question I was avoiding. I was curious about something. Ben and Amy had held hands the whole time.

"I'm kind of changing the subject here," I said. "Is there something going on between you we should know about? You've held hands the whole time."

They didn't release each other's hands, but they looked at each other for a long time. Amy finally said, "We'll see. I liked Ben a lot before this happened, and I hoped he would ask me on a date. We have a lot of talking to do." She looked at Angel. "A lot more praying to do as well. If you can find the strength to do what you did, surely I can find a little to get me through this."

Amy looked at me. "How can you forgive her for being a stripper and sleeping with another man?"

"It was part of the plan. We had talked about it before she went undercover. There was a chance she would have to sleep with him. We also knew she could die doing this, so we got married to have our time together and then we talked about everything she might have to do. She did it as part of the job, not to cheat on me. I forgave her before she ever did it. It was harder for her to pretend to like the man who killed her dad." I hesitated for a moment, remembering the times I would turn the video stream off so I didn't have to watch them. "Dad and I had many prayer sessions to help me deal with this. Without Dad, I would have gone and brought her home before she finished the academy."

"I find your actions difficult to understand. I mean... I don't know what I mean," Ben said. "I'm sorry I ever doubted either of you."

My phone chimed. I received a text message. I looked at the phone. It was from Sergeant Johnson. I pulled up the message and read it before handing the phone to Angel.

She read the message. "Two more bodies. Early reviews of the cameras have revealed some disturbing things. She'll be back tomorrow to talk to me some more."

Ben stood and Amy followed, not letting go of his hand. "I need to get Amy home. Her parents have texted her every hour, making sure she is okay. I want to talk to them, but I'm afraid of their reaction."

"Are they watching the news?" I asked.

"Yes," Amy said. "But they are finding it difficult to believe. How much can I tell them?"

Angel said, "Tell them everything. They went through this with you. They deserve to know."

We hugged them both as they left. It was awkward for them. They didn't understand the danger they had been in. Maybe one day I would show Ben a snippet of a video I recorded that showed Angel talking them out of killing them. Maybe. The one video I never wanted to watch again was Donny Ray and the Judge raping Angel. But the police will find it, and it will devastate Angel.

My phone dinged again. Another message from Sergeant Johnson.

"Angel? You'll want to see this." She had sat down on the couch and looked exhausted. I sat beside her and showed her the message.

Joint news conference at six thirty. Thought you would want to know.

Her hand shook when she reached for the phone.

"Do you want to watch it?" I didn't know whether she would.

"I think we need to watch it with our mothers, then I can answer their questions afterwards. Let Ben know as well."

"You're shaking. Are you up to it?"

She nodded her head. "I didn't eat lunch. I just need to eat something."

"Yes, you do. You have eaten little in the last week. Let's go to Mom's. There's plenty of food there, and we will visit a little before the news conference."

"Okay."

We had stopped worrying about confrontations and accusations. We knew in our hearts that Angel had done the right thing. People would question her morals and her actions, but they couldn't question the end results. She had done bad things to bring down even worse people.

Chapter 50

Angel

Dan's Uncle Vernon and Aunt Liz were at his mom's when we arrived. Several church members were there as well. My mom looked surprised to see us when we entered the kitchen, but gave us a hug and asked if we were hungry. We said we were and sat at the dining table. Dan's mom gave us hugs, but sternly reminded us we owed her explanations.

Dan's Uncle Vernon sat with us. He had a concerned look on his face. "Dan, I know I offered my legal services today, but this is way out of my territory. What the news is reporting is absolutely crazy. I've never seen this much corruption in my life."

"It's okay, Uncle Vernon. Angel was the undercover officer who did this."

I heard the pride in Dan's voice as he spoke, and it made me happy. I wasn't the only undercover officer involved, and they would find out soon. But I realized I should stop being ashamed of what I did, and be proud. Then, I had another thought and closed my eyes for a silent prayer. I was the tool that God used to make this happen. I was his avenging angel.

"There is a news conference scheduled for six-thirty," Dan said. "Will you stay and watch it with us?"

"You mean the one Homeland Security is holding?"

"That's the one," I said.

"Just how big is this case?"

Dan's phone rang before I could answer. I expected it to be Sergeant Johnson, but Dan answered, "Hello, Sherriff."

Dan listened for a couple of minutes, then said, "Thank you for calling. I'll let her know."

Dan looked at me and then at his uncle. "It's big. The FBI arrested two of Sheriff Tatum's deputies. One was Beckly; he is the one running for sheriff. Sheriff Tatum has already been asked to fill-in as interim sheriff if Beckly is convicted."

"What are you supposed to tell me?"

Dan shook his head. "He's proud of you and wants us to come visit soon. Let's watch the news conference."

We moved to the living room and hugged Dan's cousins, Mike, Sissy, and Aunt Liz before finding places to sit.

The news conference was brief, with the different branches outlining their actions. The federal and state prosecutors talked about the arrests being made and the continuing investigation. Then the FBI focused on human trafficking and the dead bodies. The DEA talked about the drugs and the connections they were tracking down. Finally, the head of the state police thanked his lead investigator, Sergeant Johnson, who was standing behind him, and her team for the tenacious work they had done in the investigation and focused on the corruption. No one mentioned undercover operatives until the reporters were given the chance to ask questions. A federal prosecutor responded by saying, "We will not disclose any information about our sources. Their lives and safety are our priority, and any attempt to discover who they are will not be tolerated."

Everyone looked at me. And I snuggled a little closer to Dan. He kissed me on the top of my head. "You're home, Cotton Top, and you're safe."

The news conference took five minutes at the most. The questions went on much longer. Uncle Vernon asked the first question.

"How much can you tell us, Angel?"

Dan's mom turned the TV volume off. I looked up at Dan and pleaded with my eyes to answer for me. I was exhausted.

He looked at me, and then at his uncle. "She's exhausted. But briefly, they knew who they were after before the investigation began. Angel just confirmed their suspicion. There are two things you will hear about a lot. The dead bodies and the video cameras."

"More cameras?" Mom asked.

"Many more cameras," Dan answered. "That's why I didn't remove the ones hidden on the farm."

I didn't want to talk, because I'd talked all day, but I knew Dan didn't need to say more. I squeezed his leg and sat up.

"They had hidden cameras all over the lodge and in the house. They used them for security and extortion. I think it's how they gained influence over the Senator. They had some compromising videos of his son."

Uncle Vernon added, "His son was with Danny Ray when your dad arrested them. That's what started the whole vendetta against him."

"I knew that. But how did you know?" I asked Uncle Vernon.

"Your dad told me. He talked to me right before his murder about representing him to get his job back if he was fired."

"Thank you for telling me," I said.

"You're welcome. And thank you for being the brave and wonderful person you are. And for bringing down these corrupt people. Your secret is safe with us."

I smiled the biggest smile. He made me feel proud of what I did. It was the first time in weeks that I felt like Angel again. I had been Angie Lewis for too long and realized I hadn't let go of that persona. Maybe I could now.

Everyone left after the news conference. It was just me and Dan and our mothers. I was exhausted, but I wanted to give them the chance to ask questions I hadn't answered last night.

Mrs. Brock looked at Dan and asked, "How much did Lloyd know about what you and Angel were doing?"

"Everything. He had to talk me out of going and getting Angel and bringing her home. He had to remind me almost daily that Angel was doing this to protect other girls, like Sarah. And to prevent other useless deaths, like her father's."

She nodded her head. "I never understood it, and he wouldn't tell me why you were acting so strange. He told me it was your job, school, the farm, and Angel being gone that was causing you stress." Dan didn't reply. He reached over and caressed his mother's arm. She reached up and laid her hand on his. "There are still things you can't talk about, aren't there?"

I spoke for both of us. "There are things I can't talk about, and there will be things I won't talk about, because I don't want to remember them. Dan knows some things, but he may not talk either."

She nodded. The television was still on but muted. She looked at it and asked, "How much of that are you responsible for?"

"Most of it," I said and remembered we hadn't told them about Wishborne. "They even arrested one of the prosecuting attorneys at our house today. Dan and I got to witness it. Apparently, he was informing his old boss, the judge, of everything that he knew about the case. They knew who I was from the beginning, but they played along because they planned to kill me eventually. The same judge denied the search warrants to search the lodge and the Ray house. But a federal judge approved them. Now the judge and Wishborne are both in jail."

"Lloyd kept telling me I should be proud of both of you. That you had made sacrifices that only God witnessed." She came to me and Dan and hugged us both. "I'm proud of you. And I'm sorry I was angry with you. I understand now why you wanted to get married. You wanted to be together before Angel went undercover." She let go and sat back down.

"That was part of it. I was afraid she might not survive." Dan answered.

"And you let her do it?" my mom asked.

"There was no stopping her." We were quiet, waiting for more questions.

"Did Ben and Amy talk to you?"

"Yes," Dan said. "We answered as many questions as possible. But it was the body count that convinced them we did what was right."

"How many did they say they had found?" My mom asked.

"Eighteen," I answered. "And that was only the ones buried there. We will never know how many others they are responsible for, like Sarah."

Dan's phone dinged. I wanted no more news tonight and prayed it wasn't Sergeant Johnson.

"It's Ben. He says he had a pleasant talk with Amy's parents. The news conference blew their minds, and her parents wanted him to say thank you for your unorthodox way of protecting their daughter."

I smiled again. The day was ending nicely. I never realized how much I needed to hear the pride and thanks from the people I loved.

Chapter 51

Angel

Dan and I had not planned past the undercover operation. There wasn't a crystal ball to show us how it would turn out. After Ben's message, he asked me, "It's been another long day. Are you ready to go home?"

I smiled and nodded yes. We hadn't talked about which house we would live in, but it felt right for us to live in his grandparents' house.

We walked slowly home. It felt wonderful to breathe in the cool air and listen to the crickets and birds, and the occasional cow mooing. As if Dan were reading my mind. He asked, "Have you been able to turn off Angie yet? Has my Angel returned home?"

I had to think about his question. "I don't know. It's like I'm stuck somewhere in between. When I'm with you, I'm Angel. When I'm talking to Sergeant Johnson and the attorney, I'm Angie. Toward the end, I was a blend of both. I knew it was over, and I was scared. Outwardly, I was Angie. Inside, Angel was planning her escape. But my plan failed.

"Can we sit on the back porch? The sound of the river helps." I looked up at him and saw him smiling. I thought about the things he had done. It was up to him to tell me; but I would keep his secret.

"It's always been a soothing sound for me," he said.

We sat on the porch swing. Dan updated me on his dad's graveside service. His shock at Sergeant Johnson bringing Amy. He told me about his conversation with Sergeant Johnson. He was afraid she had figured out that he had access to the cameras.

"How did you install them?" I asked.

"The camera shop installed the ones at the lodge. I'd already paid him for the cameras and for their installation. He sold them to Donny Ray at half the price. So, he made extra money on them. I installed the cameras at the Rays' house. It took me two days of waiting for everyone to leave long enough for me to enter the house, but only thirty minutes to install them."

We were silent for a few minutes, listening to the river and an owl hooting in the distance. I was home and safe on the swing, with Dan's arm around me and the blanket over us.

I laid my head on his chest and hugged him. "Make love to me tonight, Dan."

"No," he said softly. "Not until I know my Angel is back. I don't want to make love to Angie. She was Donny Ray's girl. I want to make love to Angel, my wife, the love of my life."

I broke down and cried. They were tears of joy and pain. It hurt to be refused, but he was right. Angel wasn't back yet. I couldn't release Angie until I had told them everything I knew. That was something Lydia didn't know. There was a difference between being a hooker and being undercover. I couldn't put the Angie persona in a closet and forget it like a worn-out work coat. It would take some time to forget the things I'd done and seen. I thought about the girl Little John had murdered. Who was she?

Dan said I tossed and turned all night, so he let me sleep in. Sleeping in meant my waking up at seven a.m. I hurt all over, and it was difficult for me to move. "Why do I feel so bad?"

"Because yesterday was the first day you've been awake all day. You'll feel better when you get up and start moving. You want me to help you to the shower?"

"I hope you're right. No, I need to do it by myself," I said.

"Sergeant Johnson called. She'll be here at eight."

"Really? I've got nothing else to tell them."

"She's bringing the FBI. They have some questions for you, apparently."

Sergeant Johnson arrived at nine with two FBI agents accompanying her.

"Good morning, Dan. Angel," Sergeant Johnson said when Dan opened the door. Then she walked in, and the two agents followed her into the living room. She introduced the two, and I immediately forgot their names. I was still hurting. Dan thought I had done too much yesterday. But I felt off. I think I was still going through withdrawal from the pain medicine.

Mom had gotten her job back with the school and left for work. Dan was making more coffee as we settled into the living room. We chatted about the farm and how serene it was while Dan served coffee and bottled water.

When he started to leave, Sergeant Johnson asked him to stay. "You may as well hear some of this. Angel is going to tell you anyway."

Dan moved to stand beside me.

"The eight a.m. and five p.m. phone calls have been traced back to Fat Man at the strip club. His club and home were searched this morning, and he's gone. We are searching for him now."

My mind raced. I had overheard D-Ray tell Little John twice that he knew who I was. The second time, he even said he was getting his revenge for his brother. "It explains how D-Ray knew who I was. Fat Man told him. But I don't see him as a drug ringleader."

One of the FBI agents spoke. "He wasn't involved in the drug business. He was coordinating the human trafficking and the money laundering for the drugs."

"Also, we've identified one of the bodies because her purse was buried with her. Her name was Audra Sams."

The name shocked Dan. "No. Dammit."

"You know her, Dan?" Sergeant Johnson asked.

"She was Amy's roommate. The one Ben and Amy went to the Lodge looking for."

I thought about the girl Little John killed. The timing was right. "Was she a brunette with brown eyes?"

Sergeant Johnson looked at me intensely. "Do you know anything about her death?"

I nodded. "Little John killed her. He used too much chloroform when he abducted her, and she died. He brought her to the lodge to ask D-Ray what to do. I checked her pulse, but it was too late."

"I remember getting your report on that. Go on," Sergeant Johnson encouraged me.

I told them what had happened. How I wanted to beat Little John senseless and how emaciated he was. I told them how D-Ray held me back and instructed Little John to plant, not bury, her in the garden.

"D-Ray said that Little John was diagnosed with a brain tumor when he was a teenager, and that the meth had helped treat it. That was the reason he acted the way he did, and he had survived a lot longer than anyone expected."

"Can you confirm he murdered her?"

"Yes. He said he thought she was gorgeous. He didn't mean to kill her."

Sergeant Johnson was typing on her phone. "Maybe not. But he kidnapped her with the intention of raping her. We can charge him for that murder along with Donny Ray's."

"You really think he killed D-Ray?"

"There were two pistols buried with Donny. One had his prints on it, and the other had Little John's. It's easy to assume he was burying the evidence with the body. I figure an autopsy will show the bullets were from the handgun with Little John's prints."

I looked at Dan. But he was still shaken about the girl. "Are you okay, Dan?" I asked.

He shook his head. "Does the family know about Audra's death? Can I call Ben?"

One agent answered, "They will have been notified by now."

"So, it's okay for me to call my brother?"

"Yes," the Agent responded.

Sergeant Johnson said, "Dan, we need to ask you to step outside and let us talk to Angel alone. Call your brother."

"Thank you." He touched my shoulder. "I'll grab my jacket and go to the back porch."

When Dan was out of the house, Sergeant Johnson asked quietly, "Angel, at any time you were undercover, do you remember being drugged?"

"No, I did some coke with D-Ray. They drugged Ben and Amy, but I don't remember being drugged."

"Okay, do you remember waking up anywhere unusual?"

"Oh! I woke up in the lodge one morning. D-Ray said I passed out at the lodge desk and he put me to bed."

"What were you wearing when you woke up?"

"Nothing; we slept in the nude."

"Angel, we've reviewed a lot of videos, and we have found some disturbing things. One of them involved you. Agent Simonsen is a psychiatrist, and she is here to help you deal with any feelings you may have."

My mind raced. The Judge and D-Ray were acting very friendly that day. I looked at the Sergeant and asked, "D-Ray let that damn creepy judge rape me, didn't he?"

Sergeant Johnson stared at me with her mouth open. I was angrier than I was upset. I was so angry that I don't remember much of the next hour, except my body aching from shaking so much.

They asked whether I wanted to see the video. No, and hell no, I didn't want to see it.

"Do you want us to be here when you tell Dan?"

"No. I don't want Dan to know. Period."

"It will come out at trial."

"Then he will find out then. We have enough to deal with now."

"You shouldn't keep this kind of trauma bottled up."

"Listen," I said. "I'm angry that this happened to me. I'm angry that the judge raped me. I wasn't the only one, I'm sure. But I knew, we knew at the beginning, that this could happen. That bastard helped them avoid all kinds of charges, and if this puts him in jail, then I'll be happy to testify. But I don't remember it."

I cried after that. I wanted to be strong, but everything overwhelmed me at once.

They left twenty minutes later. I had cried myself out. Sergeant Johnson said they were finished asking me questions for a few days and encouraged Dan and me to vacation for a few weeks. She returned my phone and had Dan's number if she needed to contact me.

I found Dan on the swing on the porch. I was still shaking with anger. It was chilly out, so he had covered himself with the blanket. He moved the blanket to let me join him, and I curled up beside him.

"It's over for now. Sergeant Johnson said we should take a vacation."

He nodded. "You look exhausted. Close your eyes, and relax."

He pulled his phone out. "I'll plan our vacation."

I wanted to smile, but there wasn't one left in me. My mind rambled, but I closed my eyes. I didn't want to tell Dan about the rape. There was a chance he already knew, because he watched the cameras. I would deal with that when I faced it in court. It will be a hard conversation, but it would be easier if it put the judge in prison.

Dan's body warmth and the blanket comforted me, and I finally fell asleep.

Our lives were turned upside down because of the decisions I made. Dan took partial responsibility because he knew I wouldn't have gone undercover if he had said no. But our relationship wouldn't have survived. I would have resented his holding me back. And Little John would still have been out there kidnapping girls, dealing drugs, and killing people.

Dan dropped his nursing classes because he had already missed too many days and asked for extended leave from his part-time EMT position so he could stay with me. They granted him six weeks, and he'd already used two of them. It would be next fall before he could restart nursing classes.

Dan insisted I see a doctor before our trip. He wanted me to have a complete checkup before we took off for three weeks. My injuries were healing, but Dan wanted a doctor to examine me and not rely on his EMT training. The injuries to my head and neck were unusual because I still had some issues with my motor skills. The doctor recommended physical therapy, but said daily activity would help more than anything.

We visited the Dalliers in Colorado, and from there we toured the Rockies from Pikes Peak and Gunnison Canyon through the Rocky Mountain National Park. Then we drove to Jackson Hole, Wyoming, and toured the Grand Tetons and Yellowstone and returned through South Dakota and saw Mount Rushmore, the Badlands, and Custer State Park.

They were beautiful and interesting, but it was good to get home after three weeks. Our farm was as nice as any national park we visited.

Over the next year, the real depositions, hearings, and the trials started. Sometimes I was called to testify; sometimes pleas were made and court was canceled. The most difficult was the trial of Little John's murder of Audra Sams. Ben and Amy were dating by then and attended the trial. The hardest part was making eye contact with Amy when I described the scene at the lodge, where I checked Audra's pulse and discovered she was dead. At the time, I didn't know her name, or that she was Amy's roommate.

The questions were tough to answer. "Are you medically trained? How did you know she was dead? Did you assault the accused, Little John Johnson? Did you neglect your duty as an officer by not reporting this incident immediately?"

That last question caused the review panel to question my actions. But they cleared me when they found out I had reported it less than an hour later. Why did it take an hour? "I was undercover and only had a few minutes to write reports when I went to the restroom." I uploaded reports to a Dropbox account where Sergeant Johnson reviewed them. Sergeant Johnson testified she sent this report to the Attorney General's office for assistant D.A. Wishborne to review. His emailed response was, *There is no evidence provided. Just a report from a psychotic, drugged-out stripper.* That email was received less than an hour after my report.

I had never liked Wishborne, and right then I wanted to see him in prison. Eventually, my wish came true because each hearing or trial added more charges against him and Judge Boone.

Ten months after my undercover job was over, Wishborne was tried and sentenced to federal prison. Judge Boone was the final one.

Chapter 52

Angel

The Dalliers had become close friends. Dan had sold them several calves in the past year and planned to sell them more. It's true, there was a fifteen-year age difference between us, and a six-year age difference between us and Hannah. But we were farm families, and age wasn't important to farmers. Farmers of all ages appreciated hard work and the many challenges each family had to overcome. Since Mr. Charlie was a deputy sheriff, the family also understood everything we were going through.

Once Dan and I opened up about our lives on the first trip to deliver Hannah's calves, they shared stories about their lives and the challenges they had faced. They were high-school sweethearts. His parents didn't care who he dated; hers didn't want her to marry into a local farm family. She had constantly been told that her family came from money. It turned out that his family was worth a lot more than her family. Her parents owned the local bank. His parents and grandparents owned a lot of farmland, a local farm implement dealership, and had invested heavily in other local agricultural enterprises. His family's wealth was invested.

They offered their help anytime we needed it. And the time was now.

The Federal Prosecutor's office had a difficult time getting Judge Boone into court. His attorneys kept filing for continuance after continuance. Sergeant Johnson finally came to us with a plan. We didn't like it, but after Angel and I discussed it, we knew we had to do it.

"Can you act your part, Dan?" Sergeant Johnson asked. Oh, if she only knew how much acting he had done.

"I can do it. The question is, can our moms do it?"

"I hadn't thought about them. Can they do it?" She asked.

"Yeah," I said. "They want this over as much as we do."

It was hard for our mothers. When Dan and I told them the plan, they reluctantly agreed. They were ready for everything to be over. Mom constantly reminded me that my decision had affected everyone on the farm. Everyone needed to move on without looking over their shoulders.

I was pregnant, and they wanted to meet their grandson and spoil him. It was the happiest occasion to happen on the farm in years, Mrs. Brock had said. But the plan would make them wait two weeks after he was born to see him.

Mom said, "If this doesn't work, I'm going to be one angry Nana."

The contractions started the day before my due date, which we hadn't expected to be accurate. My water broke at home, and we rushed to the hospital in Searcy. Dan drove with our moms in the back seat of the Escalade. I texted Sergeant Johnson to let her know. This was the part of the plan that was difficult. It was about the timing. Every childbirth was different. We planned for a natural childbirth, but we couldn't predict if I might need an epidural, or how long it would take. The worst-case scenario was that I might need a C-section, and then the plan would be cancelled because the Doctor wouldn't allow me to leave and travel.

*****

Dan

I had agreed to the plan, but I never thought it would work. There were too many things that could go wrong. Angel, Sergeant Johnson, and I talked to the gynecologist about the plan. She didn't like it, but she had followed the case since Angel became her patient, and she understood the importance of the plan. But she told Angel, "You and the baby are my first priority. If I see anything that will affect your life or the baby's life, I will pull the plug on this instantly."

Surprisingly, Sergeant Johnson agreed and emphasized the importance of making it work and keeping Angel and the baby safe. Only a few trusted nurses and hospital administrators knew what was going on. They knew our story and were happy to keep secrets and make it work.

Everything went smoothly. Angel delivered Lloyd Jonathan Brock at twelve fifty p.m. without the epidural. We named him after our dads and decided to call him LJ. He cried very little and then became quiet. His dark blue eyes stared straight at me as I held him and talked to him, then I reluctantly handed him to Angel.

Everything happened too quickly. The quiet, special moments that I wanted to share with Angel and LJ only lasted five minutes. It wasn't long enough, even though I kept reminding myself we had the rest of our lives to spend together.

I don't know how Sergeant Johnson identified the person who was sharing our information with the judge and the senator's son. But they made sure the woman, a middle-aged administrative clerk, worked that day, and they made her responsible for filling out the death certificates, fake ones, for Angel and LJ. She gave the papers to a hospital administrator, and the administrator shredded them.

It wasn't hard to play our parts. When I found Mom and Mrs. Cotton in the waiting room, I was already crying. I missed Angel and LJ already, and I didn't want to play this game anymore. I walked to them and hugged them tightly as they stood to meet me.

Ben and Amy were there, which I hadn't expected. We hadn't told them the plan, and telling them now wasn't part of the plan. Our emotions obviously confused them, and Ben asked, "What's going on, Dan?"

I broke from the hug with Mom and Mrs. Cotton, who continued to hug each other. I pulled Ben and Amy into a hug. One more lie, and I hated to tell it. "I lost them both. They didn't make it."

Their gasps and reactions told me they believed me. Amy immediately began crying, and even Ben lost it.

I was crying and was a total mess, just from the pain of having to leave Angel and LJ. I looked over Ben's shoulder and saw Sergeant Johnson sitting in a corner, pretending to read a magazine. She gave me the slightest of nods. I broke from their hug and let out a yell of anger, and turned away. I bumped into a table at the end of a row of chairs and hit my knee. It hurt. I yelled, "Dammit!" flipped the table over and walked out of the waiting room. I heard other people in the waiting room asking what had happened?

As I walked out of the waiting room, I heard Ben say, "He just lost his wife and baby."

I made my way back to the Escalade. Ben and Amy were the first to meet me there. Mom and Mrs. Cotton were walking behind them.

"Dan, I'm so sorry," Ben began. I held my hand up for him to stop talking and then pulled him and Amy into another hug.

I whispered, "They're okay. Angel and LJ are alive and well. This was an act to get the judge into court. Angel and LJ will leave the hospital in a few hours and will be taken to the Dalliers in Colorado."

Ben and Amy stepped away, and Ben asked, "What?"

Mom and Mrs. Cotton pushed in to hug me again. "How are they?" Mom asked.

"LJ is beautiful. Lots of brown hair and big blue eyes. Eight pounds, one ounce, and twenty-one inches. I miss them already," I said.

"Somebody, please explain to me what's going on?" Ben asked.

"Let's go to your apartment, and we'll talk there," I said.

Chapter 53

Dan

Television and newspaper reporters surrounded the federal courthouse when we arrived that morning. We faked Angel's death to draw out the state judge who kept avoiding trial dates. But today, he was convicted of rape because of Angel's testimony that morning. As long as Angel was alive, she was the only witness who could provide testimony against the judge, and he used every legal maneuver imaginable to avoid court. Once he thought she was dead, he eagerly showed up in court, demanding the case to be dismissed for lack of a witness. But then Angel showed up in court–alive. The federal judge denied the request to dismiss the case and proceeded with the trial. He shut down every protest from the defense and said, "This is the first time in a year we've had all parties in the courtroom. Six continuances are enough."

The defense argued that Angel was dead. The prosecutor said she obviously wasn't. Then the defense asked for another continuance because Angel was not dead.

The prosecutor then asked how they had assumed Angel was dead. There was no death certificate, no public death announcements, no public funeral. What on earth made them think she was dead?

They couldn't answer the question. The defense suddenly realized they couldn't admit they had spies in the hospital, that they had cameras on my farm. All of their sources were illegal and would be added as additional charges later. The state police had the evidence, and Sergeant Johnson had wisely fed them the wrong information to use it against them.

Sergeant Johnson had been right; faking Angel's death had drawn the judge out. She had figured out the sources they were getting their information from and gave them false information.

Angel had taken the stand and testified to having seen the judge on two occasions. On the second occasion, there was video footage of Judge Boone that showed him and Donny Ray taking turns raping an unconscious Angel.

Judge Boone's wife and daughter walked out of the courtroom upon hearing that detail. His son and the senator's son were nowhere to be found.

But their trial dates were set as well. The federal prosecutors expected them to agree to a plea deal after Judge Boone's conviction.

Sergeant Johnson watched us as she flowed with the crowd, leaving the courtroom. When she reached the back row, where Angel and I were sitting, she turned in and moved down the aisle to us. She sat down on the bench and turned to face us, with one arm resting on the back of the bench.

"Well, it's over," she said. "The judge will be sentenced tomorrow, and then he will be tried for his other charges. How do you feel, Angel?"

"I'm glad it's over. I never want to do that again."

"And we owe it all to you. But I'm curious about something." And she looked at me.

"That camera system they had. It was exactly like the one you have, Dan."

She let the accusation hang in the air for a minute. I said nothing.

"I'm curious how that happened. Any thoughts, Dan?"

I shook my head.

"And Little John swears he didn't kill Donny Ray, and that they did not install the camera system we found in the house. He claims he was set up."

I looked at her and said, "My dad asked me before he died, 'Who watches over the guardian angels? Who seeks absolution for the avenging angels?' Sergeant Johnson, you, as a state trooper, and I, as an EMT and nurse, watch over the guardian angels. It's our job to protect them so they can rest and continue their jobs tomorrow. It was my dad's job and soon to be my brother's job to seek absolution for the avenging angels. Because of you and me, our avenging Angel came home and survived. We did what we had to do."

Angel squeezed my hand. Sergeant Johnson granted us one of her rare smiles.

"I think you just answered my question. This case is officially closed. Angel, I will accept that letter of resignation as a member of the Task Force when you are ready to send it to me."

Angel nodded to her and quietly said, "Thank you." She had tried to resign several times since the undercover operation ended, but Sergeant

Johnson had insisted she stay on paid administrative leave until the trials were over. Now she would have to talk to Sheriff Tatum and decide if there was funding for her to stay on as deputy sheriff.

Sergeant Johnson rose and left us. We stayed in the courtroom until it emptied. There was one state trooper left in the courtroom with us. He motioned for us to follow him. We followed him out the back of the courtroom, out of the courthouse to where the Green Machine was parked. Angel thanked him and said goodbye.

We had spoken little since before the trial that morning. She believed I would have trouble with the revelations made at the trial that morning. The video was shown in the judge's chambers of her drugged and unresponsive, and being undressed and raped first by Donny Ray and then by Judge Boone. No one, not even Angel, knew I was aware of that video.

I drove out of downtown Little Rock and made the turn north on Highway Sixty-Seven before she finally spoke.

"You knew about their raping me, didn't you?" She asked me quietly. Her head hung forward, and she barely turned to look at me. I stole glances at her but kept my eyes on the road.

"I'm sorry," I answered softly. The tears came unbidden to my eyes. "I couldn't stop them."

"You couldn't stop them? Damnit, Dan. It's over now. Stop keeping secrets." She grabbed my right arm and pressed her thumb into the scar on my arm.

"Ow, that hurts," I said and tried to pull my arm away. She didn't let go.

"No more secrets, Dan." She said calmly. "I was there the morning you killed D-Ray. I overheard part of the conversation between him and Little John the night before. Knew what they were planning to do. I followed him to the house, and I was going to do what you did." She let go of my arm and wiped tears from her eyes before she continued.

"I saw D-Ray in the garden with the backhoe, and I hid on the road behind a brush pile. That's when I saw you step out of the house and walk to the garden. I couldn't believe it was you. I hadn't seen you in months, and I wanted to go to you. Before I could decide what to do, you called out to D-Ray, and he got off the backhoe. You talked for a few minutes, and then Donny pulled his pistol and shot you in the arm." And she punched my shoulder on the scar. "Then you shot him five times."

She stopped then, sniffled, and wiped tears from her eyes. "You shot five times, but they only found four bullet holes."

It was more of a question than a statement. This was my last secret. At least I thought I was keeping a secret. Angel had known all along and had told no one, not even me. I was devastated that she had seen me kill Donny Ray, but also elated that she had kept my secret.

"The first shot hit him in the knee. I missed the second shot. He missed his second shot."

Angel gasped at my statement.

"We shot, and it sounded like one shot. My third shot was through the chest, and I think it killed him. His body turned, and I hit his shoulder with my next shot. The last shot was when I walked up and shot him between his eyes. I think he was dead, but I wasn't taking any chances." I shivered, remembering what I had done.

It was my turn to wipe tears from my eyes then. I slowed the truck down a little. She waited for me to continue.

"I couldn't stop him and the judge from raping you, but I could damn sure stop him from killing you," I said.

Angel gave me a weak smile, wiped the tears from her eyes, blew her nose on a tissue from the box she'd been carrying all day. "That's what I thought. I went there to kill him myself, but I don't know if I could have pulled the trigger."

I pulled over to the side of the freeway and put my flashers on.

"I tried to talk him into giving himself up," I said. "He laughed at me, and said, 'No way. There's at least twenty bodies buried in this garden. I ain't doing life in prison. You're here for Angie, or should I call her Angel? She is a sweet fuck, you know.' He knew exactly who you were. Then he pulled his pistol. I stepped to the left, and his shot hit my arm. It spoiled my aim, and my shot hit his knee."

"When were you going to tell me?" Angel asked.

"I killed him, Angel. And I set up Little John to take the fall. I never planned on telling anyone. Especially not you. You've been through enough. You've been through nightmares, getting raped, and testimony that would mortify average people, and lost both your dads. If I'd known you'd seen me, then I would have said something. But I couldn't. I've tried to push it out of my mind, but it pops up every day, just like a bad weed. I will never forget it."

She touched my arm again. This time she was gentler.

"It looks like we've both kept secrets," I said.

"Yeah," Angel said. "No more secrets, okay?"

"No more secrets," I said and leaned over to kiss her. She put her finger on my lips and stopped me.

"Promise?"

"I promise," I said. The wind from a passing semi rocked the Green Machine. Angel took her finger off my lips and kissed me.

"I love you, Daniel Brock."

"And I love you, Angel Brock."

I put the truck in gear and pulled back out onto the freeway.

"How did you do it? You were supposed to be delivering cattle to Colorado. Yet I saw you at D-Ray's."

I sighed. I didn't want to tell the story, but I'd promised her no more lies. No more secrets.

"I had everything ready to go. The truck was hooked onto the trailer. The calves were loaded. Then, my phone notifies me that there is an active video recording. I caught the last two-thirds of the video where Little John and Donny are arguing about killing you. Somehow, Little John knew the Judge had raped you, and he wanted to as well. Finally, Donny laid out the plan, and Little John was happy. Donny was supposed to drug you that night, and you would be out again the next morning. Then he would let Little John have his way, and he could kill you when he was finished."

Angel sighed deeply. "He didn't drug me like he said he would. I think he had fallen for me. He was digging the grave for whoever didn't survive Little John's attack that morning."

"No. The grave was for both of you. He wanted you to kill each other, so he would be free of two problems at the same time." I was getting angry all over again, and I shouldn't have. It was over; but I wasn't sure I would ever be over it.

"When the video was over, I called Robby."

Angel interrupted me. "Why did you call Robby?"

I continued, "And Ben, and then Dad."

Angel stared at me with her mouth agape.

"I told Ben I had to work an emergency shift as an EMT. I met Ben and Robby in Searcy. Ben cleared his schedule and took the calves to Colorado. Ben thought Robby was taking me to work. I knew Robby would keep his mouth shut. He took me to the launch ramp north of the lodge and dropped me off. I told him you were undercover bringing down the drug dealers that killed his dad and that I needed to repair a camera for you. He questioned nothing I did or said. I hid overnight and slipped into the house when everyone left that morning. When I finished burying D-Ray, I called Robby to pick me up. We met Ben in Oklahoma so Robby could get him back in time to take an exam."

"The launch ramp is nearly five miles away."

"I ran it," I answered, and she nodded at me. "I was exhausted after running and not sleeping overnight, so I slept most of the way to Oklahoma."

"Why did you call your dad?"

"I started telling him everything after you went to the academy. I wasn't always thinking clearly, because I missed you and wanted to go get you and bring you home. Dad kept me focused. I wanted to make you forget about getting revenge. He must have told me the same thing twenty times. He said you were doing important work protecting people in the future who would never know they needed to be protected. Taking revenge for your father, for Sarah, and for people we would never know. I knew he was right, and he kept me focused."

The tears came unwanted to my eyes, and I took a moment to wipe them away.

"He was the only person who knew what I was planning to do that day. He was the only one who knew I had killed Donny Ray. Robby picked me up at the launch ramp again and drove me to Oklahoma. Robby was smart enough not to ask what had happened. Then, he and Ben drove home together. I'm sure Robby and Ben have figured it out, but they quit asking me questions after Dad's funeral and you came home."

"I watched you drag D-Ray to the grave he dug for me. You took his phone and used his finger to do something. What did you do?" Angel asked.

"I used his finger to type because I had gloves on, and I wasn't leaving any fingerprints. I connected his phone to the cameras I installed in the house with the ones in the lodge. When the state police looked at his phone, they found all the cameras. The cameras he installed on the farm, the cameras at the lodge, and the cameras at his house."

"How did the cameras in the house not show you were there?" She asked.

"I deleted the footage before I confronted Donny. I avoided all the cameras but one for five seconds. When I finished deleting the video, it was like it had never activated. The state police and the feds had too much video to watch. They never caught it."

"You thought of everything."

"No. I made mistakes," I said. "Sergeant Johnson caught the biggest one - the camera system was identical to mine. She wanted me to know that when we talked today."

"All your talk about your dad and absolution was your way of telling her you were on her side?"

"She knew that," I said.

Angel watched the freeway ahead of us as we passed the Beebe exit.

Finally, she spoke. "I want to go to the cemetery before we go home. I want to tell Dad it's over."

"We can do that. We can tell both of our dads together." I hesitated, holding back a tear, before I continued. "My dad had the greatest love and respect for you. He admired you for putting your life on the line to protect others."

"I didn't know that. It would be good to see both graves before we go home."

"Sure, when were you there last?" I asked.

"Right after the funeral. I promised Dad I wouldn't come back until I had avenged his murder."

"What do we do after that? Tomorrow, I mean."

"Let's start by going fishing. I want to watch the otters play. I want to learn how to live and enjoy life without a care in the world. Maybe they can teach us that."

I smiled. She had a good idea. I hadn't seen the otters since the last time we went fishing. It would be good to see my little friends again.

Chapter 54

Angel

Dan told me, "You're one of those rare people who can stand knee-deep in shit and still look to the sky for rainbows." I asked him for an explanation. "You remain positive, no matter how bad the situation becomes."

"Dad always told me, 'If you can push through the pain, and keep breathing, you can survive anything.'"

It was one week after the trial of the judge. They were starting his next trial on charges of aiding and abetting criminal activity. I wouldn't need to testify in those trials.

Dan and I were standing on the deck of his mom's house with Sergeant Johnson, looking over the Little Red River. The federal prosecutors had just left after clearing up some final paperwork before the federal judge sentenced former Judge Boone.

Sergeant Johnson was watching the river. "This is a gorgeous place. No wonder you don't want to leave here."

"Yeah, I can step out here and feel the tension flow away."

"You two are lucky. You know that?" She smiled at us. "Y'all have each other. You have a beautiful place. A healthy son. And you have me covering your asses."

"How's that?" Dan asked.

"Everything I tell you now is unofficial and off the record."

Dan and I raised our eyebrows at each other.

"I traced some cameras from the house back to a camera shop in Memphis. The owner told me an interesting story once I threatened him with all kinds of charges. He told me you paid him a lot of money to sell and install those cameras at the Rays' hunting lodge. He said he didn't put any cameras in the house, though. I assume you did that somehow, or Donny Ray really installed them himself.

"If you had installed them, that could have been the end of the case, because the evidence was tainted. But I thought about the evidence they provided and the crooks they brought down. I thought about the cases that would be dismissed and all the work that would be wasted. I stopped asking questions about the cameras. You didn't break the law by paying the man to sell cameras to someone else. And when I asked you about the cameras Donny Ray installed on the farm, you told me how you found them, but you said you didn't have access to any others. I believed you. Because I thought about my niece." She looked at me then. "You know her as Cherrie."

I gasped. I had no idea. Cherrie was the girl Sheriff Pendleton raped.

She sighed heavily. "My brother and I haven't spoken in years. He will probably die in prison at Tucker because he followed the gangs and their drugs. He killed a man and ended up in prison. I promised I would not end up like him. Cherrie doesn't know her real father. Her mother and my brother both asked me to keep that secret. I have until now. Now you know my secret; you know why I covered your ass, Dan. If you needed it covered, I don't want to know either way. And you know why I have to say thank you if you did."

"No, thank you," Dan said. I knew that was as close to a confession as he was going to make.

"One more thing," Sergeant Johnson said. "Charles Percival McAlister is a former Navy SEAL who was dishonorably discharged. He is reportedly living at a sovereign nation compound in rural Montana. He visited the Aryan Nation compound in northern Arkansas. The Feds think he is most likely the man who killed your father, Angel."

"What about Fat Man?" I asked.

"He disappeared. The DEA thinks he is in Central or South America." She looked at her watch. "It's time for me to go. Thank you, Angel. Dan."

She shook our hands and said goodbye. It was over. We had won. But what would Fat Man do? What would Charles Percival McAlister do? Was it really over?

I watched the river flowing by. Dan hugged me from behind and kissed my cheek.

"Is it really over?" I asked.

"The man who shot your father is still alive. And Fat Man is still trafficking girls. It's not over until my avenging angel says it's over."

The End of Book Two

Books By This Author

Programmed to Steal

A hacker can't always hide behind their computer screen. Especially when the person hacked is a hacker as well. Jess is determined to get revenge for her high school classmate. But she is not prepared for the quick and violent actions taken against her and her friends. Can they survive and take down the villain? Run, fight, or die. What do you do?

Fall From Grace

Avenging Angel Book One

Angel and Dan just want a simple life together. But when her father's enemies target them, their world is shattered. Thrust into a nightmare of murder, human trafficking, and violence. Angel and Dan fight for survival. Cornered and desperate, they'll have to choose: become victims or take down the monsters who destroyed their peace. Love, loss, and revenge collide in a high-stakes battle where the only certainty is that someone will die.

The End of the Road
Poetry and Selected Stories

This collection of Tony's poetry will carry you back in time. There are poems about growing up in Southeast Arkansas, and reflections on life. Poems like The Ink Pen, The Hook, and The End Of the Road will have you reflecting on your life.There are stories from his Monday Motivationals, like Growing Talent, Weeds, and The Power of a Seed, which will inspire. Finally, The Extra Kid and Carnival Ride Coupons at the Ashley County Fair are humorous true stories from his childhood and life.

About the Author

Tony C. Franklin is an Arkansas author who crafts gripping tales of crime and suspense. He is the writer behind the thrilling novel *Programmed to Steal* and the new *Avenging Angel* series, which begins with *Fall From Grace*. His path to becoming a novelist is as interesting as his plots, drawing on decades of real-world experience to create stories that are authentic and deeply motivated.

Tony's writing is grounded in a life spent observing the world around him. He grew up on a small farm in Southeast Arkansas and went on to study Agricultural Business at the University of Arkansas. His subsequent careers as an Agricultural Extension Agent and in retail management, spanning nearly two decades, provided him with a unique vantage point. He spent those years observing people from all walks of life, gaining a deep understanding of their desires and motivations. These real-world insights are now channeled into his writing, allowing him to create characters who are passionate and authentically driven.

www.ingramcontent.com/pod-product-compliance
Lightning Source LLC
LaVergne TN
LVHW020703110826
845149LV00012B/2088

* 9 7 9 8 9 8 9 6 1 4 7 5 2 *